MOUSE

THE ELMNAS CHRONICLES

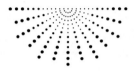

KAYLENA RADCLIFF

Science Fiction and Fantasy Publications

THE ELMNAS CHRONICLES: MOUSE
KAYLENA RADCLIFF

Science Fiction and Fantasy Publications

HTTPS://SCIFIFANTASYPUBLICATIONS.CA
A division of DAOwen Publications

The Elmnas Chronicles: Mouse / Kaylena Radcliff

Edited by Douglas Owen and Miles Cruise

ISBN 978-1-928094-53-1
EISBN 978-1-928094-54-8

This is a work of fiction. Names, characters, places, and incidents either are the product of the author's imagination or are used fictitiously, and any resemblance to actual persons, living or dead, businesses, companies, events, or locales is entirely coincidental. Jacket Art commissioned by MMT Productions

10 9 8 7 6 5 4 3 2 1

For my husband, Tim, who loves new worlds so much that he made sure I created one

CHAPTER ONE

All had been darkness. This was the first thought she knew. Where it came from or what came before, she could not say, but she saw that it endured. Bound to it, she passed through in silent obscurity; a blind phantom in a black sea.

Here the second thought struck her. *She* was. What did that mean? Well, she did not become the void. There was distinction. Otherness. Life. And it belonged to her.

And in that thought, something new entered the darkness.

There were lights twinkling dimly now, movement, shapes, voices. A face swam before her, and she recognized it as a woman's, the features indistinguishable save for two dark brows knitted together with terrible concern.

The girl opened her eyes. Grating light assaulted her senses. She squinted painfully as bright blurs sped to and fro in front of her. There was a cacophony of sound, something like chattering and murmuring, growing in volume as the world gained clarity. She shook her head drowsily, and the noise and movement ceased. The blurs coalesced into shapes and sharpened. This was a likeness of things she knew. People.

To her fresh eyes, they were strange. Peculiar light blue garments covered their mouths, continued loosely over their bodies and fell to their ankles. Only the skin from the bridges of their noses to the peak of their foreheads showed, and their heads, too, were covered in light blue cloth. Some held shimmering tools in their white-gloved hands, and others carried and concentrated on what appeared to be writing tablets. Each of them fiddled with strange instruments, things that beeped and buzzed and blinked in patterns. With routine calculation, these people in blue approached her, prodding and pinching, waving the instruments about her while uttering a manner of noises unknown to her now hearing ears.

Presently, one of them pulled the garment down from his mouth, revealing a light brown face with tight lips.

"*Gree'da andth Mahkthi?*" he said to her, his brow furrowing.

She shook her head and he frowned impatiently.

"*Mahkthi,*" he repeated, this time a little slower and louder.

"I… I don't understand," the girl replied timidly. Her crude, harsh words, though she spoke them in a high and clear voice, fell upon the still air like a dish clattering to the floor.

"Ah," he replied, clicking his tongue and shaking his head. "*Thi'randth Elmnas.*"

Turning aside, he whispered urgently to the others in the room, and immediately, they dispersed. She lay alone.

What is this place? The girl blinked, bringing the room into focus, and swept it curiously. It was a short survey. Four bare, dismal gray walls stared back at her, their monotony broken by a tired, white ceiling and the closed wooden door. Featureless, except for the half-supine cot on which she lay. Gazing down, she gasped in surprise at her knobby, pale legs and what appeared to be her naked, ashy body, barely covered by a loose, paper-thin sheet. Impulsively, she made an attempt to lift her limbs, but she fell limp even as she tensed to move. Her head thumped painfully with the effort. Though she was not willing to succumb so quickly, a slight wiggle in her toes and a curl of her fingertips was about all she could manage.

The door clicked open, and she swiveled to see a new man enter. Older, with hair graying at the tips and keen, dark eyes, the unmasked newcomer strode inside with stiff stoicism. He adjusted his impeccable white frock self-importantly, smoothing a wrinkle from the carefully pressed collar buttoned to his throat. Approaching her in silence, he pored meticulously over the tablet he held out loosely in front of him. She watched him quizzically as he hummed and frowned at the device. Finally, he turned his attention to her.

"You know this speak?" he asked, his words halting and stilted as he stumbled over them.

Relieved, she nodded gratefully. He spat out the words as if he ground rocks against his teeth, but she could at least communicate with him.

"Good, good," he said. "You know where you are?"

She shook her head.

"You know your name?"

She searched her mind for this, a memory of her name, but nothing came. It should have been there, close enough to feel, but it slipped just beyond her grasp. She searched his face for an answer, but he simply waited, his eyes trained carefully on her every expression. Again, she shook her head.

"Hmm." The man scrutinized her, mumbling indistinguishably. He placed a hand on his clean-shaven jaw while flicking and striking at the tablet with the other. What was he doing? The girl arched her neck and peered at its glassy surface curiously. Frowning at her interest, the man set it face down at the end of her cot. Instead, he reached forward, touching her with icy hands that made her skin crawl.

"Not be scared," he said. "I am *physnion.* Healer. I check you, make you okay."

Hesitantly, she assented, and he produced instruments from his deep, white pockets. She waited patiently as he squeezed her limbs and shined lights into her eyes and ears. He stepped back, put his instruments away, and cleared his throat.

"You hurt bad," he started. "No remember what happened. Trauma victim. You from different land, all people there gone. Dead. But we help you. We make you learn, do good. You be okay."

Panic twinged in her belly.

"Please, can you tell me what happened?" she asked anxiously. "Where I came from? Why you brought me here? Is there anyone else like me, who might remember?"

His face wrinkled with confusion as he assessed her question.

"We find you, make you safe. You be okay here." The man finally replied. He offered what was supposed to be a reassuring smile, but there was nothing reassuring about it. There were words she wanted to use to describe it–calculated, or frozen, but nothing quite fit the chill that ran down her spine.

"You be strong soon. You work, learn." He smiled again, patted her arm, and made his way to the door. "Healers come now. Help you."

When he left, the people in blue returned. They heaved her from the bed, her limp feet hitting the cold floor with a dull smack. A tingling sensation traveled up her legs as the men half-carried, half-walked her along. Though aching and resistant, the muscles began to move, and slowly, slightly, she could feel some strength return.

More gray walls met her outside the room, and her toes dragged across a smooth, black floor. The people in blue guided her as quickly as she would go down the long corridors, all lined with closed doors. She lingered. Were there more like her, waking from darkness only to be cast into one far greater?

"*Vaamnaa, Un-qwa-sah!*" Her impatient guide hissed, and he shoved her forward.

In time, they reached an open doorway, and behind it, a vast room full of mirrors, glass panels, and dazzling machinery that the girl observed uncomprehendingly. There, more of the blue people descended and prodded at her, placing her on scales, hanging her with wires and weights, putting hands in her mouth, and shining lights in her eyes. The girl resigned herself to silence, hoping to catch some meaning of their fluid, lilting tongue. She understood nothing, of course, but their furtive whispers and suspicious glances betrayed their fear that she did.

A hand pushed her forward, and she found herself in front of one of the mirrors. She gazed curiously at the face that appeared there. Tan and thin, but rounded, with a small nose, pink lips, and wide-set stormy gray eyes, hollow and large with hunger. Matted, dirty blonde wisps of hair framed the face, fell to her shoulders, and hung over her eyes. Two round ears poked out beneath the absurd mess of tangled hair. She surveyed the rest of her tiny, gaunt frame that was all awkward joints and protruding bones. An image came to her mind–a man made of sticks hanging in a green field–but it passed quickly, disappearing to the nothingness from where she had come. The girl reached up to touch her face, to look longer, but more hands moved her on roughly, ripped her meager sheet from her, and stuffed her under a lukewarm stream of pounding water.

Before the girl could so much as yelp, someone scrubbed her unceremoniously, hit her with a blast of hot air, and pressed a pile of garments into her shaking arms. Whimpering and startlingly exposed, she got the hint, pulled the clothes over her damp skin.

When she had finished, a woman in blue approached her.

"Hello," she said with comforting fluency. "I'm here to check one more thing. It will be alright, I'm a healer."

She gently took hold of the girl's hand and turned the palm downward. There, sitting just below her knuckles, was a small patch of discolored flesh, slightly raised from the rest of her hand. The skin puckered around a small, precise scar, where a rectangular lump bulged from beneath the surface. The healer prodded the lump with a metal utensil, causing a tremor of pain to shoot through the girl's hand. As she flinched away, the healer offered a terse apology before continuing to poke at it.

"I needed to make sure it was healing," she said. "Do you know what this is?"

The girl did not reply, but rubbed her hand gingerly.

"We call it a *du'icuas*. It means, 'wage card,' but it's how we know who you are around here. You can use it to let yourself into the buildings, and when you start working, collecting your wages. You will understand more once you get acclimated."

The girl frowned at the alien object poking obtrusively from her hand. *And who am I?* she wondered as the healer woman turned her attention to her tablet, scribbling what appeared to be notes on the object's ever-changing surface. She leaned over as silently as she dared to catch a glimpse, and on the screen there appeared an image of her own face, and next to it, characters she recognized as numbers. 146.

Aware of her audience, the healer motioned over the surface of the tablet, and it turned black before the girl's eyes.

She rounded on the girl with a stern look. "Now listen to me. There are some rules you must obey. The most important is to do what the healers and others in charge ask of you. They only want you to be safe, as there are… dangers, beyond our walls. You also will not speak this language we speak now outside this room, or there will be consequences. Do you understand?"

"Oh," she said softly, surprised. "Why?"

"Because it is uncivilized and suited only for beasts," the healer replied with a withering glare. "Do you want to be treated like a beast?"

Cautiously she shook her head, recoiling at the woman's sudden and unmerited contempt.

"Good." The healer smiled, her face so serene the girl believed she might have imagined the last exchange. She cringed as the healer leaned in and lifted the girl's sleeve. Her bare shoulder stung as the woman pressed down lightly upon it.

"That's healing nicely, too. If you have any issues with your new wage card, your mark should be enough to identify you."

Lifting her arm, the girl examined the tender shoulder. She expected foreign symbols or words, but even upside-down, she could read it: 146.

"Now then," the woman said. "This place is your new home. It is called the Misty Summit Healing Camp. Here you will learn to work. It is how we will teach you to become functional again after your trauma, and if you recover, you will be free to go. The work will be hard, and you have much to learn, but only this will make you better. Do you understand?"

The girl didn't, but nodded anyway. She detected a hint of annoyance as the woman sighed and made a sweeping gesture toward the door.

"It is time to meet your barracks ward. Shall we, *Un-qwa-sah*?"

After administering their tests, the healers hurried the girl called

146 down the corridor. There, out a small door, a vehicle waited. Arms hoisted her over the side, dropping her into its flat bed. A thick, numbing darkness draped itself over her, and it seemed as senseless as the slumber she had just escaped. She searched it, begging the black to reveal something, anything about this confusing world. It gave her nothing. The vehicle roared to life and lit the darkness ahead, glaring into a foggy shroud that swallowed everything beyond a few feet. It lurched forward and the girl clutched her seat as they bounced along in the night.

Presently, the vehicle came to a lighted path, and in a break in the fog, the girl made out a building looming ahead. Just as quickly as she had been loaded, several hands deposited her at the door of the bricked-up structure, visible only by the lighted post just outside. She was still gaining her balance as the vehicle rollicked off into the darkness, leaving her alone in its shadow. A knobless, sealed door rose before her. The girl ran her hand over the smooth exterior, seeking out the secret of entry, but the door showed no intention of intimating it. Gaping stupidly at the building, she ducked when the door suddenly whirred and slid back with several loud clicks.

Lurking within was a squat, unkempt woman wearing a dirty, pink smock and a mean scowl. The scowl deepened as she regarded the girl.

"I'm... I'm sorry," the girl tried, but a meaty arm swung forward and yanked her inside. The woman—the barracks ward—dug her fingers into the girl's bony shoulder, dragged her upright, and faced her toward the room. Other than a few barren cabinets by the ward's bed (distinguishable by its extra comforts), the room was filled with rows and rows of bunks, all stacked uniformly against the high walls. Pairs of eyes peered over the steel frames, glistening in the light that streamed in the barred windows from the lampposts outside. The ward turned the girl back toward her, bellowing unintelligible commands and gesticulating violently. Uncomprehending, she shrugged her shoulders and shook her head. The ward responded with a disgusted grimace and, with a sharp cuff, sent the girl tumbling to the floor.

The girl managed to pull herself weakly from the floor, its grit clinging to the bruise forming on her cheek. The woman towered over her, pointing a swollen finger at the bunk as she continued to scream.

She may have understood little, but she understood this. Scampering down the rows of bunks, she took a bed as far away from the snarling, red-faced hag as possible. The pillow was thin and the blankets thinner, but she buried herself beneath them, hoping desperately she would not hear the ward pounding after her. Minutes passed, however, and soon, heavy snores rose from the great woman's corner.

With a breath of relief, the one called 146 closed her eyes for the first time since her waking. The familiar darkness settled in around her, offering what comfort it could in the alien world full of voices and perils unknown beyond it. Still, she found no respite in its embrace. The moments since her waking repeated with terrible urgency, every detail of her frightfully bizarre day flashing vividly in her mind. She felt its panic, its need to recover what was lost, but even now, she knew she would not find it here. There was a terrible dread that filled her, that made her sweat even in this cold room under threadbare sheets. She had to get out.

146 was quiet as she extracted herself from the tangled bedspread, holding her breath at each telling rustle. She would not stay here, not in this place, and she would be gone before anyone knew it. Scanning the shadows and, detecting no signs of movement among the rows of bunks or changes in the overall sleepy breathing of those around her, she slipped carefully out of her cot.

Her bare feet made contact with the cold floor. The door to the barracks, only several strides ahead of her, beckoned to her, and she imagined what freedom might be like beyond them. She rushed forward, the strength of her will carrying her beyond the limit of her atrophied legs. In moments, she arrived at the door, the barracks ward snoring on her left, and escape just within her reach. With an outstretched hand, she leaned tentatively toward it, searching in the semi-darkness for the release mechanism that opened it to her before. Out of the corner of her eye, however, something moved.

She wheeled around, only to be met with a pair of glistening eyes, staring at her from the bottom bunk of the cot closest to the door. Squinting, 146 could distinguish the shape of the girl on the bunk. The other shook her head somberly and gestured to the door. 146 turned back to it, her hand still stretched out in hopeful ambition. Just beyond her fingertips, the mechanism glinted enticingly. She reached out, close enough to graze it, but before she could, a shuddering hand rested on her arm.

The glistening eyes were right behind her now, opened wide with fear. She shook her head more vigorously this time and pointed to something at the top of the doorframe. 146 looked up, and sure enough, there was another mechanism there, only she couldn't tell what it would be used for. The wide-eyed girl behind her stabbed one finger toward it emphatically. Then, with a sweeping motion, drew the rest of them across her neck. She tugged at her arm once more before backing away.

And now, she understood. Whatever opened the door would also let the ward know the door opened, and after experiencing the beastly woman's wrath for something rather trivial, she shivered to think what kind of punishment would be in store for a crime much greater. It was clear. There would be no escape. 146 made her way slowly down the rows of bunks back to her own. She slumped into it dejectedly, dread and despair swelling painfully in her chest.

The girl had nowhere to go. Even if she did, who would want her? Dead, she remembered bitterly. Gone. No one to claim her, to tell her the story she could not recall, to give her hope of being someone once. No, she was a number, a nothing in a sea of nameless faces.

She curled up in the creaking cot, knees hugged tight against her chest in defeat. Soon her heartbeat slowed, the gripping panic subsiding with her newfound realization. There was nowhere to go but here. Drained of emotion, she turned over, nursing the emptiness that replaced her despair. Even so, she abandoned hope, watching as the dim glow of the spotlights streamed through the high windows and cast long rectangles in between the rows.

But in the light just beside her bed, something new, something alive, skittered out of the shadows. She studied it fastidiously, its familiarity drawing her in though she had no words yet to categorize it. The creature twitched its whiskered nose up at her, its bulbous, black eyes studying her in return.

Out of her locked memory a small word escaped, and her mouth moved automatically.

"Mouse," she whispered.

With a flick of its naked tail, the little beast shot back into the shadow, disappearing into a crack in the wall behind the girl's cot.

She watched the crack for a while, and when the creature did not return, she smiled.

CHAPTER TWO

146 stared at the twisted springs of the cot above her, slouching dangerously into her already cramped confines.

In the stretches of sleep she did manage, nightmarish images bombarded her, only to deteriorate each time she was startled awake. Each episode left a terrible ringing that ricocheted between her ears, drowning out the disturbed silence of her quarters. Long after the ringing died away, however, the sense of familiarity lingered. She was missing something.

146 examined her limbs in the semi-darkness. She flexed her feet and stretched her arms, testing their mobility. Other than a little weakness in her muscles, no doubt exacerbated by the searing hunger in her stomach, she sensed none of the physical trauma the first healer insinuated.

What had she *actually* suffered? Presumably, whatever had taken her people. *My people*, she suddenly remembered. *Are they really gone? Am I the last? And if so, why am I here?*

The occupant in the cot above her stirred, and the sagging middle lifted momentarily before settling closer to 146's head. She sighed. Absent mindedly she rubbed her temples, trying to make sense of this new world. She drew her hands back in shock as a sharp stinging erupted from them. The screaming pain subsided as quickly as it come, but it left her with an eerie sense that something was very wrong. Why couldn't she remember what it was?

146 rolled to her side nervously, her gaze darting around the room with suspicion. Shapes began to grow out of the darkness, and she surveyed her miserly sleeping quarters. Rows of cots resolved, stacked against the walls and in uniformed order throughout the room. The rectangular, high-ceilinged barracks stretched out before her, interrupted by the tall barred windows every few yards along the walls.

Figures slept fitfully on the cots just as she had, twisting and turning beneath their scanty sheets. 146 gazed at them in confusion. *So many. Why so many?* There was an idea that rolled around in her head; things burning, people screaming, insidious red fogs slithering along rubble-strewn streets. These images faded abruptly, and the girl was suddenly unsure she had imagined anything at all. At any rate, their sleep appeared no more restful than hers; from around the room came sounds of creaking springs, low whimpers, and forlorn sighs. *What is this terrible place?*

The gray gloom of an approaching dawn mingled with the bright spotlights outside, its sickly glow streaming into the middle of the sterile room. As 146 squinted at the windows, watching the sky fade from a coal black to a desolate gray, grating, fluorescent lights overhead suddenly whirred to life.

She sat up in surprise, wincing as she grazed her forehead on the upper bunk's rusted springs. Heads around her lifted sleepily. There was a quiet murmur as the heads turned to watch the great boulder of a woman, the barracks ward, lift herself from the bed by the door. No sooner had her feet touched the floor did she begin croaking what 146 could only assume were orders.

The barracks ward stalked about the room, angry tirades spewing from her thin red lips as she dealt hard blows to anyone remaining beneath their meager covers. The girl was standing by the time the ward reached her. She took in the woman in the light who, though not much taller than she, was roughly an arm span wider and could easily suffocate her between a rolling belly and a large, rippling arm.

The ward drew herself up to stare down at 146 and brought her face close, her double chins trembling as her mouth became taut. She was pale and hideous, the night's rest having done little for her appearance or demeanor.

"*Brethan andth bithnii, Un-qwa-sah,*" she breathed menacingly. "*En Sa, Milgrim, shah kek ath ro.*"

She lumbered on to harass other girls, leaving 146 in stunned confusion. There was now a bustle of activity in the room as girls around her moved to the other side of the barracks. 146 watched them curiously. They were of varying ages, some maybe as young as eight while others, older than she, were nearly reaching adulthood. Pulling clothes and shoes from a set of lockers along the wall, they dressed in full view. The girl shifted uncomfortably but worked her way toward the lockers anyway. Presently, she found one with her own numbers scratched rudimentarily into its metal casing.

146 swung the door open, revealing a set of unwashed blue coveralls, some threadbare undershirts, and a pair of ankle-high leather boots. Sighing, she pulled the shirt on and slipped into the coveralls. They hung from her body much like a blanket might hang from a broomstick. The boots, of course, fit about the same.

"*Uz ra,*" a polite voice said behind her.

She whirled around. A girl her age stood there, a soft, friendly smile on her umber-colored face. Her thick, black hair fell in a loose braid down to her waist. Even beneath the ill-fitting coveralls she betrayed the shape of a woman, her skin smooth, her penetrating brown eyes wide but pleasant. She whispered again, the language neither the tongue of 146 nor the healers, and held up a smaller pair of boots. They were in worse condition, with holes in the toes, but judging by their size, 146 would have better luck with them. She slipped off the oversized pair and exchanged them for the smaller one gratefully.

"*Un-qwa-sah,*" she said, pointing to herself.

The girl smiled.

"*Un-tre-sin,*" she offered, lifting the sleeve of her shirt to reveal the numbers "135" emblazoned in black ink.

A loud buzzing cut through the subdued murmurs of the barracks. Girls streamed rapidly toward the door, now unlocked by the ward. She stood by, arms crossed as she spat on the floor.

The girl called 135 waved for 146 to follow. 146 fell in with the others, making sure her passage by the ward was buffered by at least two other bodies. The ward's narrowed eyes followed her as she went along. 135 gestured slightly toward the woman, muttering, "*Milgrim*," with a shudder. *That word. That must be what the woman is called.* It was fitting, of course. Only a name that foul sounding could describe her. 146 nodded in acknowledgement and shuffled out the door.

Morning had done little to improve the girl's understanding of her surroundings. Weak light from an unseen source filtered through layers of gray and red-tinged clouds. They hung low and cast a sickly, orange glow on all she could see, which wasn't much. A thick mist swirled around her knees, obscuring the ground and filling her nostrils with a putrid, choking film. The others around her pulled their shirts up over their faces or began tying scraps of fabric across their noses. She followed suit and herded along with them.

146 shambled along, aware of the uneven, slippery surface beneath her feet. She looked down, able to catch a glimpse of a cobbled path as the many plodding forms disturbed the mist's preferred current. Soon the path began to climb, and large forms came into view and loomed ahead. The incline leveled out, leaving behind much of the mist. Now it crept silently over their toes and sank into the cobbles.

Her breath came easier and sight clearer as the group crested the hill. They arrived in a relatively flat, empty square, full of strange shacks and buildings. There were signs tacked to them with foreign characters; words, she assumed. As a small mercy, symbols accompanied the words, denoting the function of each building — food, drink, and other various supplies. This must be the market, where her *du'icuas*, the wage card, worked. 146 scratched at the lump on her hand, momentarily distracting her from the pleading of her empty stomach.

Past the market and to her left stood a long, low building. 146 squinted at it to discern its purpose. A door opened, revealing a tidy woman draped in blue cloth and carrying a flickering tablet.

Disjointed screams and moans escaped from the crack of the slightly ajar door, as well as the stagnant smell of sick and death. 146 halted in shock. The neatly groomed woman returned her stare, eyeing 146 suspiciously. She stepped back and slammed the door, shutting up the ghostly wails inside. The girl hurried on.

The path inclined once more and crested another slope. At its apex rose a massive, metal structure. Concrete shafts towering out of the complex billowed black smoke into sky. Here the crowd of milling girls mixed with others – diverse men and women of all ages. 146 silently observed the churning mass of people. Noticeably absent were boys. Hardened, creased, and stubbled faces of men met her instead. She drove her hands deep into her pockets and hunkered herself alongside 135 as several of them leered at the young women.

The path narrowed, and along it rose tall, barbed fences, effectively driving the incoming herd in a chute toward the complex. Signs with large ominous print hung from the fences at intervals, and beyond the fences stood groups of men smoking pipes, talking and laughing in their unfamiliar tongue. Their sable, starched uniforms stood out starkly against the drab gray landscape. Cruel-looking truncheons hung from their waist, but the long-barreled weapons of glinting, obsidian steel slung over their shoulders drew the girl's eye in fear and fascination. Instinctively, 146 did not allow her gaze to linger long upon them.

She turned her attention instead to the curious shimmering pedestals also stationed along the path. These were made of smooth, metallic rock, refined and polished so each one glinted on every surface. The glossy rock formed an hourglass-shaped base, its top a flat, reflective plane. From that surface, four arching spindle-like prongs sprang up into an oval shape, and lightning-like energy shot from prong to prong. As she passed by, 146 could plainly see what appeared to be a semi-translucent person, hovering between the spindly prongs.

Startled, she stopped short. Yes, there was a face there, contained within the globe. A reposed olive-skinned woman, with deep, dark eyes, a high forehead, and flowing, raven hair, gazed out serenely. She wore a heavily embroidered red and white robe around her shoulders and an intricately decorated onyx pendant on her neck. 146 stood in

awe of her dignified beauty, and then, the woman spoke. The words, though still incomprehensible to the girl's ears, rolled melodically, soothingly, from the orb. 146 relaxed, the weight of her fear and confusion gradually lifting. Growing brave, she reached out to touch the orb. Her fingers passed through the image like smoke.

Though mesmerized, 146 sensed she was not alone. She looked up. Two of the black-clad men observed her keenly, their hands straying to their truncheons. She winced at a hand on her shoulder.

"*Lin-adaah,*" 135 urged.

146 thought she could guess what that meant. She straightened up and slipped back into the untidy line, her new friend beside her.

They plodded along for a few minutes before the narrow space between the barbed fences opened into a sort of courtyard. By the time the girls reached it, the area was already teeming with people. The line surged, then stopped altogether. And there, they waited.

What's going on? She hopped, pushed, and peered about the crowd impatiently. There wasn't much to see. A blinking red light, which hung on the outside of the complex and above the heads of the crowd, was all she could make out. Exasperated, she glanced over at 135, who stood by with expressionless patience. In fact, it seemed the others here waited in much the same way; 146 could only make out a few whispered words and the soft rustling of shifting feet. She alone disturbed the eerie still.

A click, beep, and mechanical whir echoed through the courtyard, and the blinking light turned green. The crowd moved forward. Ahead, 146 could see a large metal bay door. On either side of the door hung a square box, which chimed affirmatively when those who wished to enter waved their right hands in front of them. 146 examined her own hand curiously and wondered if this peculiar ritual would hurt. Several of the uniformed men observed these proceedings fastidiously, watching with narrowed eyes as the boxes counted each obedient arrival.

135 had ended up on the left side of the door and was nearly at the box. 146, finding herself on the right and several people behind, cleared her throat nervously. *Oh no,* she realized. *I'm on my own again. What if I do it wrong? What will they do to me?* With this thought, her

eyes grew wide, and she struggled to suppress the sudden panic squeezing her chest. As if sensing this, 135 inclined her head covertly toward 146. She waved her hand by the box as she did, and allowed a wan but reassuring smile. Then, with a subdued nod, she disappeared into the complex.

146 arrived at the door. Two of the black-clad men guarded the entrance, and they looked on in austere annoyance. She avoided their gaze timidly as she raised her right hand and offered it to the strange box. A nearly imperceptible tingling radiated from the skin above her wage card. The box beeped in reply. Before she could let out a sigh of relief, however, the guards stepped menacingly in front of her.

"*Un-qwa-sah!*" the taller one demanded.

146 looked up fearfully. Two hard, brown eyes pierced her from beneath the shadow of the man's helmet, worn low over his brow. His countenance bore a perpetual grimace, accentuated by the thick line of stubble sweeping across his chin.

"*Un-qwa-sah!*" he yelled again, pointing at her sleeve. 146 looked at it dumbly before realizing the command was, in fact, a question. She nodded.

"*Vaamnaa,*" the other barked, and they grabbed her by the crooks of the arms and pulled her into the facility.

Inside, the building spiraled far down into the bedrock. 146 took in its immensity and chaos. There were multiple levels of the facility, each one carved like shelves along an arcing path that descended into the depths below. Presently, they came to the path itself, and she gripped the lone railing that guarded the crude blocks of stone cut into the steps along it in terror. The guards pushed her down the steps impatiently. She chanced a glance over the edge, and hot air rushed up to meet her as she peered down to the bottom. There, sooty workers fed a blazing furnace, and wide, cauldron-like smelters, filled to the brim with some molten metal, erupted glowing bubbles and bursts of red flames.

Everything 146 could see flurried in activity. Across the chasm she could make out levels, snaking with people as they heaved pulleys full of raw ores and wheeled carts of crates between them. She scrutinized the carts. Cylindrical barrels, bearing a significant resemblance to the weapons slung to the backs of the men escorting her, overflowed from many of them. The path wound around, and 146 glanced backward, watching the crates disappear through partitions within. She wondered where they were headed.

They reached a flattened opening along the path, which stretched into a massive level burrowing deep into the mountain. The bay was divided into uniform sections, where groups of workers toiled at machines of various kinds. Whether out of fear or absorption in their tasks, the workers pointedly ignored the new arrivals. Though the air here was not as hot as along the cavern wall, it was thick with dust and intolerable clamor. She covered her ears, but nothing deadened the industrious cacophony of the clanking, whirring, grinding, buzzing machines.

Here they stopped. One of her escorts seized her arm roughly. It was the other man, and 146 cowered as he brought his face close to hers and barked unintelligible commands. She couldn't hear a word, and it wouldn't have mattered if she could. He pointed toward the back of the room as he shouted. 146 looked in that direction, following his jabbing finger to a closed-off partition among the jumble of tables, machines, and unheeding people. Fidgeting in his grasp, she nodded with conciliatory vigor.

When he was satisfied he had yelled all he could, he shot her one last scowl before releasing her. The two men turned heel and hurried away, leaving 146 alone and confused. Rubbing her arm, she waited awkwardly as the workers there gave her sideways looks. None offered any help. Her eyes began to fill with tears, but she desperately wiped them away on the collar of her shirt.

A woman came through the partitioned area, pushing an empty cart through the narrow aisles between machines and people. The short, bronzed woman grunted as she set down the cart and slicked a sweaty lock of frizzing hair back into her thick messy bun. Smudges of black grime dappled her from her forehead to her boots. Noticing 146, she let out a frazzled sigh, wiped her hands on her long black apron, and approached her.

"*Un-qwa-sah?*" she shouted over the noise. 146 nodded.

"*Thi'randth ka macth a'reh.*" the woman shouted again, pointing.

The girl shrugged and shook her head. At this the woman sighed again and rolled her eyes.

"*Ven.*"

146 followed the woman, who guided her through the partition. Beyond the curtain the sound faded–almost to silence, it seemed, to the girl's assaulted ears. There was a station here, where a thick, wide, wooden table filled most of the room. Unrecognizable parts and tools covered most of it, and one machine sat dormant on its edge. Suddenly, a gravely but powerful voice boomed from the other end of the room.

"*Que'ya, Galena?*"

146 gasped as she took in its source. An enormous man leaned over the table, his broad shoulders nearly matching its width. Staring curiously from beneath two white, bushy brows, his brilliantly green eyes gleamed in the semi-light of the enclosed room. Round, blotchy cheeks protruded above the grizzled shadow of a beard, reminding the girl of someone who had just come inside from a long afternoon in an icy, winter breeze. Shaggy white and gray hairs covered his head, but patches of tired red betrayed the vibrant color of his youth.

With another sigh, the woman launched into an impassioned monologue 146 could neither decipher nor follow, but assumed was at least in part about her sudden appearance. The man held up his broad hand. Her words, strangely enough, simply died away.

"*Grata, grata,*" he said quietly.

She looked at 146 in annoyance, and with a harrumph, left the partition.

The girl stood in terrified silence as the man shuffled out from behind the table, rising from a low stool like a mountain rising from the horizon. She stepped back as he approached, his massive frame towering several heads above her own. He offered a disarming smiled.

"*Gree'da andth Mahkthi, neua un?*" he asked gently.

She continued to shrink back, shaking her head. A stray tear spilled out of her eye, rolling down her hollow cheek. Then, she saw something on his face she had not seen since she arrived: compassion.

"Aw," he said, kneeling down so he was at her height. "*Nam ir asaa.*"

Before she could stop herself, 146 whispered, "I'm so sorry, I don't understand!"

She clapped her hands over mouth in horror. To her surprise, the man's face lit in up in cherubic delight.

"You speak the forbidden tongue!" he whispered excitedly. "So do I *neua un* - little one - so do I!"

CHAPTER THREE

S he watched dumbly as the giant of a man rambled on in hushed tones. He waved his massive hands, his blanched face growing rosier the longer he spoke. *He's speaking to me, and I understand! How can this be?* If she remembered correctly, they did not look much alike. But then again, she didn't quite belong among the others here, either. She looked at her own hands. It was noticeably darker than the man gesticulating before her, but not the olive tone of the guards or the healers, and lighter than the deep brown of her friend 135 or the bronze of the woman who brought her here.

Her new companion, however, noticed none of this. Whatever their differences, it didn't matter to him. He continued as someone who had finally returned home after a lifetime away.

"I can't believe it, yeh know! To finally meet someone who speaks what's forbidden–ah, well, yeh ain't alone anymore. Don't you worry," he said. "I can teach yeh everything you need to know. The language– they call it Gormlaean – it isn't so bad once you get the hang of it."

"I'm sorry," 146 finally interjected. "But... who *are* you?"

"Ah!" he chuckled. "Look a' me, forgettin' my manners. The number is... eh, 24, I think. But everyone here calls me *Rood*, Red, in the common speak."

"Red?" she replied quizzically.

"Yeh, yeh. Only the supervisors call you by number. Among the rest of us, though, you need a name. And since no one comes to Misty Summit with one, yeh get to pick one all brand new! What's yours then?"

The girl brought a hand to her shoulder, brushing it carefully, thoughtfully. New words, places, and possibilities swirled in her mind. Maybe, she even ventured to think, this nightmare would be over soon.

The image of the small furry creature escaping through the dreadful barrack's wall suddenly swam into her thoughts. There were other strange images that came to mind as well – the same sort of creatures, hopping suddenly from a bag of wheat, slipping into cracks in the floor. Now swarming, fleeing over scorched dirt. Feelings of revulsion accompanied the old pictures in her head, but as she thought of them now, she felt something new. Appreciation for their nimbleness, their clever survival? No, it wasn't that. Hope. It was hope.

"I think I've got it," she smiled, looking up at Red. "What's the word for Mouse?"

Red slapped his thigh and laughed. "*Meeko!* Yeh know I think that'll do. Mouse it is, little one. Come on, I'll show you what we do here."

The girl, now called Mouse, spent the rest of the work day under Red's tutelage. Their assignment, as she soon discovered, was rather tedious. Each day, Red explained, they were given boxes of small parts, and it was their job to inspect them. Anything that didn't fall into specifications underwent a rigorous rescue operation – each piece to be shaped by the tools splayed across the wide table and the machine, a deburrer, sitting at its end. The unsalvageable went into a box headed to the forge.

Along with the job, Red taught her words and important phrases she'd need to know to get by. It was only bits and pieces, but Mouse was a quick study. Even so, her world still did not make sense. *Rehabilitation camp,* she thought, unable to suppress her skepticism. *If we're not prisoners, why lock us in? Do they think we're dangerous? What's so wrong with me? With Red?*

These questions never left her lips. They felt too perilous, even here in the solitude of her mind. But Mouse could not contain all her curiosity.

"Is our language the only one that's forbidden?" she asked as they sorted parts. "I know of one girl, 135, she spoke to me but it was not in Gormlaean."

Red nodded. "You won't hear much, but some speak with other words, they do. The supervisors hate it, but they don't forbid it – not like ours. And I'll tell yeh something else. Only common speak is heard above a whisper, unless you'd like a visit from the Enforcement Squad."

"The men dressed in black, with the weapons, you mean?"

"Yeh," said Red softly. "Them. Be careful 'round them... and the rest of the lot in charge. And there are others to be mindful of too..."

Red frowned at the table. There was sorrow in his eyes, deep, abiding, consuming. *How much has he seen? What has he suffered? And for how long?* Mouse shuddered at the possible answers.

Still, the moment passed, and he brightened when he looked up at Mouse. "Tell yeh what. Keep yer nose clean and you'll do alright."

She gave a muted nod. The more she learned about this place, the more she wondered how long she might survive it.

A loud ringing suddenly permeated the cavern. Red stood abruptly and began to gather up any remaining parts.

"Galena'll be in shortly to get our crates," he explained. "That's the lass who brought yeh in – the foreman."

Sure enough, the frazzled woman from before came as predicted, pushing an empty dolly. She huffed and sighed, but Red grinned playfully. Mouse was sure she saw Galena smirk as he began loading the dolly, whistling lazily as he did so. Mouse helped where she could, but the old man was even stronger than he looked. For all her puffing and straining, he had barely broken a sweat. He pulled the heavy crates out and onto the dolly with ease. Mouse stepped back, wheezing, as Red continued. Catching the sight of the backs of Red's massive arms, she gawked at the jagged scars starting at his elbows, crossing and disappearing beneath his left sleeve, and continuing to his collar. Their raised outline snaked through his stained, deteriorating shirt.

"*Grata*," Galena said sincerely, directing her gaze to both Red and Mouse.

Roused from her surprise, Mouse gave a humble nod in return. *More questions, but another time.*

Another bell pierced the air. Galena hurried out of the partition.

"Shift's over," Red whispered. "Time to eat. Follow me."

Red and Mouse worked their way out of their production zone, as the area was called, among a throng of other laborers completing their shifts. They came back to the sheer walkway carved into the rock. Mouse watched as people flowed out from their zones. How many people were here? Hundreds, it seemed. She wondered what the capacity of this place was, and why her assigned number was so low. *That is a good sign, releases must happen often.*

The stream of workers wound back up through the facility, reaching ground level. A dead sort of light filtered in as they made their way out toward a separate bay door from where she had originally entered. Mouse could see the incoming shift at the other door; the fresh force only halted their trained steps to register their cards at the access ports. They disappeared to their respective zones within, lost in the haze of ever-burning fires and the roar of sleepless machinery. Production, it appeared, never stopped here. There were always bodies to fill each level and station. No one looked her in the eyes as she passed.

Ahead, access ports on her exit whirred to life as the retiring shift straggled out. Enforcement squad guarded the door, ensuring only those who were permitted could leave. Mouse followed suit, pointedly staring ahead so as not to draw their attention. The port beeped. She hurried through, relieved to find herself another number in the crowd.

The door let out onto another path, also lined with the strange hourglass-shaped rocks and fencing. Mouse glanced behind her, searching for Red. In the shuffle to exit the plant, she had lost him. She tried to pause, but the crowd trotted hurriedly along. To where, of course, wasn't exactly clear either. Presently, Mouse could see where they were headed; as the path sloped away from the facility, it declined toward and emptied out into the market. With most of the mist burned off from the morning, Mouse could see the flat square stood atop a clearing on a mountainside. The ground, covered in a short, brownish grass, fell away on its sides, where various paths cut in. The paths disappeared into the fog further down the mountain, but a hazy glow along them marked the way. From up there, Mouse appraised the layout of the complex.

On her left, beyond the path to the plant and the fence there that hemmed her in, was another clearing. This one, however, was perfectly smooth and black, shimmering with a metallic gleam underneath the spotlights around it. Enforcement Squad, supervisors, and foremen milled about it. A great smooth machine perched in the clearing, perfectly aerodynamic, and cut from the same metal as the ground it rested upon. It roared and hummed to life, rising with fluid ease from the platform. Mouse watched in awe as it gained altitude and revealed large glowing sapphire discs on its underside. They rotated, spinning faster and faster until the motion seemed to cease altogether. The metallic creature climbed, cresting a thick, steel wall on the left side of the complex. The sentinels on the wall waved it on with red, gleaming torches, and it roared over and disappeared into the mist beyond. Mouse glanced quickly to see what lay to her right, but there was only more mountain, falling down and down until the ground was swallowed in the impenetrable fog.

She continued on to the market, no longer forlorn as it was when she first passed. Each building was now unshuttered, and people thronged around the different kiosks. Enforcement Squad members patrolled the perimeter, ever observing. Dozens of workers clambered around the one marked for rations, while just as many flocked to another stand, marked with an image of a pipe on the opposite side. There was a haze of curling smoke around it as men stuffed handfuls of dark leaves into their pipes and lit them greedily. They smoked in a wide arc by the stand, looking more content than Mouse had seen anyone appear since she woke up. She watched as new arrivals raised their hands to a black surface emitting a single ray of red light. An affirmative beep merited a handful of the leaves; a stringent buzzing caused the vendor to scowl and shove the disappointed customer away. Mouse considered the satisfied stupors of the lucky smokers, but headed to the ration kiosk instead.

The ration vendor appeared to work in much the same way. As Mouse stepped up to the counter and waved her hand in front of the black access port, her stomach growled in anticipation. Her mouth watered when it beeped affirmatively. The surly man behind the counter looked down at her disdainfully and handed her a sealed, square container. There were words on it, but she couldn't read them. Mouse looked around in confusion. The crowd pressed in, pushing Mouse away from the kiosk. *What am I supposed to do with this?*

She turned the container over in her hands as she walked to the common area. There was some space here, though people still huddled in groups, some laughing loudly, others talking in furtive whispers. Mouse ignored the needling eyes of the men she passed. In the midst of the clamor bobbed a familiar head of black, braided hair, glinting beneath the market's lampposts. Mouse weaved her way toward her excitedly, slipping through the jostling crowd. When she was close enough, she whispered, "*Un-tre-sin!*"

135 jumped as she spun around, her deep brown eyes wide, comely face flushed and anxious. She exhaled sharply as she looked at Mouse.

"*Ah, Un-qwa-sah,*" she said, relieved. 135 waved her hand invitingly, and Mouse followed her to a set of empty chairs on the outskirts of the market.

"Thank you," Mouse said in Gormlaean as they sat, to which 135's face lifted.

"You learn!" she exclaimed, her accent heavy. "Good!"

"Um... a little," Mouse answered shyly, struggling to remember the words. She turned her attention to the odd container, still infuriatingly unopened.

135 giggled and gently took it from her. She pulled a hidden tab on the corner, creating a small hole. Handing it back, 135 lifted her own container and hungrily slurped its contents. Mouse nodded gratefully and tipped the rations toward her lips. A thick, tasteless paste drained into her mouth. She grimaced and pulled it back in disgust.

135 laid a sympathetic hand on her knee. "*Taku.*" She gestured toward her mouth with pinched fingers. "*Taku, tahj 'alquuw.*"

She raised her arms and closed her fists, coiling muscles for emphasis. Mouse sighed, and satisfying the aching in her famished, distended belly, she gulped down the rest.

Across the market, Mouse caught sight of Red. Mouse observed curiously as the crowd swayed and parted for him. He walked with purposeful, regal strides, stopping every so often to exchange words with those standing nearby. She couldn't determine what he said, but he leaned in with an intimate confidence, leaving them with a handshake or a pat on the shoulder as he moved on. Men and women alike either nodded deferentially or allowed quiet smiles to grace their otherwise despairing faces. Red looked up, smiling as he passed Mouse on his way to the smoking stand. She hopped up after him and took her place behind him in line.

"There's not much I know yet," she breathed in the forbidden language, just loud enough for him to hear. "But I think people trust you. You're a good man, aren't you?"

Red turned, scoffing.

"No, I don't think I could be," he whispered in reply, shame filling his eyes.

"Why do you say that?"

"Whatever I did... whatever I can't remember... well little one, I'm here, aren't I?"

"So?"

"Maybe some of us deserve this place is all."

Mouse silently considered this, struggling to find words to console him. Words failed. She felt it – the weight of whatever she was – pressing down on her chest, screaming she deserved the shame of her language, her people, of death. She knew he felt it, too.

Red sighed, turning again to say something, but stopped short. He stared past Mouse, his face contorted, fists clenched in rage.

"What is it?" Mouse questioned apprehensively.

"Slim," he muttered accusingly, and that's when Mouse heard her whimper.

She whirled around. Behind her, a short, pale man stood behind 135. He pressed himself against her, his left hand clutching her hip as his lips grazed her ear. Tears stained her flushed cheeks as she struggled, but his other hand yanked her braid with humiliating deprecation.

Mouse pirouetted wildly, searching the crowd for hope of help. The Enforcement Squad looked on with lethargic disinterest while those nearby shuffled away, involving themselves in suddenly urgent conversation or in studying the laces on their boots. There was only one other witness, and he was barreling toward the scene with indignant fury.

"Stop it, now," Red growled.

The man Slim glanced up and froze. Red came to a lumbering stop before him, dwarfing Slim's slighter frame. Mouse couldn't understand as Red spoke, but his words were hot and laced with venom. Slim did not reply, but his eyes burned with hatred. For a moment, neither moved. Even 135 stopped squirming.

Finally, Slim relaxed his grip, and Red backed away, allowing 135 to shimmy out of his arms. But a sinister grin spread Slim's ugly mouth, revealing crooked blackened teeth. Her eyes grew wide in horror as he whispered once more in her ear. And before Mouse knew it, 135 was sprinting across the market, Slim's cold laugh hounding her as she ran.

The market froze. Every voice ceased, every breath held tightly against hearts stopped in chests. Not one sound, except for the pounding of 135's boots.

The Enforcement Squad weaved among them now, black blurs shoving through the crowd in stasis. Gun barrels winked under the lights of the market. The guards were shouting. Commands Mouse now recognized. Stop. Halt. Shoot.

"Stop," Mouse mouthed weakly. The air caught in her throat; she had no voice, no warning to give. But 135 sprinted on, heedless. *Why won't she stop? Please, just stop.*

Mouse watched helplessly as one guard dropped to his knee. The sniper took aim. His rifle erupted, its blast screaming through the air like a white, hissing snake. And just as 135 reached the edge of the market's plateau, it burrowed into her back and burst through her chest. She disappeared over the edge, falling forever into the fog below.

He lowered his weapon. Mouse blinked into the gathering dark.

CHAPTER FOUR

It was still and silent when Mouse woke, startled to consciousness by the sound of her own breathing and the urgency of a familiar dream.

She forced herself into quiet introspection. Frequent but ever elusive, the dream quickly deteriorated. She wracked her brain, making a note of every detail before each slipped away. There was the face, she knew this – the woman's face, always indistinguishable, except for her perpetual concern. Mouse sighed in exasperation. This was all she could ever ascertain. The woman, the face, the concern. Like so many nights before, it was gone, leaving her with a head full of questions and a wild thumping in her veins.

Too awake to settle into sleep again, Mouse propped herself up on a skinny elbow and brushed a few untamed hairs out of her eyes. Shapes grew out of the darkness. There were the rows of cots, the bare floors, and the white washed walls, slowly but surely crumbling away with the wear of time. The only thing that had changed was the number of restless girls in each sagging, rusting bed. More had arrived, just as Mouse had, to stay in the Adolescent Barracks. More numbers without names, ebbing and flowing in endless succession. Some moved onto the Women's Barracks as they aged out of these quarters, but more simply disappeared from Misty Summit altogether. There were rumors, of course; rumors they had been integrated successfully into society, but Mouse knew better. People didn't leave Misty Summit because of good behavior.

The Summit. Home sweet home, she scoffed. *And how long have I been here? Months? Years? Lifetimes?* It was hard to say. Each day ran headlong into the next, and it was difficult to distinguish the longer she breathed the mountain's sulfuric air. In that time her body had grown; even hidden beneath the ill-fitting clothes and hindered by meager rations, it was taking on a more womanly form. It was a fearful thing, growing to maturity here, but all that really mattered was she had survived. For now.

She examined the room quietly, wondering what nightmares affected the sleeping silhouettes around her. Not one of the girls here, she noticed, could sleep without stifled moans, tears, or whispers. Many times she thought to reach out, shake their shoulders, and tell them, especially the new ones, all would be well, but Mouse didn't have much of a gift or liking for that sort of deception. So many had gone, like shades melting into the dark, always leaving an emptiness behind them she could no longer pretend to bear. They thought her reserved, or aloof, maybe, but they had not yet seen her world.

Still, the question of the face bothered her, and it would have been nice to share it here, while the memory was still fresh. She pondered the possibilities alone instead. *Who is she? My mother?* It could be. Some did become mothers here, and she must have had one. But she had also seen the way mothers and children were; how intensely they loved right up into the time the children were taken away. And Mouse could not recollect that attachment, that great pain. There was only the burning curiosity of never knowing. It was this apathy that made her wonder if the woman was her own wild creation – a pathetic, hopeless fantasy fueled by desperation and desire. Neither of the explanations satisfied.

The face, she feared, was another question lost to an answerless past, a prisoner of her own uncertainty. Mouse sighed and muttered a curse to whatever capricious god or unfortunate accident had made her to be so inquisitive. Not much got to her anymore, but this one dream, this irresolvable question that demanded a satisfying answer, was driving her insane. *Well, so what?* Mouse thought bitterly. *What if she's my mother? She's gone. Either she's dead or she didn't want me.* Mouse wound up here, after all, at the Misty Summit Healing Camp and Manufacturing Facility, where the vast multitude of the useless, unable, and unwanted lived in broken resignation. Then again – oh! That abominable curiosity! There was no way to know for sure, not without proof, without solid evidence of what was or what is. Mouse clenched her teeth, annoyed that this same curiosity too often strengthened an already brutish resolve. Even so, elusive as the truth was, she would always be determined to find it.

Mouse peered carefully past her bedframe to the door as the gloom of the early morning waned. Milgrim snored on in horrid contentment, the only person whose sleep remained unplagued. Mouse had two theories to explain this. One, Milgrim was too stupid for the sort of sophistication that spawned existential fear. The other, she considered her abusive dominion over little girls the happiest of callings. And why wouldn't it be? There was no threat to her reign from the supervisors, and no end of girls to punch, kick, spit on, or throttle.

Yes, Milgrim's self-given duty was to beat every new rabble into submission. Even so, she never lost her particular distaste for Mouse, and used every opportunity she could to show her. Thanks to Red, Mouse picked up Gormlaean quickly enough, if only to predict when Milgrim meant to cause her harm. Of course, that was Milgrim's most natural inclination, but knowing when her curses carried special vitriol was immediately useful. She could avoid the inevitable maelstrom of blows that would follow. Most of the time.

The beast stirred.

"Get up, you lazy filth!" Milgrim barked. She ripped the thin sheet off one unfortunate girl with one hand while striking her with the other. Whimpering, the poor girl slunk to the floor and darted in the opposite direction. For her size, Milgrim maneuvered with surprising stealth, and though Mouse might be considered clever, the woman had managed to catch her off guard at times. She hated that. Lights flicked on and Milgrim strode purposefully about the room, encouraging any hesitation with a murderous glare. Today she was on the warpath, eager to get someone on her bad side. Mouse was even more eager to stay off it. Already dressed, she hopped to the ground and raced to the door.

Mouse stepped out of her quarters into the damp morning air, thick with the mist that perpetually shrouded the mountain. She breathed in as deep as she dared, the sensation akin to covering her mouth with a wet towel dipped in sulfur. Mouse resisted the urge to cough, pulled her shirt over her lips, and drew in shallow breaths. This was going to be a dismal day. On some rare occasions, Mouse could see far enough to just make out the edge of the summit, and even the rest of the mountains in their range, rising in jagged slopes beyond the barracks. On those days she could barely taste the air, the walk to the plant an almost leisurely stroll. Today, however, she would be happy just to see her hand in front of her face. The mist coated her in a fine layer of moisture and soot, and for a panicked moment, she had the impression it intended to crush her. She shook the feeling, jammed her hands into the pockets of her coveralls, and trudged aggressively on the cobbled path.

Her steps quickened as she ascended, ever aware of the peril of solitude. The Women's barracks were close to the edge of the summit, away from Enforcement Squad numbers, and too close to the Male Barracks for her comfort. Not that the Squad's presence conjured any genuine feelings of safety, but at least Slim and men like him didn't prey on girls openly when they were around. Usually. Even so, men at Misty Summit were a great deal fewer than the girls and women, and men, it was said, had needs. Their actions were to be expected.

She glanced over her shoulder as she crested the hill to the market. Her quarters sunk into the mists, and no one had yet followed her. For now, she was alone. Her thoughts strayed back to her dreams, her memories of a life past. She only had fragments, and when she pieced them together they never made any sense. There was the woman, yes, but there were sounds, smells, sensations of touch that awakened and resumed their slumber instantaneously, as if something, someone were pushing them down. Mouse looked again at the mists behind her, and she felt them enter her mind, ever obscuring whatever was below.

Trekking through the empty market, she ignored the stands and the angry aching in her belly. Today, if she were lucky, would be the first time she ate in three days, thanks to Milgrim. Rescinding wages was her favorite punishment, besides bludgeoning. Mouse looked down at her boots and considered eating a few strips of leather to get through the day. Not worth it, she decided. The body would survive a little while without food, but it was useless without a good pair of shoes.

A rumbling on the landing strip garnered her attention instead, and Mouse watched with interest as a large, metal-plated hovercraft powered up and glided out of the transport bay. Hurriedly, Mouse pulled a creased, dirty piece of paper and pencil from the front of her coveralls. The hovercraft whirred loudly, the radiant blue discs spun and vibrated with their momentum. She examined the rough schematics she had drawn during the last transport and sketched in some minor adjustments. The craft thundered away, weaving magic about the mountain top until it was a distant rumble. *Now, if I had just five minutes inside.* That was all she would need - a few minutes to walk around, throw some switches, and touch some buttons. And like every other machine on the summit, she'd master it.

She continued her climb, arriving at the chute near the entrance of the facility. There was a crowd now, jostling to get inside the courtyard. Mouse slowed her pace, not particularly anxious to join the fray. She scanned the signs on the high fences as she ambled, now able to read them as she passed: DANGER: ELECTRIFIED FENCE. Reading was not discouraged here, for those who could read were allowed to do the work that required it. And that privilege came with a small wage bonus. Her groaning stomach nearly convinced her to take the aptitude test, but every other fiber in her being warned her against it. Don't stand out, they said. Better to live hungry than to not live at all.

"Can you believe them?" an Enforcement Squad officer complained to a supervisor beyond the fence as Mouse passed. "Sauntering in here, telling us how to do our jobs. If I had a bronze piece for every time a Party Representative—"

"Watch your tongue!" the supervisor hissed in reply. "Or they'll cut it out of you!"

Mouse slowed, pretending to tie her bootlaces just ahead of the conversation. The supervisor continued in a subdued tone. She strained to listen.

"The Coalition just wants results, that's all. We're very close…"

As naturally as she could, Mouse stood, not daring to linger in earshot any longer. *So the Coalition was here.* She glanced at the closest holograstone containing the image of the lovely serene woman smiling out with deep, dark eyes. Her embroidered red and white robe and intricate onyx pendant gleamed luxuriously from the glowing orb, making Mouse feel naked and shameful under her stately, sightless stare.

This, she had learned, was a Coalition Party Representative. The rulers of her rulers, a dignified people of grace, beauty, and refinement. Mouse had never seen a *real* one, but their faces always filled the holograstones, explaining plant procedures and safety measures, ever reassuring the trauma victims of Misty Summit their work was the road to recovery, the path to freedom. The Representative continued on stoically as Mouse listened.

"As always, our concern is for your safety. It is only within the bounds of the Misty Summit Complex that such safety can be guaranteed. Therefore, travel to and from the mountain is restricted to Coalition approved personnel. Reports have confirmed sightings of Mistwolves several miles from the gate of the complex, so keep in mind the appropriate safety procedures…"

Mouse shuddered. She had never seen a Mistwolf, and hoped she never would. If the stories were true, it meant she faced a gruesome death. According to them, these creatures inhabited the vales below the summit. They were said to be enormous, with gray coats that concealed them easily in the mists, gifted with an intelligence that could only be matched by their insatiable hunger. They traveled and hunted in packs, making them all the more dangerous to any poor creature caught wandering in their vicinity. Some said they were a force not even the Coalition were able to control, and others that they were demons from the old days, and as such no one could kill one. Mouse even heard if any poor soul were to look the beast in the eye, the sight would torture him into insanity.

"It's true, you know."

Galena, Mouse's production zone manager, strode up beside her. The woman rubbed her eyes sleepily. "I never believed it, not until last night."

"What are you on about, Gal?" hollered another woman joining them. "Them beasties ain't real. No way I believe it, I'd bet ya half me wages."

"Then you'd be a poor meal before they ate you up anyway, you grimy old hag!" Galena shot back.

Others gathered, their curiosity piqued.

"Alright then," the challenger said, crossing her arms. "Let's hear it."

"Mist was thick as boiling metal last night," Galena began, launching into her tale. "Dark as coal and hard to breathe. They called me back to help unload the transport that came, you see, down in the bay. And it was a full load, not to mention two Reps along for the ride."

"Yeah, we already heard about that, Gal, last shift told us when they came i' the morning!" a voice piped up in the crowd.

"I ain't done yet!" Galena growled, glaring at the guilty interlocutor. "Anyway, so the driver, he says to me, 'I seen a pack of Mistwolves on my way up, they followed us to the base of the mountain. Lost 'em in the fog though.' It was then—and I swear on this old rock this is true—I heard the howling. Oh, it was a sound I never heard before, you can believe that. A sound like… like words in the howls, all hungry and terrible. They were talking to each other, not a doubt in my mind that they were! Froze my blood solid."

"Did you see 'em?" someone asked earnestly.

"Well, I wasn't standing on the wall, was I?" Galena answered sarcastically. "Of course not! But I'll tell you what. You won't ever find me out on night shift again, not even if they gave me triple wages."

"More for the rest of us then!" the original challenger scoffed, gaining murmurs of agreement from some of the crowd. The murmuring hushed as the complex's loudspeaker crackled above them.

"Proceed to your workzones immediately," it ordered.

The crowd dispersed obediently. Mouse followed behind, images of snapping, dripping jaws filling her head all the way to the access ports.

CHAPTER FIVE

A wall of hot, sooty air smothered Mouse as she entered the plant. The production zones writhed with harried workers, crates upon crates of parts passing between hands, loaded onto carts, and hoisted up pulleys. Shafts of slick gun barrels filled many crates to the brim, reflecting the vermillion glow of the cavern's dim light. Others contained assorted hardware and pieces, but Mouse thought she could guess at their purpose. *More guns.*

There were people everywhere, impeding Mouse's progress to her own zone. Many, she realized, were still working from the night before. She pushed her way through as the interior loud speaker whined above the noise of the facility.

"Last shift laborers of zones one and four are dismissed. Zones two, three, five, and six will exceed normal shift capacity until further notice. For your safety, routine physicals will be performed on select laborers throughout the next few weeks. Thank you for your cooperation and admirable attention to duty. Remember, work is freedom, and you hold the key."

The loudspeaker cut out abruptly as the shift-ending whistle screeched over it. Some dead-eyed workers shuffled exhaustedly by, but the rest continued their furious toil, ignoring its persistent wailing.

Mouse quickly calculated the bodies remaining in each zone. The plant had to be at three times normal capacity. And, she noticed, the place crawled with supervisors.

It was easy to pick them out from among the common rabble. Though not as polished as the healers or as stiffly uniform as the Enforcement Squad, supervisors confirmed their status with clean trousers, unblemished boots, and shaved faces. Badges with names, real names, identified them, and most of them bore a closer resemblance to the Party Representatives than of those clad in worn coveralls and stained shirts. They held themselves with an air of menacing self-importance, and those who did not cower beneath them paid for their impudence dearly. But today the supervisors flitted like nervous birds about their zones as they barked orders and harassed those slow to obey, betraying the urgent fear behind their hard, sulky grimaces.

Mouse waded into the flow of replacement forces, which was more or less at a standstill as dismissed shifts straggled out among them. She looked up curiously as a flash of bright blue caught her eye.

It came from outside of the spiraling levels of production zones and on the walkway just above the massive storage and receiving bay to the right of the great cavern. Here were the testing rooms and offices of the healers, the Healing Ward, sealed off from the rest of the plant by a thick glass panel and heavy door. On any given day, Mouse could make out the shapes of smocked men and women behind the glass panes, undefiled and secure in their sterile environment, but it was never very clear what they were doing there. Still, even in her curiosity she never lingered. Only some returned from the Healing Ward, and of those who did, their minds did not return with them.

Warily now, Mouse watched as the flash of blue, a healer in his clean lab coat, descended the metals stairs from the walkway. He nodded to the Enforcement Squad personnel guarding its entrance and strode methodically toward the production zones.

Workers scurried out of his way as he drifted through the crowd, leaving a wake of empty space behind him. Mouse stifled a shudder and moved aside, doing her best to shelter among the others. She wasn't fast enough.

The healer's hand brushed past her own. He withdrew it hastily, looking down his nose at the unlucky offender. Mouse's breath caught in her chest. She pressed against the person behind her, cornered, but he barely registered her presence. The numbered masses of Misty Summit meant nothing to him; at least, not until their number came up. He coughed in disgust and moved on, his search continuing.

The healer stopped in zone three, the mid-zone where many of the parts were processed and packaged as hovercraft cargo. The crowd around Mouse cautiously filled in behind the healer as he approached a quivering man there. Mouse could only guess at what was being said, but the laborer mopped his brow with his sleeve, nodded in resignation, and accompanied the healer back to the unknown. Again the crowd parted, its silent apprehension unnoticed amid the plant's normal mechanical roar. The two walked through unheeded, a frozen and calculated smile on the healer's face as they went.

After they had passed, Mouse dared an inconspicuous look. They clanked up the metal stairway, through the heavy door, and to the sterile, white corridor beyond. She watched their forms distort and blur behind the glass, wraiths in blue descending upon them. And then, they were gone.

The crowd thinned out now as workers broke off to their assigned places. Mouse drew a long breath, the humid air doing little to calm her senses. This unlucky laborer wasn't the first to disappear for a "routine physical," and Mouse knew he wouldn't be the last. She stooped to retie her boot, her racing heart refusing to slow. The questions that entered her mind now, questions she wasn't sure she wanted to answer, kept its rhythmic thump galloping about her ribcage. *Who was next?*

Mouse squeezed her eyes shut and shook her head, dispelling the thoughts as best she could. It wasn't much use. The numbing fear pulsed in her fingertips, adrenaline-soaked sweat beading on her temples. Her neck began to prickle, and the sensation of hairs standing on end rippled down her spine. It occurred to Mouse, however, that these sensations were independent of her internal turmoil. No, she realized, someone was watching her.

She stood briskly and wheeled around, catching a pair of shrewd, cold eyes staring her down. The owner of the eyes, none other than

Slim, leaned jauntily against the closest structural pillar as he toyed with a twisted metal rod. Mouse's own eyes narrowed and she returned the stare resolutely, defiantly. An ugly smirk turned up the corners of Slim's mouth, but he relented, slipping his hands into his pockets and slinking away.

Unnerved, Mouse watched him disappear into the recesses of the cavern. It was not long after 135's last breath that Slim dogged Mouse, gliding along in the dark, waiting like an opportunistic bottom feeder for her to make the fatal mistake of being alone. He had other quarry, of course, but Red's protective interest in Mouse intrigued Slim all the more, for what man does not want what he cannot have? She often imagined his shadow even when it was not there, and in the empty spaces between the plant and the barracks, fear was her constant companion. Still, it kept her wise, pragmatic, alive. One did not last long without it.

After a time, Mouse felt she could safely turn away from the pillar where Slim had stood. Down she went, nimbly weaving through the stragglers of the night before who shambled up the steps. She arrived at her zone, full of crates, parts, and people, and picked her way along to her partitioned corner.

Red looked up briefly as she entered, sighing as he plucked more pieces from his current crate.

"Sit yourself down," he grunted. "Looks like we'll be busy today."

Mouse acquiesced silently, pulling up her own crate with a grimace as a bleary-eyed Galena wheeled in a dolly of five more.

Galena yawned. "Oh look, you're finally here. No supervisors down yet, but turn out as many as you can before they come meddlin'. Get to it."

Mouse made a show of prying at a crate with a crowbar until Galena hurried out, muttering about the blasted Party Reps. As the partition closed, she dropped it, picked up a round part instead, and spun it disinterestedly on the tabletop. It teetered and toppled noisily, and Red eyeballed her over the edge of his magnifying glass with an air of grandfatherly disapproval.

"Alright, alright, I'm on it!" Mouse replied. Red smirked and continued silently scraping at the small part swallowed by his massive hands.

"Is the deburring machine busted again?"

"Yep," he sighed. "Blame the last shift."

"Well, that won't do. You'll be at that forever." Mouse hunted under the wooden table before pulling out a hidden cache of tools. As she had done many times before, she set to work on the machine.

"You better be quick, little one!" Red boomed over the machinery.

She smiled mischievously. "Keep an eye out and time me."

Though plant policy mandated only appointed engineers had permission to repair the machinery that kept the Summit going, Mouse never could keep her hands off them. It began on a day when production was slow and supervision limited. A surge of curiosity and courage caused her to tinker with one of the ancient, long-deceased machines gathering dust behind her partition. Like a complex puzzle, she tore it apart and pieced it together perfectly, finding and fixing the broken component in the process. From then on, she cautiously sought out limping machines, restoring them to working order in stolen, secret moments. Even so, no one mentioned or noticed the forbidden practice. Maybe it was ignorance, or maybe the machines would never be attended otherwise, but even Galena turned a blind eye to the miraculous recoveries of every damaged vessel within walking distance of Mouse's station.

She chanced a furtive glance over her shoulder as she rapidly pulled the cover of the deburrer away from its metal body. "I had the dream again."

Red didn't look up but raised his bushy brows attentively. "The woman again?"

"Yeah," Mouse grunted, digging around in the deburrer. "It's the eyes, you know? Like she saw it all coming. But I can never get past that. I can't know if it's real."

"More will come," Red assured her. "If you're lucky enough to stick around like this old man, that is."

"Anything new for you?" Mouse asked hopefully.

"Well, not much, lately," Red said cryptically. "Still, that little girl in the field, crying out to me. Still the great big yellow light shining down, and then... the fire. But they're clearer now, every day just a bit clearer, and it only started with the girl, you know."

"I'm sure she's out there, Red. We'll find her some day."

With a snap, Mouse put the machine's cover back in place and tightened its bolts with deft dexterity. She toggled the switch, satisfied to hear the gears whirring rapidly.

"Done!"

Red grunted in approval. "Quicker than last time, I'll give yeh that."

Mouse beamed at the work well done. She turned to gloat, but words left her as she caught sight of the old man. Red hunched dejectedly over the table, every line on his face furrowed deeply as he stared hard at his worn hands.

"Red," Mouse said softly. She moved to his side. "What is it?"

Red turned his piercing gaze toward her, focusing with the same intensity he had formerly devoted to his hands.

"Do you really think yeh can do it, Mouse?" Red asked. "Find her – the little girl – that is?"

"I think *we* can," she answered slowly.

"She won't be so little, you know. I've been here too long for that."

"Red," Mouse whispered. "What's this really about?"

"The Party Representatives," he replied with a hoarse whisper of his own. "There's a reason they were here, little one. I've heard things, and they're not good."

"The physicals," Mouse added breathlessly. "It has to do with them, doesn't it?"

He nodded grimly. "They're taking us, one by one."

Mouse stared down at her boots, her mind straying to the conversations and events she witnessed before arriving that day. Yes, it was true, and it had been like this since day one. She had a made a point not to dwell on these truths, to move on, and feign ignorance; to survive the only way she knew how. But the reality confronted her, gnawed at her, and as Red whispered it, she knew she could no longer push away the questions that threatened their fragile existence.

"What are they doing to us, Red?"

He shook his head. "I can' say. But whatever yeh think, I'm tellin' you it's worse. With those Reps showin' up, I can tell yeh one thing, I don' think it'll be long before–"

"Don't say it," Mouse interrupted. "It'll be fine."

"Little one," Red sighed with resignation. He reached for her hand, his calloused fingers engulfing her petite ones with a firm but tender clasp. "This old man's lived long enough to know what's coming."

Mouse squeezed her eyes shut, forbidding the hot tears to flow. Red held her hand a little tighter before placing his other over top, slipping something hard and sharp into her palm. Mouse ventured a peek as he released her hand. It was a flat and small rectangle, made of materials she didn't quite recognize. There were strange, metallic designs etched on the outside, connecting in lines and circles. On its backside she observed tiny, teeth-like prongs. Only one thing she knew fit that description.

"A wage card?" she guessed.

"Something like it," he said sagely. "But so much more. Now you listen to me – don't let that outta your sight, not even for a minute."

Mouse nodded solemnly and placed it carefully in the front pocket of her coveralls.

"When you're done here today, go see my bunkmate, Twitch. You'll find him by the blackleaf stand. Jumpy fellow at times, but decent. Ask him for my things, he'll know what you mean."

"Can't you tell me why?" she asked.

"You'll know, in good time," Red answered. "Oh, but there is one more thing, little one. There's a place, on the other side of Misty Summit, where I go to think sometimes. It's by the west wall. Yeh ought to try it out yourself to clear yer head… maybe even tonight, if yeh think it'd do you good."

Mouse frowned, opened her mouth, and promptly shut it again. Red's attention was once again on his work, his expression as impassive as always. *Why the west wall?* She ruminated. It was an unspoken rule, but the workers weren't allowed on the far side of the complex. Some said Mistwolves could breach the walls there, while others swore it was the stinking pit where those who disappeared slept forever. In that place beyond the male barracks, falling into the mountain's mists below, those with an ounce of sense did not stray. Whatever business

Red had there, Mouse was sure her survival depended on not taking part in it.

She flipped on the deburring machine and worked through her crate, alone with her thoughts. So absorbed she was in them that Mouse had not noticed the wraith in blue beyond the partition, drifting closer and closer until it was too late.

CHAPTER SIX

Mouse could not move. Her blood ran cold inside her as the machine whirred on, grinding the metal nut in her hand to a fine, metallic dust.

The healer who entered their zone wore a white coat over his blue garment and instruments dangled out of its pockets. He smoothed his short, dark hair and furrowed his groomed brow, both of which complemented a clean-shaven and well-cut jaw. Keeping a wary berth he approached.

Red, for his part, shrugged off his presence until the man stepped just beside him. Even on his stool, Red's shaggy head remained level with the healer—a fact not lost on either of them. Red pointedly ignored the man until he addressed him

"Worker 24?" the healer denoted in a commanding tone.

Red stiffened, turning ever so slightly in acknowledgement.

No, don't take him. She thawed enough to move, slowly, methodically, and shut off the deburring machine. Her breath caught in her throat as she fought her limbs for normalcy.

She walked haltingly to the table and picked up the examination glass, chancing a covert glance in Red's direction. His face was stoic as the healer spoke quietly to him. Determination, not resignation, etched the creases around his eyes. To Mouse, he appeared more a warrior leader now, ready to fall beside his kinsmen in the lost battle. There would be no retreat or surrender, only death in defiance.

In the moments that followed, Mouse began to comprehend the conversation taking place.

"...and so you will need to accompany me to the healing ward for your physical," the healer finished explaining. It was polite enough and he mustered a smile, but his knuckles were white as they gripped his tablet, his shoulders rigid as the small tendons on his neck rippled beneath the skin.

Red nodded beyond the partition, where, as Mouse quickly realized, two Enforcement Officers stood with hands draped loosely over their batons.

"No need to bring out the welcoming party for little ol' me," he said with a smirk.

The healer's eyes narrowed shrewdly. "Some workers are more averse to routine checkups than others. Everyone here benefits from the presence of order. We wouldn't want an unnecessary misunderstanding now, would we?"

"I understand yeh well enough," Red replied coldly, his hand coiling about a nearby crowbar.

The healer stepped back in alarm as the Enforcement Squad made their way in. One officer rapidly produced a rifle. Mouse stared hard at her work, but was all too aware it was not leveled in Red's direction, but hers.

"Your appointment is on my schedule and will proceed as planned," the healer demanded. He inclined his head thoughtfully at Mouse. "I can make it my last one for today, with your cooperation."

Red's grip slackened. With a nod from the healer, the officers stepped behind Red, their truncheons pressed into his back. He stood, towering above them, but he didn't resist. Mouse could not breathe.

"I think yeh'll find my results unsatisfying, sir," Red's icy threat came as they guided him away.

"We shall see," the healer murmured as the partition's flap closed behind him.

For a long time, Mouse didn't move, frozen in a terror she had never known. The production zone around her still buzzed and clinked with the life of the other workers continuing on in oblivion. Aware she was not breathing, she steadied herself against the table and opened her mouth to catch the air. The taste of dust and metal caught her in her ribs, and she coughed and covered her mouth to keep from being sick.

Ice again clogged her veins as the scene replayed in her mind. What could she do? For a moment, an insane impulse to charge after them surged through her. Red had gotten her out of so many messes of her own; wasn't there a way to get him out of his? But the impulse passed, and an awful emptiness swallowed her. *There's nothing you can do,* she thought in despair. *He's gone, and chances are, you're next. This is it.*

Mouse collapsed onto her workbench and mindlessly pulled the crate toward her. She could not think, not now. And yet, without direction from her brain, her hand wandered to the front of her coveralls and patted it reassuringly. Beneath the panic, another voice persisted.

No, this isn't it.

Her hand rested on her chest, its heaving calmed as her wits returned. She lifted her hand and peeked in the pocket, studying its contents. The wage card that was not a wage card. Twitch. The west wall. Now Red's words echoed clearly in her mind, and suddenly it made sense. *Instructions. Not suggestions.* If Red had a plan, its success depended on her getting out. It was not much to go on, but there might be hope – maybe even for Red. All she had to do now was find Twitch.

The screeching of the shift-end bell took Mouse by surprise. Her heightened sense of danger had caused the time to pass unevenly; excruciatingly slow in her solitude and in sudden, rapid succession each time Galena entered the partition to remove and replace crates. Indeed, it was not Galena she expected, but the wraiths of the healing ward or the black bludgeons of the Enforcement Squad.

They never came. As the bell sounded, the loudspeaker crackled to life.

"Attention, laborers. Zones will return to usual capacity unless otherwise noted by your foreman or Supervisor. All shifts should proceed under normal schedules."

Mouse blinked back tears.

Falling into the relieved crowd of exiting workers, she made her way to the community market, walked hesitantly into the graveled square, and carefully watched the crowd. She dared not ask around for a description of the man she sought. Instead, she hoped the "jumpy fellow" characterization would make him an easy find.

A few workers lingered in the nearly deserted market. She had better luck of picking him out in this thinner line-up. Still, there was no telling who could be watching. Mouse threw a quick glance over her shoulder, just in case. No one paid any mind to the boyish girl hovering around the square, and so she proceeded, winding her way through a small group of hungry workers gathered impatiently around the rations vendor. Slowing as she neared the outside of the group, she chose her place carefully among them and scanned the crowd.

Her gaze settled on four men as they loitered by the blackleaf kiosk, already enjoying their purchases. One man, standing furthest from the vendor, looked the part. He was easily into his forties, maybe older, though Mouse couldn't always tell. Everyone looked older than they were here. He had a gangly profile, thin and weak next to his brawnier companions. Straw-like hair sprouted from his balding crown and hung limply on his shoulders, fighting a losing battle with age and stress as it slowly slid off his head. His long, sallow face bore a wary countenance, which was home to a pair of sharp, deep-set eyes that constantly roved the market. As he smoked from a pipe, he shifted from foot to foot, watching.

Mouse drew a deep breath before stepping out of the crowd. Red's opinion notwithstanding, she got the feeling Twitch was only decent when he had to be – and Mouse was not the intimidating type. *Well, there's not much you can do about it now. Here goes nothing.* Mouse shuffled toward the blackleaf vendor. She managed a few paces before he had spotted her, his shifting eyes finally resting. The others also watched as she drew closer, needling her with a cruel amusement.

"Twitch," she attempted with some authority, cringing as her voice wavered childishly instead.

"Who's asking, then?" he said, smoking nervously.

"Mouse." She then quickly added, "A friend of Red's."

Understanding dawned on the man's face. He pulled the pipe from his mouth.

"Right. Collecting his things. Sentimental reasons, yeah?" The man winked, and her skin crawled.

"Um... yeah."

"Right, right." Twitch looked from side to side before continuing. "And you've got something for me then?"

Another wink, at which she wrinkled her nose indignantly. "You want payment?"

Twitch smirked. "Well, that's usually how these things work."

The men with Twitch snickered, to which Mouse responded with a glare.

"Fine," she said, not bothering to hide her frustration. "Blackleaf to your heart's content."

"Aw, I was hoping for a kiss," Twitch replied with a wounded simper, answered by a renewed chorus of snickers from his cronies. "I guess that blackleaf will be pleasin' me longer, though."

"That's what I thought," Mouse spat in disgust. She hoped Red had the sense enough not to confide in this man as she approached the kiosk.

One brief transaction later, and Mouse handed her entire day's wages over to Twitch in a wrapped, brown package.

Twitch's eyes lit up.

"That'll do it! Follow me."

Twitch nodded to his companions and turned toward the Male Barracks. She hesitated, every animal instinct she possessed pleading with her to walk the other way.

Twitch limped down the path for a minute before glancing back impatiently.

"Hurry on up, little girl!"

Mouse put her hands in the pockets of her coveralls and followed.

Evening was falling upon Misty Summit as Mouse and Twitch walked to the Male Barracks. Paired with the heavy mist creeping up the mountain, the darkness was suffocating. Mouse could not see Twitch in front of her, but she could hear the sound of his shuffling gait as he kicked into the gravel and stone along the way. The occasional luminary along the path served as her only guide besides him. Each cast a hazy glow in the evening mist. She hated not being able to see, but comforted herself with the thought that no one else could, either. Twitch also seemed to appreciate this as he scraped along. There was one thing they both had in common: neither of them particularly relished being noticed.

Mouse felt the ground level out as she followed, and even in the thick mist, recognized the great spotlight ahead. Twitch's shuffling ceased, and she stopped a few steps behind him.

"You still there, yeah?" Twitch's voice cut through the fog.

"Yeah, I'm here."

"Alright then. Wait here, and I'll be coming back to you with Red's things. You might want to stand off the path a bit—no telling who'll be coming this way tonight."

"Okay, I'll be here, by the light."

Twitch's dragging footsteps grew softer as he shambled away. The soft click of a door and a voice she didn't recognize told her he had made it inside. Quietly, Mouse withdrew from the path to wait. She wrapped her arms around herself and shuddered. It was too far, too dark, too risky. She had never been on the path Twitch took to the Barracks; the main path leading from the heart of the market hit each of the sleeping quarters on the way, so the workers had little reason to use this one. Mouse peered around fruitlessly, hoping to gain her bearings. In the mist, her internal compass failed her. She would have to follow the path back up to the market if she wanted to get back, and hope no one else met her along the way.

A long time passed before Mouse heard the clicking of the door and the familiar shuffling gait. The footsteps approached the luminary she waited by, stopping a few feet away.

"Psst!" Twitch hissed in the mist. "Still hanging about, little girl?"

"Still here," she replied shortly, miffed at the pejorative. "That took you awhile. Was there much to bring?"

Twitch's silhouette materialized as he approached. She could only see his face when he stood right under the lamp next to her. Holding a pillowcase in his left hand, he gave it a shake, which subsequently rattled.

"There was a good amount, yeah."

Mouse breathed a little easier. Twitch was a coward and a cheat, but he had at least made good on their deal. She reached forward to grab the bag. Before she could do so, Twitch pulled it out of her reach.

"Ah, not so fast," he said.

"I came through on my end," Mouse said flatly. "Your turn."

"Yeah… see, that's the thing," Twitch said, searching the empty air nervously as he swung the pillowcase around. "With people just disappearing, getting sick, or what have you… I've got to be sure I'm making the best deal. You understand. We made a pretty decent one, sure, but then again, if I play my cards wrong, I won't be here to enjoy tomorrow."

"But you agreed!" Mouse insisted.

"You need to understand, sweetheart–I'm a businessman. And, well, a better opportunity presented itself." He shrugged, almost apologetically. "That's just the way it works."

"What did you do?" Mouse nearly shrieked, her heart pounding. "Did you tell the supervisors?"

"No," a familiar voice answered, cutting through the fog. "He told me."

Another silhouette formed out of the mist behind Twitch and approached the dim light of the luminary. Mouse recoiled as Slim swaggered toward her, leering from the shadows.

CHAPTER SEVEN

"So, the little mousey has come out to play tonight," Slim mocked, an ugly sneer curling his lips. "Didn't expect to be caught in the game, did we?"

Her mouth hung open, fear choking the breath out of her. He had finally cornered her, and there would be no one to rescue her this time. How stupid she had been! No doubt Slim caught Twitch going through Red's things inside the Barracks, and scared the coward into telling him why. She did not know whom she resented more – Twitch for his pathetic notion of self-preservation, or herself for ignoring her instinct. Settling on the former, she cast a murderous glare at Twitch, who shrank back like a whipped dog. At another time, she may have pitied him, but now, she could think only of his betrayal, and she let herself go numb with rage. Anger offered her some strength, relaxing the hold panic had taken before. Then, a moment of clarity. Slim might do heinous things to her, things that not even the Healers or Supervisors would do, but at least he would never have the pleasure of tasting her fear. And if anything, he would not have his way easily.

"So what did you offer him?" Mouse returned icily. "His worthless life and some blackleaf to betray his only friend's last wish?"

Twitch winced at the mention of Red and stared hard at the

ground. Though she had turned her glare toward Slim, she caught him shrinking shamefully out of the corner of her eye.

"That was basically all it took, yeah," Slim replied nonchalantly. "But what else was he going to do? Grow a backbone?"

He laughed openly at the idea. Twitch managed to cower so low to the ground he nearly disappeared.

"No. The only backbone that one's ever had was that lumbering troll. His 'only friend,' as you so sweetly put it. And if I'm not mistaken… you two have that in common."

Mouse refused to dignify Slim with a response, even if it was true.

"Now, Twitch here made a choice. A dirty little one, yes – but poor ol' Red's gone. He knows the game's changed. He knows who's in charge now. And that's a lesson I intend to teach you tonight."

"It was you," she said, the horrific realization overcoming her. "You tipped off the supervisors, didn't you? They took him... because of you."

"He got what was coming to him," Slim growled. "Getting to enjoy the supervisors' protection is a nice added treat, isn't it? And now that Twitch here has been so kind as to gather up the criminal's personal affects, well, looks like I'll be their darling for some time."

Slim turned to look at the whimpering wreck beside him. "Don't you agree, *friend*?"

Twitch wrung his hands and looked over Mouse. Such wretchedness and great misery swelled behind his eyes, and Mouse thought he might throw himself off the mountainside if he could. His face twisted grotesquely. Might he still be vulnerable to his convictions, weak as they were? Red had believed there was something good in him after all. Maybe she could prove him right. Mouse turned to Twitch, her arms open in appeal.

"Red told me you were a decent man. He told me he had only been able to trust two people, and that was you and me."

Twitch eyed the ground. Mouse pressed on. "Now, he asked you to do one thing. One little thing, for the man who had protected you, cared for you, befriended you." Mouse thought she saw his eyes grow wet, but she could not tell in the dull light. It was now or never.

"I'm just glad that wherever he is, he's not here to see this… he'll never know how gutless you really were."

"Shuddup!" Twitch suddenly burst out. He shoved his hand forcefully through his pocket, grabbed his pipe, and tried to light it. His hands trembled so violently he could barely strike the match.

"I done my part, Slim. I'm leavin'."

Slim's sniggering stopped as he shook his head, responding with steeled savagery. "Not yet. You haven't finished helping me."

"Aw, come on, Slim, I've done what you said, I don't see what else I have to do." Twitch retreated, but Slim grabbed the front of his coat and yanked him to his side.

"You're going to hold her. Until I'm done."

Twitch looked from Slim to Mouse, working his quavering jaw. Finally, with a helpless groan, he dropped the pillowcase containing Red's things by the lamppost.

"I'm sorry," he mumbled stupidly. Mouse gritted her teeth, preparing herself for the fight she would lose.

To her amazement, Twitch threw himself upon Slim instead, shrieking.

Slim stumbled and crashed to the ground, grunting with surprise. Limbs flew in all directions as they grappled. Mouse froze, astonished.

"Get away!" Twitch cried to her. "Run!"

Presently, Slim kicked through the chaos, effortlessly toppling his uncoordinated attacker. A metallic flash gleamed in the lamplight before it plunged into Twitch's ribs. He howled in agony.

Lights around the Barracks burned through the mist. Slim swore, a great wailing sound penetrating the fog. Yanking his shiv from a gasping Twitch, he wheeled around to face Mouse. She cradled the pillowcase tightly, gaping, paralyzed by the sight of the dying man. Slim flashed her a psychotic smile, and over the wailing of the alarms she could hear him calmly say, "Oh, I'm going to enjoy killing you."

Slim lunged forward, only to stumble as Twitch stretched out a blood-soaked hand and clung desperately to one of his ankles. Disgusted, Slim kicked off his slipping, weak grasp. The distraction, however, was all that Mouse needed to escape. A string of obscenities followed her as she tore off into the darkness. Mouse had no idea where she was headed, but she would get there fast. On impulse, she swerved toward her Barracks, but as the blaring sirens grew louder, she remembered where she was: trapped between Milgrim and the Enforcement Squad, and Slim. She skidded just short of the halo of light surrounding her Barracks and pivoted away, turning instead toward the west wall.

The lights behind her became hazy orbs as she fled, and she lost herself in the shadows of the mountain. Wet grass and earth slipped beneath her feet, every blind step a gamble. Would the ground betray her as well? She sped on, hesitantly presuming upon the kindness of the fickle dark to hide her. Suddenly, Mouse's feet found firm, flat ground.

The lights and sounds were now far off, distant like a bad dream. Maybe, on a night like this, no one would know where to look for her. She labored to breathe as she ran, the taste of soot filling her mouth and nose like sand. Adrenaline surged through her, begging her to flee, but she could not.

Mouse slowed to a jog, the clamor and spotlights swallowed up in the mist beyond her. She stopped, painfully aware of how loud she was in this sudden stillness. It was the pillowcase; it jostled noisily any time Mouse moved. She twisted the case closed and wrapped it tightly around her right arm. Now she looked around intently, searching for a landmark she might recognize, but the night had masked everything only steps away. This was no place to stay, and yet, there was nowhere to go. Mouse lingered, unwilling to commit to any one course. Her breathing, still ragged from her flight, shattered the silence, and Mouse got the feeling she was trespassing here.

It was strange, Mouse thought, to be so close to danger, and yet feel so far removed from everything at the same time. It was the air, which was lighter here and no longer tasted of soot nor lay heavily on her skin. She could breathe so easily. For the first time, Mouse could see freedom in this darkness, and taste it on the whispering breeze now stirring the haze. Fingers of churning mist receded briefly to reveal a small, glowing orb only a few feet ahead. Mouse crouched low, scrutinizing the light carefully. The light was weak, winking briefly as the mist obscured it.

Curiosity outweighing her caution, Mouse advanced toward the dim light at a crawl, sidling through the darkness in silence. It towered over her as she approached, its position high on an unseen post or pole. Wisps of mists swirled in the soft breeze, momentarily revealing the large, shadowy object before her. *Now what could that be?*

Mouse proceeded, crouching, hands held out in timid apprehension. Her fingers scraped rough, aged stone, crumbling as she disturbed it. A wall, she realized, but not like the wall surrounding the complex. At the entrance of Misty Summit, the thick, metal behemoth stood fifteen or so feet high and was wide enough for the Enforcement Squad to station posts around the clock on its top. This ancient but formidable barrier was fortuitously vacant, but from what she could tell, still too tall to climb.

She sighed. Where was she now? Mouse stood up and followed the course of the wall, running a hand against it as she walked along. The rough imperfections and weathered grooves of old stone caught the calluses on her fingers; the sensation strange yet comforting after spending her known life handling the metals of the plant. Though the mist had begun to roll off of the mountain, the night deepened, darker and heavier than when she had first slipped away beneath its cover. For the moment, she was secure in its obscurity.

The gully by the wall was worn, and Mouse detected ruts in the packed and hardened ground. It was a sure sign that Enforcement Officers regularly patrolled the area, by vehicle and foot. By some stroke of luck, Mouse was between patrols. *But not for long.* She continued tentatively, making sure to keep an eye and ear out for anyone nearby. Her tired, sore, limbs begged her to slow her pace, or even lie down and rest them, but every phantom sight or sound in the darkness urged her on. By the time she would be aware of a patrol, she realized, it would be too late.

The wall fell away from her trailing hand. Mouse stopped immediately, peering into the dark to make sure she had not missed a turn. It continued straight on in the direction she was headed. Confused, she ran her hands over the surface of the stone. Sure enough, something was missing. Though the darkness concealed it well, there, just where the stone should have been, was a crumbled gap in the wall. Mouse turned to face it and again ran her hands against its edges. The gap was about a foot or so wide – not wide enough for her to fit her shoulders in straight on, but if she turned herself sideways, she was sure she could squeeze herself through it. It had collapsed down into a v shape, widest at the top and smallest at the bottom. *Maybe if I could climb up into it, I could get a better look at where I am.*

Bracing her hands along the inside of the eroded wall, she heaved one leg up, attempting to push off with the other foot and then straighten her leg to stand. The gap was high, but she grunted with approval at her first successful attempt. She stood inside it, now high enough to get a good look around. Only tendrils of the mist hung about the summit now, and she saw some distance into the complex. Lights glimmered from far off, but she did not hear the sirens. Her flight had taken her down the side of the summit, into the feared trenches of the west wall where bodies went to rot. Thankfully, she had not seen any – yet. She gazed upward; the lights sat like little lanterns high up on the mountainside as the black earth sloped gently away from them. Mouse and the west wall were obscured in the summit's shadow, its natural darkness a welcome comfort. Pushing herself further into the crack, she twisted to explore the other side. The wall was surprisingly thick, maybe almost as thick as the rest of the complex's barriers. She squeezed and jimmied herself through until she could peer out the other side.

Mouse gasped in awe. Even in the darkness, she witnessed the outside world for the very first time. The cloud cover over the complex continued out into the vast sky before her, the angry, red glow muted but still illuminated the landscape enough for her to survey its enormity. An entire mountain range stretched out to the horizon before her, spreading jagged shadows on an already dark world. It made a rough semi-circle around a great valley steeped in a thick blanket of fog. From here, Mouse could also see the slope of Misty Summit. Rocky outcroppings and small boulders dotted the mountainside, all the way down into the valley where they disappeared into the mist. Small, gnarled trees grew among them, breaking up the barren landscape with knotted roots and shades of grayish green. A thin brook originating from another part of the summit snaked down into the valley, glinting like a fiery writhing worm beneath the dark crimson sky. Mouse gazed long at the world before her, unable to decide if it was ominous or peaceful. It struck her that the only thing she had ever seen in her life, that she could remember, anyway, was the inside of the complex. Stepping slightly outside of it, however, even if just for a moment, stirred up feelings she could not recall nor explain. She wondered now if the tales of the Mistwolves had been just that—a lie to keep her and her fellow workers crippled by fear and cut off from any hope of experiencing life beyond these walls. And, if that were true, she had nothing to lose.

That's well and good, but what if it is true? Galena's story quickly came to mind. Even if she was exaggerating, Galena had heard something, and that something was still out there, lurking in the shadows and the mist, waiting. Mouse considered the possibilities once more. Getting torn limb from limb and eaten alive was no better than a violating death at Slim's hands. And yet, the unknown horrors suffered by the taken niggled in the back of her mind. It was a bleak choice. She squeezed herself back to the middle of the crevice to think, sinking down until her knees touched the broken wall in front of her. Wedged in and alone, Mouse wished she could see enough to look through Red's things in her relative safety. Maybe there was something there that would help her, if only she could reach down into the sack and find it.

Just beyond her crevice on the complex's side of the wall, a soft rustle whispered in the grass below. As carefully and quietly as she could manage, Mouse shifted herself toward the opening and peered out. In the darkest hours of the night, nothing moved, save for the mist ebbing away from the summit. Mouse breathed a soft sigh of relief. Solitude.

A pale hand shot into the gap and grabbed Mouse by the shoulder of her coveralls. She yelped as the hand dragged her down, her face scraping the gritty wall. Mouse braced herself within the gap as best as she could, digging in, and frantically fighting against the relentless pulling. Slim's pallid, wild face appeared in front of the opening.

CHAPTER EIGHT

"Looks like I found you." Slim said, a ferocious and deranged grin upon his lips. He drew in tired, shallow breaths, sweat dripping from his forehead and foam bubbling at the corners of his mouth. Blood, brambles, and mud covered his torn clothes, as if he had clawed his way out of the ground just to find her. His fist clenched the fabric of her coveralls tightly, furiously pulling at them to bring her closer. Mouse let out a frightened squeak as she fought against his grip.

"Thought I wouldn't be smart enough to realize you'd come out this way, did you?" Slim snapped, jerking her violently. "Well, I was! I knew ol' Red must have something pretty valuable in there, or else he wouldn't have made sure you got it. And you knew it too… that's why you ran this way. Didn't want the others to find you with it? Didn't want anyone to know?"

"Let go of me!" Mouse cried. "It's got nothing to do with you!"

"No?" Slim growled. "You listen here! Do you know what I'm gonna do? Do you? I'm gonna do a little magic, see…"

Slim tugged harder, prevailing, and she slowly slid toward him. She could see the whites of his eyes glowing with sinister satisfaction in the darkness.

"Once I pull you out of there, I'm gonna have my way with you.

By the time I'm done, you'll be begging to die." Slim's eyes gleamed ravenously as he spoke. "Then I'm gonna wring the life out of you, I'm gonna watch you die, slow and painful. But don't you worry, lovely, I'll make sure this sack of yours is safe with the Enforcement Squad. You'll be making Slim their hero after all."

Mouse whimpered as Slim dragged her toward him, his face now level with hers. He gawped at her, licking his lips hungrily as he drew her closer.

"Shh, shh, shh now. Don't make a fuss. You'll ruin the fun."

The palms of Mouse's hands began to tear and bleed as they slid against the stone, failing to stop her descent to certain death. She searched the crevice frantically for something, anything that could save her, when her gaze fell upon the pillowcase, still wrapped tightly around her arm. It hung heavy on her, grinding painfully against her wrist as she tried desperately to pull away from Slim.

With a swing of her arm, Mouse slammed the contents of the case onto the top of Slim's head. He bellowed in surprise and pain, his grip loosened briefly. Slim swayed and toppled backward for a moment, but it was enough for Mouse to pull herself free, scurrying back into the gap. The crumbling rock scraped at her arms and face again as she dragged herself through the crack, but she felt nothing but the exhilarating rush of freedom. At the other end of the wall, Mouse stared out into the black, unknown world from which she had retreated only moments ago, terrified of the consequences. As Mouse glanced back through the crevice just as Slim was hoisting himself up into it, those consequences were much less concerning now.

Just as she had, Slim found it fairly easy to slip himself through the crack in the wall. Frantically, she looked down, swiftly judging the distance to the ground. This side of the wall was much higher, the ground beneath hard, rocky, and unforgiving. Even so, broken ankles or skulls were small matters if she wound up dead first. With a deep breath, Mouse got herself as close to the edge as possible, and closing her eyes, jumped.

She landed on her feet, but pitched forward upon impact and fell on her hands and chest. The blow knocked the wind out of her. Mouse rolled to her side, dry heaving. The sky above her swam a little as the pain swelled, but it subsided in time for her to see Slim's head poking out from the gap above her. As quick as she could manage, she rolled back to her hands, pushed herself up, and began sprinting headlong down the mountainside.

The gnarled trees and great boulders blurred and faded into darkness as she whipped past them, her downward momentum carrying her further along the slope than her tired, aching legs could on their own. Her knees buckled in complaint at every forceful plant of her foot. Still she continued her dangerous descent, too afraid of falling to stop or look back. Scattered sticks, loose stones, and overgrown roots laid treacherous traps for her. By some miracle she went on, only narrowly avoiding a trip or slip that would have her tumbling down the mountain. Over the sound of her own body crashing through the undergrowth, Mouse could hear Slim close behind. He roared murderously down the summit, his footfalls and breaths heavy.

Mouse made quick work of getting down the mountain, but Slim gained with every step. Her lungs burned and legs began to crumple, but she did not stop. Terror whipped her onward even as the mountainside plunged into the sea of mist in front of her. She could lose him in the mist, as she did before, but there was no telling what was waiting for her beneath its pall. With no time to think, and no option to go back, she took a leaping stride into the shroud. Fog settled on her skin as it swallowed her whole. The taste of sulfur and grit filled her mouth and she stopped short, coughing and struggling to breathe. Mouse looked intently into the fog, but it was useless. Wisps of white seethed in every direction, heavy like a drape upon her shoulders. It was this heaviness that nearly overwhelmed her, catching the breath in her throat and pressing tightly against her. Mouse tried to breathe normally all the same, hoping her wheezing breaths had not already given her position away to Slim or anything else lurking in the haze. She pulled the collar of her cotton undershirt up over her mouth to stifle it. This served to filter the air, and for the time being, it relieved Mouse of its distinct taste. Calmer and no longer gasping, Mouse proceeded deeper into the fog.

There was no mist like the one that now enveloped her. She passed through, its thick, opaque layers like parting curtain after curtain. It muffled the sound of her very footfalls from her own ears. Mouse could only wonder if Slim had actually followed her. She listened for a moment; there was nothing. Maybe he could not hear her, either. Then again, he had found her all too easily only moments ago, even after she had eluded him half the night. Mouse picked up her pace, attempting to walk in a straight line. Though rendered deaf and mute by the mist, she kept on, hoping against hope that she would not cross paths with her pursuer. Beneath her feet, the terrain changed, exchanging the rocky soil for short grass and sparse undergrowth. The tiny teeth of thorns and brambles snagged at the legs of her coveralls as she passed. A heavy hush blanketed Mouse as she continued into the valley. Nothing but the air stirred around her.

Silence. Had Slim lost her? Maybe, but Mouse could not shake a base fear that there lay a greater danger in the quiet. It was this quiet that was all wrong. Many nights in the Barracks, she had often laid awake, listening to the sounds of various creatures in the dark. She had not expected to see them in the mist, but she thought she might at least hear something. Yet everything around her fell deathly still, just as if these same creatures collectively held their breath, hushed and hidden from that which lurked within. Presently, the scent of sulfur and soot she had come to know so well mingled with something else, something foul and stomach-churning. There was only one smell she could compare it to, and that was the stench of that terrible house along the market she encountered her first day on the summit, the Disease and Injury Unit. *The smell of death.* A prickle of fear ran down her spine. What horrors did she blindly wander toward?

The sound of heavy footfalls floated dully on the thick air. Mouse halted mid-stride. Slapping footsteps stopped abruptly, any echo dying immediately in the dense air. From what sounded like miles away a loud cackle erupted, and she could hear Slim, yelling through the fog.

"What are you playing at, little girl?" he shouted with sadistic amusement. "Ready to give up, yet?"

Mouse turned round in a panic, but she could not see two feet in front of her, let alone wherever Slim stood. Could he see her? Or did he just hear her breathing? Mouse crouched and held her shirt over her mouth. A cold laugh reached her ears.

"Ah yes, it's been a long night, but you've learned an important lesson... Slim always gets what he wants."

Without warning, the foul odor now permeated the air. She gagged, the suddenly pungent stench overwhelming her senses. Slim must have smelled it too, for he choked as well.

"Aghh, what is that? Hey! Get back here!"

Mouse furrowed her brow, thoroughly confused. His mocking tone suggested he had once again cornered her, and yet Mouse felt he was very far away, too far away. *Does he see me, or only something he thinks is me?* Mouse made herself as small as possible, gripping the ground with quivering hands. The mist, suddenly turbulent, displaced above her, and the prickling shiver returned to race down her spine. Mouse swiveled her head as slowly as she dared.

Just beyond the opaque curtain of mist loomed a shadow, dark and vast, moving stealthily to her right. A sense of crushing terror came crashing over her, and she bit her lip to resist the overpowering desire to scream. The shadow turned away, fading once again into the mist. She nearly collapsed in relief, but steadied herself as she heard Slim's pounding footsteps again, though farther from her than before. They stuttered to a halt.

"You're done. I've got you," he said.

Low, rattling growls disturbed the heavy air. Mouse more felt than heard them, and panic rose in her throat. *Keep still!* She thought desperately, fighting the impulse to flee. She could hear Slim shuffling his feet, stop, and turn about. An unnerving silence filled the space between them and lingered, broken by a sudden, ear-splitting scream.

Shadowy masses rushed past, the mist cresting and falling like waves around her. Mouse covered her ears and cowered close to the ground, unable to stifle the sounds of Slim's shrieks of agony. The only sound that could drown that horror out was the clamor of barks, snarls, and howls that followed. Then, a sickening crunch, and Slim's screams ceased. Mouse covered her mouth, the ripping of flesh and cracking of bones raised bile in her throat. It would not be long, she knew, before they sensed she was there. Even with the hot scent of blood in the air, the monsters were bound to smell her. Mouse inched to her feet, listening for any changes in their growls that would indicate they had heard her. The Mistwolves continued to gorge noisily. Mouse moved, she hoped, in the opposite direction. As the feast went on with no regard to her presence, Mouse turned swiftly and ran.

For a moment, Mouse could hear nothing but the sound of her own breathing rushing past her ears as she sped through the darkness. But the frenzied din of feeding ceased. Behind her, several deep barks answered vicious snarls and other unearthly utterances. A fear even unlike that which she just experienced took hold, for in that moment she knew Galena's tale held true – these beasts were speaking to one another.

Shapes loomed and faded as she ran past, giving Mouse the impression the fog was beginning to dissipate. A chorus of haunting howls penetrated the mist. The monsters were close, and they were drawing closer. Adrenaline surged through her, giving new strength to her exhausted, failing body. And yet, to her right and left, Mouse could make out the massive lupine shadows of the Mistwolves. They loped effortlessly beside her, so close she could distinguish the sound of their shallow panting from the soft padding of their paws. *They're playing with me,* Mouse realized. *And they're just waiting for me to give up.* Those aching legs begin to wobble beneath her, and she knew it would not be long now before they would have no more to give. Mercifully, she did not have to wait to collapse in the creatures' midst – the ground betrayed her now, seizing her boot as she rain over the plain. She catapulted out of it and hit the ground at a roll, skidding several feet from her dislodged footwear. Her body somersaulted, kicking up dirt, dust, and straw that subsequently clung to her coveralls and hair. Quickly, Mouse turned over and around to face her end. She was not going to die lying down.

The haze of the mist cleared rapidly around her, but a wall of it remained steadfastly from where she had come. Her eyes grew wide as two shapes lurked just beyond the curtain.

And then they appeared.

CHAPTER NINE

Two Mistwolves padded out of the heavy wall of mist, snarling at Mouse as they approached. From their paws to their hackles, they stood at least two feet taller than she, and they were twice as long. Though a little thin with hunger, their sinewy haunches coiled powerfully beneath their fur. In awe and terror, Mouse watched as they snapped and barked at each other, their great, shaggy heads swinging from side to side. Two cold, black eyes sat deep beneath the brow of each wolf, and their ears swiveled and twitched with anticipation. They sniffed the dank air with their short, broad snouts, drinking in the smell of sweat and fear that permeated Mouse. Below their snouts, great, powerful jaws larger than her torso hung slightly open, and each displayed an impressive set of curved, yellow teeth. They were still stained from their last gorging, and their mottled gray and black coats were matted and dripping with the moisture of the humid air.

The Mistwolves continued to bark at each other. At another time, Mouse might have found the exchange fascinating – it sounded just as if they were arguing over what to do with her. She looked into their black, roving eyes – intelligent, stony, hungry. Those eyes watched her intently. They shuddered their colossal bodies, snapped razor-edged jaws, and stamped impatiently. Though each massive paw the size of a shovel, still the beasts lumbered toward her with impressive stealth. There was no creature more streamlined to slaughter than the ones converging on her now. These were the things of nightmares. A sudden and silly desire to laugh came over Mouse as those black eyes and gaping maws stared her down. How had she survived even this long? Had they sensed her presence this whole time, and as chance would have it, Slim was simply the first to die? And with their appetites at least partly sated, did they amuse themselves now by prolonging the hunt? Mouse gulped weakly, and unable to help herself, vomited.

They waited, milling around a short distance off. One of them let out a few short barks, and then turned its shaggy head to look behind it. Another shadow approached. Padding into the clearing, another Mistwolf, larger and older, stepped between them and growled authoritatively. He turned his great head to reveal a broken, seared ear and vacant eye socket, and shook his shaggy, black-and-brown flecked coat with pride in their presence. The first creatures whimpered and tucked their tails between their legs in deference. It snarled savagely and bared sharp, stained teeth. *This is it.* Mouse thought as she sat upon the ground, too weak to even stand. She raised her chin, searching for something, anything other than those ripping jaws to fill her mind. And on the horizon, past the bearers of death, she found it. Day was breaking.

Every morning on Misty Summit was one obscured by the veil of thick clouds, but high above them, even on days when the mist was impenetrable and oppressive, daybreak fought to make itself known. It was the hidden light beyond, illuminating the world with day, piercing the fog, even when she could never truly see it. She knew this was the natural world's quiet promise and comfort: even night had to yield to the day, no matter how weak its light might seem to be.

And, as she faced the darkness and its monsters, hope stirred within her, the sliver of orange-tinged gray rimming the world as it spread through the cloud-masked sky. The feeling was strange, but also wonderful, nostalgic as a memory, and it filled her with some intangible longing, peace, and strength. The Mistwolves gathered themselves now in attack formation, but here Mouse found her legs to stand, ready.

Fangs glistening and jaws dripping with anticipation, they began their onslaught. Mouse stared defiantly, unable to keep from back-pedaling but facing them all the same. She could already feel their hot breath creeping over her skin as they drew closer. *Here come the teeth.*

She tripped backward over something that felt like a thick, metallic rope. A wall of pikes rose from out of the straw, and Mouse shrieked as they flew up around her. Shining, blinding spotlights, affixed to the pikes, took aim at the wolves. She blinked in disbelief as the beasts halted dead in their tracks, emitting an arsenal of angry howls and snarls at the lighted posts. Mouse scooted away, watching as the wolves yelped and scratched at their ears. Slowly, but surely, they retreated, growling as they re-assimilated with the mist. Their shadows disappeared, and soon, so did their howling, dying away to empty echoes as the mist swallowed them. All that was left was the unusual buzzing emanating from the pikes.

Mouse stood shakily. The lightening sky above revealed a brand new world below, and Mouse stumbled about it dreamily. *Am I really alive?* She rubbed her eyes and patted her arms and legs hesitantly. Only she and the pikes remained. They glared brightly into the wall of now receding mist – the last vestiges of a nightmare Mouse could not believe she had survived.

Mouse walked around the sharp sentinels and paused, considering their mysterious ability to stave off Mistwolves. Jamming her hands in her pockets, she came around to the front of the posts, observing them quizzically. Each pike was about seven feet of cylindrical metal. A circular spotlight radiating a painfully bright glare shone out from the center of each post. The row of pikes itself was not actually that long; it did not even stretch further than a few yards. Mouse wandered around to get a better look at the display, kicking her bare ankle against the taut rope responsible for her fall before.

She looked down to examine it, discovering a thick, heavy cord suspended a few inches from the ground by short, wooden stakes. Searching along its length, she could see the cord and the supporting stakes stretched far beyond the posts and snaked across the field she stood in. The section she had tripped over appeared to be vibrating. *Ah! It's a tripwire.* She must have triggered it during the attack.

Mouse gazed beyond the posts, which guarded the middle of a great field. Short, yellow-green grasses and various kinds of low-lying bushes and brambles covered the expanse below the mountain. There was straw strewn about, concealing, she imagined, more of the strange barrier. She searched along the trajectory of the pikes to the outcroppings of small, bushy trees lining the horizon some distance away. Trees were few and far between on the summit and the surrounding mountainside. Mouse faced the summit once more. As the mist burned off with the dawning of the day, she could see where she had come from that night. Part of the field was still veiled, but rising from above the mist was the mountain that had held her captive for so long. It was not the largest in the range, but the slope was steep. The rocks on it became more and more numerous as they climbed up the mountainside, until they abruptly stopped at that old stone wall. Heavy clouds cloaked the rest of the summit from her eyes. She hoped that meant no one up there could see here, either.

Lost in thought, Mouse gazed up at the mountain. For the first time, she saw a world other than Misty Summit. It was hard to believe, and even harder to have any idea of what to do. After all that she had been through, she had not considered the possibility of survival – but here she was, alive and relatively unscathed. Remembering why she had gone through all this trouble in the first place, Mouse lifted the pillowcase, still wrapped securely around her arm. It was covered in filth, but intact as it jangled against her. With her other hand, she checked the front pocket of her coverall, sighing in relief to find the chip card safely inside. What to do now? She wanted to go through Red's things, but doing so where she had narrowly avoided death did not seem wise. Mouse needed to seek refuge somewhere. But first, her bare wriggling toes reminded her, to find her boot.

She spotted it a few yards away, jutting out from a dip in the plain. With a grunt, Mouse unwedged it, wondering if the extra distance the tumble put between her and the Mistwolves was what ultimately saved her life. She sat down. Just as she finished re-lacing her boot, however, something jabbed her in the back.

"Now, don't do anything crazy," a voice said behind her. "Stand up and turn around. Slowly."

Mouse complied, raising her hands and turning to face her captor. She was surprised to find a lean boy with warm bronzed skin and strong arms, about her age or maybe older, nervously looking down the end of a long barreled rifle. Taller than she, but not by much, the boy straightened, no doubt hoping to appear imposing. Despite his obvious discomfort, he nestled the weapon against his broad shoulder with expert ease. Messy black hair fell defiantly over his ears and eyebrows, curling slightly at the ends to allow him to see from two bright, honey-colored eyes. He dressed plainly, wearing a short-sleeved, cotton shirt, hide trousers, and muddy, leather boots. His only other accessory, a steel dagger, glinted at his hip.

"Oh!" the boy said, surprised. "I'm sorry, I thought you were a boy."

He stammered in mortification. "That's... ah, not really what I – um – meant, I just... uh..."

"Don't worry about it," she said, relieved to see a friendly face. "But if you feel bad enough, you can lower that thing."

"Oh, right." He put the gun to his hip and scratched his head in embarrassment. "I guess you're not a bandit then, huh?"

"A bandit?" Mouse chuckled. "No. There's nothing out here, what would anyone be after?"

The boy nodded toward the posts. "The tripwire's made of pure Kyrthite, of course."

Mouse frowned. "Kyrthite?"

"Oh, you know, super-conducting metal... powerful and durable. Very expensive."

When no comprehension dawned on Mouse's face, he shrugged. "You must be a city girl, huh? Say, what are you doing out this way, anyway?"

"Um... I, uh, just lost my way, I guess." Mouse shrugged, hoping she offered a nonchalant smile.

The boy raised an eyebrow curiously, but, instead of pressing the issue, held out his hand. "I'm Berr-Toma Breythorn. Call me Toma."

"I'm Mouse," she replied awkwardly, returning the gesture.

"Mouse?" he asked. "Well, that's different."

"I guess it's kind of a nickname," Mouse replied. "You know, from… the city."

"Right," Toma acknowledged slowly.

He continued to eye her, inspecting her as one would a strange creature. And what a strange creature Mouse was – standing in a barren field in her work attire, covered in dirt and sweat and sick, clutching a jangling pillowcase and looking, she imagined, thoroughly out of sorts.

"Any chance you could tell me where I am?" Mouse asked, evading the boy's steady gaze.

"Wow," Toma chuckled, brightening. "You really are lost, huh? Right now, you're standing on the property line of Breythorn Farm. The only place stubborn enough to hold a border with the Mistlands."

"This place is a farm?"

"Yes – well, not right here. We just own this land. The Mistwolves don't come past here." Toma frowned. "Although, they have been getting bolder. It's why I came out here, actually. We've got an alert set up at the farm that lets us know whenever the wire's been tripped. We have to come out and reset it, you see. I'll be honest, I wasn't expecting to find anything still alive out here, let alone, well… you."

His cheeks flushed, and for the first time, he broke his gaze. Mouse tilted her head, sizing up the boy before her. She could not remember a time she ever met one her age; only grown men populated the Summit. They were hard, cold, predatory. Excluding Red, of course. But it was not so with Toma. Warmth filled in his eyes, a lightness and innocence Mouse found both perplexing and refreshing. She did not know what to make of all that stammering and stumbling over words, though, and so continued the conversation.

"What scares them off?" Mouse asked. "The pikes don't extend very far. Is it the lights?"

"Exactly. Mistwolves don't come out during the day if they can help it, or they only travel in the mists. Don't know why, but they hate bright light. We've seen them avoid it as much as possible, and they definitely won't stick around when it catches them off guard. So, that's part of what the posts are for."

Toma walked over to the pikes and placed his ear up against one. "Now, you hear that buzzing? That would be the frequency emitters. As soon as the wires are tripped, and the lights go up, the emitters get going as well. It runs a frequency they can't stand."

He bent over and fiddled with a knob on the bottom of one of the posts. The lights suddenly switched off, and the posts lowered back onto the ground. Frowning, Toma stood up and kicked straw over top of them. "I'm starting to wonder if they really work, though. You weren't here, were you? When the wire was tripped?"

She nodded, wide-eyed. "They were after me, actually. I – well, someone was after me. He chased me into the mist. I only got as far as I did because... they got to him first."

Mouse shuddered as she recalled Slim's lasts moments. "I ran while those things were... eating. They sensed me though. I couldn't see a thing, the mist was so thick, but I heard them, just panting, running right beside me. Then I fell, over there. They came out of the mist and charged at me. Then the lights came up, and they were gone. I can't believe I'm still alive."

Toma looked at her, aghast. "They came out of the mist?"

"Yeah," Mouse replied. "I got a good long look at them, too. They were huge."

"I don't believe it. But you're here. My, how did you make it? To actually show themselves! No one I've known has seen them that close and lived to tell about it, that's for sure. That was nothing short of a miracle."

They stood silently for a moment, looking back at the mist. If only Toma knew how many miracles Mouse had experienced that night. He placed a sympathetic hand on Mouse's shoulder. "You have a place to rest for the day?"

She shook her head wearily.

"You look like you could use it! Why don't you come back to the farm with me? My mom's a great cook, and we've got warm water and a room to spare."

Mouse hesitated. Trusting strangers had not gone so well for her lately. And yet, his kindness was a welcome change. And there, while alone, she might actually have a safe and private place to go through Red's things. She offered Toma a tired smile, suddenly aware of every one of her aching muscles.

"Right now, I can't think of anything better."

CHAPTER TEN

Breythorn Farm lay just beyond the clearing, hidden behind the rows of squat trees at the end of the field. Buildings dotted the property, including a large silo, a wooden barn, and a stone cottage sitting at the furthest end, huddled between two gently sloping hills. A wooden fence with wire looped around the top surrounded the inner property, and Toma opened a thatched gate to get inside. Some domesticated beasts Mouse didn't recognize wandered about within, snuffing and picking at the dirt. Toma led Mouse on a path through a group of long, glass-roofed buildings. He pointed out the features of the farm as they passed.

"These long sheds are greenhouses," Toma explained. "With things not growing outside like they should, we've had to find some creative ways to keep the farm going. We've got a few more pigs wandering about here, and some goats and chickens, and two good horses, too. Over there, our irrigation systems, barn, and there, that's the silo."

"Why don't things grow outside?" Mouse asked before she could stop herself.

"No sun, of course," Toma said.

Mouse regarded Toma blankly.

"You know, the sun? Big yellow light in the sky? Hidden by the clouds ever since the end of the Last War?"

Mouse shrugged, helplessly. Toma stopped walking and gave her a long, hard look.

"I don't like to ask too many questions of strangers," Toma started. "Your business is your own. But... you're not telling me something. Now, I'm not saying you're a liar, but I'm getting the feeling there's more to it than just you're not from around here. I'll need to know what's going on straight away before I bring you inside."

Mouse sighed. She wanted Toma to help her, but where could she even begin? His world was already proving to be vastly different from hers. How could she expect to him to understand what had happened, let alone believe it? He watched her intently, his honey eyes scrutinizing skeptically. Sure, he was no Twitch or Slim, but she still knew nothing about him. Blind trust had gotten her into enough trouble so far. Then again, he had been kind, and from what she could tell, honest about himself. She owed him that much, at least.

"Okay," Mouse relented. "Is there a place where we can talk?"

Toma looked around, and then pulled Mouse over to one of the greenhouses. He unlocked the door and held it open for her.

"This should do. Come on in."

Mouse walked into the greenhouse, overflowing with great, leafy plants bedded in troughs of soil. A row of bright lights, similar to the ones that had saved her life earlier, hung over the troughs and bathed the plants in a warm glow. Nozzles sprayed a fine mist throughout the greenhouse. Mouse could feel it sprinkling lightly upon her face, cooling and refreshing her skin. It was so unlike the mists she had come to know. Toma shut the door behind them.

"Alright," Toma said, crossing his arms. "Tell me everything."

Taking a deep breath, Mouse started at the beginning, recounting everything she could remember from her first day at Misty Summit. She told him about the complex, the people who lived there, the dreams that plagued them, and the disappearances and fates of the taken. With a heavy heart, she told Toma about Red and his last day. Finally, she related the events that transpired the night before – her meeting with Twitch gone horribly wrong, Slim's pursuit and attack,

and her escape through the old wall down the mountainside. She fell
silent as she came to the Mistwolves.

"And... you know the rest."

Toma had listened respectfully to her story, but wore a troubled
expression as she spoke.

"You've come from the prison?" he said, hesitantly.

"No," Mouse replied, confused. "I came from the Misty Summit
Complex. Where the manufacturing plant is."

"That's the prison, Mouse," Toma said, his voice low. "For some of
the worst folk, too."

"The Healers told me I was a trauma victim when I woke up
there," she replied slowly. "They said that's why I couldn't remember
anything. I learned a trade there, to use in the real world. Every one of
us was told the same thing."

Toma continued to regard her suspiciously, which annoyed her.
She was telling the truth, wasn't she?

"I'm not a criminal," Mouse added defensively.

"Okay," Toma said calmly. He pointed at the back of her right
hand. "Then what's that?"

"What? Oh." Mouse looked down at the pink scar on her hand
and the slightly raised rectangular lump beneath it. "It's a wage card.
All of our information is transmitted onto it, and at the end of the
work day, we can get whatever we need. Food, supplies, access to the
plant, that sort of thing."

"Listen," Toma began cautiously. "The only people I've known
who've had those scars were people who had been to prison. I've seen
the scars on some of the bandits before, after they get caught... The
Coalition tells us to look for it whenever someone comes by we don't
recognize."

Mouse placed her face in her hands in consternation. "So Red was
right, wasn't he? It isn't just a work facility. It's so obvious now..."

She laughed in spite of herself. "Oh, how could I have been so
stupid? And what a perfect prison, too. We didn't know how we got
there... and how could we leave? The Mistwolves, the Enforcement
Squad... But Red knew. Red got it right."

Mouse closed her eyes, the pain of Red's disappearance all too fresh in her memory. She opened them, only to see Toma giving her a hard stare.

"What?" Mouse snapped, frustrated. "You don't believe me?"

"How can I? You've got the chip!" Toma sighed. "I should've looked for it, but I didn't. You... didn't look the type."

With a doleful expression, he stood and turned toward the door.

"Please wait," Mouse whispered. Without thinking, she grabbed his arm and held tight. "Please. I don't know what you're going to do, but hear me out. I'll admit it, there were horrible people there. I didn't lie about that. But even they did not remember who they were before they came to the Summit. Maybe they were prisoners. They sure acted like it. But just look at me – what in the world do you think I'm capable of? I was a little girl when I was sent there. What crime could I have committed that landed me in a place like that? Just... look at *me*, Toma."

He swallowed, searching her eyes. "You're asking a lot of me. It's not the most believable story I've ever heard."

"I promise, I'm not lying to you. I'm telling you everything I know," Mouse said, at a loss. She held out her hands in resignation. "I know it must sound crazy, but I'm here, alive, aren't I? Against all odds, you know that. Besides, I *know* there is something bigger going on here. More than the fact that they're lying to us and making us think we're not prisoners. And if there's more..."

Mouse looked away, unsure of what to say. Toma had no reason to believe her – and the fact that she could not remember anything did not help. What if she really was a criminal? What if she deserved to be at Misty Summit? Mouse shook the thought out of her head. It did not matter. If she was a criminal before, she was someone else now.

"Toma, you might be right," Mouse assented, sighing. "Maybe I was someone other than who I am now. I don't know. I wish I did. But even so, you or I will never find out if you turn me in. And what if the truth is something else? Either way, don't you think I deserve to know? What happened to Red, what happened to me? Who I really am?"

"Oh... I don't know." He shuffled his feet. Uncertainty clouded his previously resolved expression. "Like I said, the story is a bit hard to swallow."

Toma walked in a wide arc around Mouse, examining her. He put his hand to his chin to think.

"Then again, I've never met a Coat who wasn't a liar."

"Uh, a Coat?" Mouse asked. "What's that?"

"That'll be the Coalition, on account of the coats they all wear. Long, black coats with the Coalition Insignia on it, you can't miss it. But don't let them hear you say that," Toma added in a low voice.

"And you don't like them," Mouse inferred.

Toma let out a short laugh. "That's an understatement if I ever heard one! Do you know anything about them?"

Mouse searched her memory, gathering all the things she had heard from the holograstones.

"Some things. At the complex, they were the only people that the Supervisors and Healers were afraid of. That's how I could tell they were in charge. We had this device, called a holograstone, and there was always this woman in it. She was dressed in such beautiful red robes – so clean, so unlike everyone at the Summit. She also wore this pretty carved necklace. She called herself a Coalition Party Representative and would talk about the dictums."

"Yep, that sounds about right. Dressed in finery, at our expense," Toma scoffed. "Listen, if what you're saying is true, you know, about you not knowing a thing, then boy, are you in for a fun surprise!"

"What do you mean?" Mouse questioned. "What are they like?"

Toma sat himself on the ledge of the trough, relaxing. "Ah, well, you see, the Coalition is our government. Been that way since even before Last War. Pah!"

Toma waved his hand in annoyance. "These fat, greedy Gormlaeans already got *everything* and they have to have all of Reidara, too. The people of the Dell had to have been better off before the Coats came. Happier, at least, to be left alone!"

"Gormlaean..." Mouse mused. "As in the common tongue?"

"Yeah, it's the country that's north of us. Where the Coalition comes from. And this, where you're at now, is Maiendell."

"I see." Mouse frowned. "But how did your country get to be ruled by Gormlaen?"

Toma sighed. "It's been this way for many years, long before my father was even born. He says we used to have a king, but things weren't going so well. Times were hard. Our people were dying. And so, we joined up, and it's been that way in the Dell ever since."

"But you don't think it's better."

"I know it's not better," Toma declared definitively. He shook his head, annoyed. "We're nothing to them. And what belongs to us they claim as their own. I can't tell you how many times the Coats visit the farm to take *their* cut. It seems like more and more every time."

"So now they rule you."

"Yup, along with the rest of the world, I think." Toma nodded. "Coalition nations are Heibeiath, that's the desert country on the other side of Gormlaen, and Elmnas, the mountain lands of the far north."

Her ears perked up at the mention of Elmnas. Her home.

"What can you tell me about Elmnas?" she asked.

"Not much." Toma shrugged. "Well, not much that I know to be true. It's all myth and legend, big, wild, and mysterious. Honestly, I don't even know if there are actually people up there anymore. I've never met an Elmling before."

"Well, tell me what you've heard, anyway," Mouse pressed.

"Alright, here goes. According to legend, Elmnas was a place like no other. It was ruled by people called the Guardians, these mighty warriors who fought with swords. It is said they fought like gods and could rain fire down from the sky to destroy their enemies."

"Swords?"

Toma chuckled. "Some story, right? The legend goes on to say that they all just disappeared. Coalition swooped in and 'civilized' them. If you ask me, it sounds like primitive tribal stuff. Maybe they thought the stories would keep the Coats away."

Mouse pondered Toma's words, wondering what truths lay within the myths. Her thoughts returned to that first day at the Summit, when the healer told her all the people she had known were dead. Was it true that something awful had happened to these Guardians – her very own people – and now they were extinct? Maybe she was the only Elmling left. She didn't want to think about it.

Mouse turned back to Toma, only to realize he was still talking.

"Yeah, it's been hard," he said. "We wake up fighting off bandits and Mistwolves, and come back home to fill their outrageous orders, all stamped with the approval of the CP. My family tries to live as good citizens of the United Dominions, but the Coalition pushes their luck. As for me, I've never trusted them. Any Coalition Guards or Representatives who've come here have all been liars and thieves."

Mouse gave him an empathetic pat on the arm.

"I'm sorry, Toma."

"Me too," he replied. "Still, it's always been this way, hasn't it? What can we do? We're just farmers, my father says. None of us could save the sun. We just read the bad omens and try to survive."

"Do you know what happened to it?" Mouse asked.

"No one really knows." Toma shrugged. "Some say it was natural, others say it was the war. Some of the old women still swear the dark spirits escaped their pits and now rule the air. What I do know is the skies turned red, the world shook, and so many things died. After that, the war ended and no one ever saw the sun again."

"Do you remember it? What it looked like?"

"I don't, it was before our time," Toma said grimly. He leaned over the leafy plants, looking at them tenderly. "My grandfather used to say everything grew tall, and all the fields around here would be blooming in the late summer sun. Rows and rows of big green plants. He says it was something to see. But nothing grows right anymore."

Mouse watched as Toma meticulously checked the settings on the nozzles and the lights hanging overhead. His brow furrowed as he worked, deep in thought.

"Then the mists came," Toma explained. "During the Last War, I've been told. And in the mists, the Mistwolves. People would go out to work and never come back. Eventually, the Coalition sent out dictums on how we could protect ourselves, but by that time our people had them pretty well figured out."

Toma shook his head. "And no one has answers. Where did they come from? Something doesn't add up, you know?"

"I'll tell you what," Mouse said, unraveling the sack from around her arm. "It sounds like you need to find some answers, just like me. Maybe we can find some of them here. It all belongs to Red, and I'm sure he's got something for both of use. If you don't turn me in or tell anyone who I am, I'll share it with you."

With a sigh, his wariness dissolved, yielding into a grin.

"Okay," he brightened. "I think I can live with that."

"Good," Mouse beamed, relieved. "Because I didn't have a plan B! Shall we take a look?"

Toma nodded.

Just as Mouse was about to divulge the sack's contents, however, the door to the greenhouse creaked open. Mouse bundled up the bag abruptly and looked up. A small girl of about eight stood at the greenhouse door, gawking wide-eyed at Toma and Mouse. She twirled her long, dark hair, which fell to her waist, and stamped the mud out of the leather boots laced up to hem of her cotton nightgown.

"I thought I saw you come back," the girl spoke softly. "Mama says breakfast is ready and to come inside. Who's that?"

"This is a friend, Mina. Go on in and tell Mama that we're coming."

The little girl cast one last long look at Mouse before running out the door.

"My little sister," Toma explained, a little self-consciously. "Well, this will have to wait. Come on."

CHAPTER ELEVEN

Mouse followed Toma back to his family home, kicking at the mud as they went along. They arrived at the front step of a cozy stone cottage, which puffed welcoming clouds of smoke from its long chimney. Mouse had never been to a family's house before, having only known the Barracks and Housing Units. In fact, the whole idea of it made Mouse a little nervous when Toma opened the door for her and beckoned her to come inside.

"It's fine," Toma assured her. "We put up visitors and travelers here all the time. No one's going to think anything of it."

She stepped into a small room, where dirt-caked boots lined the floor and coats hung from wooden pegs attached to the bare wall. Toma kicked off his own boots and placed his gun against the wall before hopping up the two steps that led to a short hallway. Mouse followed Toma through the hall, where he stopped at a doorway on his right and motioned for Mouse to join him. She came up next to him and peered in the room. Six sets of eyes gazed back at her.

"Oh! Hello!" a woman called cheerily from within. She resembled Toma, slighter and shorter, and smiled with warm, almond-shaped eyes. The man next to her, sporting the same messy hair as Toma, bowed his head politely. Weathered and dark, he appeared to be in his early fifties. Three boys had packed themselves on the bench on the far side of a long, wooden table, and all of them stared at her shyly, hiding their faces behind the edge of the table. Mina peeped out from behind her mother, her inquisitive, large eyes probing Mouse. Breakfast must have just been set before them, for the food still steamed and simmered in their bowls. It occurred to Mouse it had to be rather early in the morning. She rubbed her eyes, the memory of her darkest night wearing on her.

Toma put his hands on Mouse's shoulders. "Everyone, this is a new friend. She goes by Mouse, and she's from the city. Mouse, this is my family. My father, Berr-Teo, my mother, Sheimee, my brothers, Jorem, Kendir, and Henlin, and of course you've already met Mina."

The children waved hesitantly from behind their plates. Sheimee smiled and beckoned to Mouse.

"Please, sit. We have only just started, and there is plenty to eat. Have you been traveling far?"

Toma stepped in for her. "Yeah, she was on the path to Anders, but had lost her way. When I went out to reset the posts, I ran into her and invited her to come back."

"I see," said Sheimee. "We are glad to have you. Stay as long as you need – the route to Anders is a long one, especially on foot."

Berr-Teo scanned her, puzzled. "Child, where are all your things?"

"She had a little trouble along the way," Toma blurted. "Bandits, of course. Took everything, except what you see. She was only trying to bring some salves to her grandmother, who's been ill for a while now."

"Oh, I am so sorry," Sheimee empathized. "Thieves! They've become a bit of problem lately. Really though, no shame, attacking anyone who comes up the path. Most travelers haven't been warned properly of the danger. You make yourself comfortable, and we'll help you get on your way. I don't think we have any salves to spare, though."

Sheimee turned to go through the cupboard behind her.

"It is a travesty," Berr-Teo agreed. "Every time we get a visit from the Coalition, I've urged them, again and again, to set some guards on the route, but they have yet to listen. They will regret it when they lose their transports to those marauders."

"Until then, we'll need to be careful," Sheimee continued. "Speaking of which, Toma – when you went out, was anything missing?"

"No, everything was in order," Toma reported. "But we might want to keep an eye to the mists…"

The subdued chatter around the table ceased. Berr-Teo acknowledged Toma's statement with a nod.

"Yes," he said. "That has not gone unnoticed. But there is no need to panic. I have spoken to the Coalition about some secondary defenses."

Toma's siblings exchanged worried glances as his father sat to eat.

"Please," Sheimee said soothingly to Mouse, turning from the cupboard and defusing the silence. "Have a seat. You look hungry."

"Thank you," Mouse replied gratefully, sliding onto the wooden bench.

Bowls overflowing with unfamiliar foods sat steaming before her, their wonderful smells mixing sumptuously. *Real food!* Mouse thought with uncharacteristic giddiness. *I can't even remember the last time I had gruel, and this? This is a banquet!* Her stomach groaned in anticipation.

Toma hopped over the bench to sit next to her, smiled, and then immediately dug into his meal. When at Misty Summit, Mouse had always eaten privately and quickly – there was never a guarantee she would eat again that day, and always the fear persisted someone would take what food she had. Out of habit, she nicked the closest thing to her – a few rolls – and stuffed them into her pockets. The Breythorn family, however, took no notice and continued to eat heartily, conversation muted by the breakfast feast.

Now that Mouse knew she was a prisoner there, it became clear life on the Summit was anything but normal. She watched closely, nonplussed by the foreign interactions of the family in front of her. Sure, Red had been like a father to her, but he was the only person she would readily call family. She had distanced herself from everyone else, living like a ghost among them, seeking always to be unremarkable, unnoticed. In this way she had survived – alone, for the most part, but safe.

And yet here, Mouse witnessed a new set of realities, one where codependency and interaction were the norm. Jorem and Kendir for instance, were having a contest to see who could fit the most in their mouths, to Sheimee's clear disappointment. One stern look from her and the boys ceased, glumly poking at their plates.

Mina had skittered around the table to sit next to Toma, gaping up at him with great admiration. Smiling, Toma put his arm around her bony shoulders and shook her with brotherly affection. Henlin, on the other hand, anxiously asked his father if he would take him to ride the horses today, at which Berr-Teo grinned, ruffled his hair fondly, and said, "I see no reason why you can't." Mouse immediately thought of Red, and inside her the knot that had grown since his disappearance tightened with anger and despair.

"You must be exhausted," Sheimee said, misreading Mouse's reservation. She nudged Toma. "Why don't you show our guest to her room? She's had a long night, and I'm sure she's looking forward to getting some rest."

"Oh, yeah, of course," Toma said, grabbing a fistful of small fruits before standing. "Come with me!"

Mouse followed Toma out of the room and to the end of the hallway, which met with a narrow set of stairs. He leapt up them ahead of her.

"Well come on, then!" he whispered, waving her along. "If we're going to see what's in that bag, we better do it now! Before I have to go out and do any more chores!"

"Oh, right," Mouse replied, scurrying up the steps after him. She followed Toma into the modestly furnished room at the top of the stairs. Neatly turned sheets framed the single bed, despite the Breythorns having no warning of impending company. An old but comfortable chair welcomed her from the corner, and beside it, resting atop a worn vanity, a basin of fresh water promised to cleanse Mouse of the night's grime. So Toma had not exaggerated – they played host to stray travelers often. Toma closed the door quietly, and then flopped in the chair.

"So let's see what your prison pal's got in the sack."

Mouse's withering glare wiped the smirk off his face. Satisfied, she displayed the pillowcase and rattled it. "Red told me that if anything were ever to happen to him, that it was absolutely necessary for me to get my hands on his personal things. He told me that I was to look for… something… specific."

She unwrapped the pillowcase and proceeded to dump its contents onto the bed. Random items tumbled out, including an empty matchbox, a crude, wooden pipe, and a pile of metal parts Red had taken from the plant for some reason. Mouse winced as she remembered slamming it all onto Slim's unsuspecting head. No wonder he was so angry. She scanned the items for the old leather wrap.

"Ah, here it is." Mouse pulled the tattered leather case out of the dirty, cotton shirt it had been wrapped in. It was a single piece of cracked, malleable leather, folded inward into a square and creased around the edges. Its edges were worn and barely holding, as if it had been wrapped and re-wrapped countless times. A thin, black cord, crisscrossed over top, holding the entire ensemble closed.

"What is it?" Toma asked curiously.

"Well… I don't know," Mouse replied. "He told me that whatever was inside was really important."

Mouse tugged the cord loose and laid the case on the bed, unfolding it carefully. Toma got up and stood behind her, watching her progress over her shoulder. She pulled the leather away to reveal crinkled pieces of heavily notated paper.

"That's odd," Mouse said, squinting at the loose pages. "I didn't know Red could write."

Toma reached over her and grabbed one as Mouse carefully spread on the bed. "What is this?"

"Let me see."

Toma wave a page with a detailed drawing. She snatched it and studied the sketch.

"It looks like… the complex," Mouse said. "From the top. Look – here is the wall, the gate where the transports come in… here's the plant, where we work… the market… the Healing Ward… oh, and over here, the Barracks. I don't know what these lines are, though…"

Mouse traced the dotted lines that ran from the Male Barracks to different points in the complex. Each one had an "X" at the end, and

Red had written initials and times by most of them. One line, however, was solid, and an arrow pointed to the far side of the complex. Mouse recognized it immediately.

"The west wall!" she exclaimed, astonished. Excitedly, she flapped the page and pointed animatedly at it. "See here – this solid line with the arrow? This was where he told me to go. I got out at the gap."

"And what are all these initials and times for?" Toma asked, tracing the lines on the sketch.

"Hmm… Enforcement Squad. Looks like markings of their stations... and these must be times for patrols. See?"

"Strange," Toma said. "The patrols along the west wall don't seem to be regular. I wonder why."

"Because you don't go to the west wall," Mouse muttered. "Unless a man makes you."

Shock replaced the confusion in Toma's eyes. He opened his mouth, closed it, and chose instead to stare at his boots. Mouse watched with her own confusion and surprise. Was it not like this everywhere?

Recovering, Toma reached down and handed Mouse a sheet covered in tiny print.

"Should we see what the other pages say?"

Taking it, Mouse probed the sheet carefully. Squeezed in the top corner, she could make out a scribbled, "Dream Log," along with a date. Reading on, she recognized the dream Red had often described. Below it, Red had included a list of it, variations and random words, which seemed to have come to him throughout his many nights at the complex. He had written and re-written the long version of the field dream as the details of it developed, and in the margins he had scribbled "Grigus Gildar" repeatedly. At the bottom a phrase had been scrawled frantically in large hand – "TAKE IT WHERE THE LIGHT TOUCHES TWO GIANTS." Mouse frowned at them, unable to make any sense out of it.

"Toma." She nudged him and pointed to the page. "Do any of these words mean anything to you?"

He glanced up from the page he was studying and squinted at the words over her shoulder. "Hmm… well, I've heard of Grigus. Yeah, I think he was the leader of the Elmling Raids."

"What are the Elmling Raids?" Mouse asked.

"When I was a kid there was some trouble in Gormlaen. Some warriors were coming down from the mountains and raiding villages. They came pretty far south, too. I remember Coalition soldiers passing through the farm on their way to the western ridge. There were a lot of them, burning and stealing as they went."

"I wonder why he remembered that."

Toma shrugged. "Maybe he was a raider with Grigus."

Mouse stared hard at the words, trying to imagine Red as a vindictive rebel, slashing and burning and killing with remorseless precision. The raised, pink scars running the length of his back and arms seemed to confirm the narrative, but the man in her memory could not fit in that world.

"Where is Grigus now?"

"Dead, I guess." Toma shrugged. "My father says the Coalition killed most of them. They never got this far, though. We never heard about the Elmlings again."

Mouse meditated on the fragile pages in her hands, the fragments of Red's past coalescing with her own. Elmnas. Could his memories guide her there? Could this be the key to her own revelation? Or was she better off not knowing the truth? If his crimes earned Red his place at Misty Summit, then maybe, so had hers. Did she deserve the life she remembered?

Mouse recoiled at the thought. No, it was bigger than her, wasn't it? Her mind drifted back to her waking moments, to the venomous hatred of the healer when Mouse spoke the language of Elm. To Milgrim, berating and harming her at any opportunity. To the disdain of the healers to those who bore more resemblance to her than them. And suddenly, Mouse realized her crime.

A tap on her shoulder brought Mouse back to the present.

She jerked, startled. "What is it?"

Toma held up a page and read it aloud. "Accounts of the Taken."

"Let me see that." Mouse grabbed the page and read it as quickly as her mind could comprehend.

"Listen to this, Toma. 'A', taken two days after we discussed recurring dreams. She dreamt about the Healers, needles in her arms. 'A' returned three days after that. I came to her after work. 'A' did not know me, did not see me. Glazed eyes, mechanical movement. Inhuman. 'B', much like 'A'. Did not approach 'B' upon return, but observed. Same condition. Stood behind 'B' in market. Small scar at base of neck.' He drew it, here."

Mouse lifted the page to show Toma. Red had sketched unique characteristics of the taken beneath his first two accounts. Below it, Red had continued to record his encounters. Mouse read on.

"'C', 'D','E', transfers from other depts. Sups. getting suspicious. Watched the taken, did not engage. All have scars. 'E' fell sick in the Barracks and was taken to Healing Ward. Followed 'D' back to Barracks. Behavior is peculiar. Taken's actions suggest outside control."

"Outside control?" Toma asked incredulously. "What does that mean?"

"I don't know," Mouse admitted. "But I've noticed it too. Some people... well, they were sent to see the Healers. Most don't come back. Those that did weren't the same. Like they could not do anything without being told to do it. And what Red said about their eyes is true, too. They were so empty. Have... have you ever seen someone die? There was this girl in the barracks once. She started shaking. She couldn't stop. I went to her, I tried to help... There was this moment, right before it was over, when she looked at me, but she did not see. And then she was gone. That's what their eyes are like."

"How– how often did this happen?"

"Not often," Mouse replied softly. "Until this week."

Toma shook his head in disbelief. "So they're experimenting on the prisoners? Do you remember if they ever did anything like this to you?"

"Whatever they did to me, it wasn't that," Mouse answered. She lifted the hair that fell over the back of her neck. "See? No scar, right? The more I think of it, they never took girls like me. At least not yet. Maybe they needed us to work. But the old ones... well, they were the first to go."

"How awful." Toma shuddered, shaking his head at the thought.

"Test subjects and slaves… but for what? What were you making there?"

"Lots of things. Rails, hovercraft plating, gun barrels…"

"Guns!" Toma exclaimed, banging his hand on the bedside table.

"You don't seem surprised," Mouse said.

"There have been rebellions throughout the United Dominions, a lot of them," Toma explained. "We don't see it much here, being so close to Gormlaen, but we get news. Some say it's not going well for the Coalition. Of course the Coats keep telling us they're taking care of it, there's nothing to worry about. But it all makes sense. The farm tariffs, the constant transports, the random Coat patrols, they're gearing up for a big fight."

Toma jumped up and paced the room before sitting again. "Is there anything else here?"

Mouse shuffled through the pages. Beneath the pile of scraps littered about the bed, one last page caught her eye. She snagged it and waved it before him.

"What does it say?" Toma grabbed the sheet, tilting his head in bewilderment as he searched it. "What are all these scribbles?"

He handed it back to Mouse, who scanned it quickly. Her eyes widened with understanding.

"These aren't scribbles, Toma. It's… I think… Elmling." She laughed in amazement. "And I can read it!"

"How?" Toma asked. "You're from Elmnas?"

"I didn't tell you before, because I wasn't sure, but when I first woke up at the Summit, I couldn't understand a thing. It was what brought Red and I together. I spent so long forgetting what I knew, relearning everything. But it's all still there – and now, now I might be able to use it."

"Well, go on!" Toma elbowed her, excited. "Read it and tell me what it says!"

"Little one," she translated. "If you read this now, you have had the pleasure of meeting my friend. Sorry." Her heart beat a little faster. This could be the page that tied everything together.

"Red used to call me little one, only in Gormlaean," she explained. "Leave me here. I'm not coming. Don't wait. One thing inside holds you back. It's only good for blackleaf. If you don't find it, someone will. Take my gift to where the light once touched the twin giants. Find our people, they will know what to do. This is all I know so far. Sincerely, your friend."

Toma squinted at the page along with Mouse. "What's he talking about?"

"The gift... He always knew he wouldn't make it," she mumbled. She reached into her coverall pocket and held the chip card aloft.

They sat in silence, studying it for a moment.

"Well," Toma finally said. "What is it?"

"The wage card that is not a wage card," Mouse whispered. "Red wanted me to keep it safe, at all costs."

"To bring it to your people," Toma added. "The Elmlings, if they're still there. But why?"

"I don't know," Mouse confessed. "I've never seen him so serious, though. If what he says is true, they'll know what it does."

What secrets could this card possibly hold? Carefully, she slipped it back into the pocket. Toma picked up the page again, frowned, set it down, and stroked his chin thoughtfully.

"How about the rest of it?" Toma asked. "One thing inside holds you back? Does that make any sense to you?"

"Oh, um... let me see." Mouse examined the words, mumbling them over and over again.

"So what's something that's inside you, but is only good for blackleaf?"

"Well, he knew I never got any blackleaf. One pack could eat up your wages for the whole day. I always told him it was never worth it to go hungry for the night, but he would just smile and say, 'Yeh have your dinner, an' I have mine'." Mouse chuckled. "Never made any sense to me, even if it seemed to make the prisoners feel better. Well, if I had been there as long as him... maybe then I'd see it differently."

"Wait. What did you say about the packs of blackleaf again?"

"That one pack of it could eat up your wages for the day. Why?"

Mouse mulled the statement over as Toma gave her a knowing look. "Oh! Right. The only thing good for blackleaf at the complex is our wages. At least, that's what Red and everyone who smoked would have said."

Mouse smiled. "As you can imagine, the food was… well, certainly not your mother's cooking."

Toma grinned appreciatively. "I'll make sure to tell her it's better than prison food some time. So, your money is the thing that's only good for blackleaf. And your money… it's on that card of yours, right? But holding you back? What do you think that means?"

Mouse tapped her index finger against her lips, considering the statement's ambiguity. *My wages are on my card, of course. How could they be holding me back?* They did not seem to hold her back. In fact, they were the only thing that kept her alive on the Summit. Each day they were transmitted to her card. Each morning, she waved her hand over the reader to check into the plant. And each day, her superiors knew exactly where she was, who she was, and what she was owed. The card was more than a receptacle for her income; to the Supervisors, the Coalition… it *was* her. *Do they know where I am now?*

Mouse's heart skipped a beat as the sudden realization slammed into her. She looked up at Toma, trembling.

Mouse held up her hand, revealing the rectangular lump just beneath the surface of her skin. "It means we're not safe here."

CHAPTER TWELVE

A ll the fear Mouse had abandoned at the threshold of the Breythorn home came surging back. She quaked as Toma stood uncomprehendingly by, barraging her with questions.

"What's wrong? What are you talking about? What's the chip have to do with this?"

"Don't you see?" Mouse cried. "My wage card – it's more than that. If they somehow know where it is, they know where I am. They'll find me."

"I am an idiot!" Toma said, slapping his palm against his forehead. "It's a tracking device. Of course it is!"

Mouse struggled to control her shallow breathing. "You've heard of such a thing before."

"Definitely," Toma replied. "Hunters and trappers use them to track game sometimes. Which means…"

"Someone's using this to track me." Mouse searched the room wildly for a solution, but she could not possibly find one in enough time. She had been away from the complex for far too long now – they had to know exactly where she was. A Coalition transport could be at Breythorn Farm any minute. Out of the corner of her eye, Mouse saw the glimmer of Toma's knife, still hanging from his hip.

"Give me your knife," Mouse demanded.

"You can't be thinking–"

"There's no time. When they get here, they'll know you've helped me. I'm not about to drag you into this! I'll make a run for it once I'm through."

Toma shook his head. "You won't get far. I'm in this now, whether I like it or not. I'll give you the knife, but you're not going anywhere. I'll… I'll think of something."

The blade gave off a dull shimmer as Toma pulled it from the leather holster around his waist and handed it gently to Mouse. She gripped it awkwardly in her left hand and tentatively approached the pink scar. Gritting her teeth, Mouse pressed the point down. She stifled a whimper as the sharp point poked a small hole, and several drops of bright, red blood burst forth onto her skin. There was a stinging sensation spreading through her hand, and Mouse found she could no longer hold the knife steady. She could not ignore the droplets of blood pooling on her hand and splashing on the floor.

"Wait – let me do it," Toma said. "Close your eyes… It should hurt less that way."

Mouse dropped the knife into Toma's hand and squeezed her eyes shut.

Toma wasted no time. Mouse bit her lip to keep from gasping as he cut into her skin. Pain and numbness grew and spread fluidly through her hand and wrist, intermingling peculiarly with the draining of her blood as it dripped down her thumb and fingers. Finally there was a tiny clink followed by the sound of ripping cloth. She opened her eyes when Toma began to tenderly wind a strip of linen from the sheets of the bed around her hand.

"Don't look at it," he advised as he finished. He walked over to the basin to rinse his hands.

"What did you do with the chip?" Mouse asked, searching for it on the floor. She swayed at the sight of the spreading puddle of blood there instead.

"It's in the basin, we'll worry about where to –" Toma stopped short as a light rumbling came from just beyond the windowpanes.

"They're here," he said, hastily grabbing her good hand. "Come with me."

He pulled her down the hall and pushed her into a small, dusty closet at the end. Closing the door, he whirled Mouse around to face him.

"Whatever happens, you have to stay in here!"

Toma gave her a long, hard look with his golden eyes, which even in the low light of the closet sparkled brightly. It was hot inside, and Mouse could see tiny beads of sweat forming on his forehead slipping down the end of his nose. Her hand throbbed in pain and the sticky heat of the broom closet was almost unbearable, but Mouse was amazed to find she was no longer afraid.

Toma reached over her head and pulled on a string from the ceiling. A ladder fell down behind her with a loud rattle.

"Go on, climb up," he urged. "I'll close it after you."

Mouse turned and scrambled up the rickety ladder into an even dustier, hotter crawlspace. Flattening her body against the wooden boards of the ceiling, she wedged into the space, barely big enough for Mina, let alone Mouse. She was already sweating profusely when Toma carefully closed the trap door behind her.

"Remember what I said. Don't move a muscle."

The door snapped shut, cloistering her in the darkness. She could hear Toma close the closet door and jog down the hallway. All this time, the rumbling outside had grown louder. The house trembled at the approach of the hovercraft. It thundered just outside before it guttered and stopped completely. A sharp knock rapped against the front door, which coincidentally, was right below Mouse's hiding place.

"Now, if they think they can get blood from a stone…" Sheimee huffed irritably below her.

Mouse heard the door swing open.

"Hello," Sheimee said warmly, easily disguising the displeasure in her voice as if she had done it many times before. "If you're looking for supplies, you'll have to come back next week. I'm afraid we gave you all we had ready at the last shipment."

"Shipments are not our concern," a deep voice answered. "A highly dangerous criminal escaped from Misty Summit Prison last night. You are harboring the fugitive here."

"You can't be serious!" Sheimee exclaimed incredulously. "Why, we spend half the day beating back bandits! How dare you!"

"We will need to be coming in, Mrs. Breythorn," a female voice demanded. "If you do not impede our search, the Coalition will look favorably upon your cooperation. Am I clear?"

"Of course," Sheimee replied, the frustration edging into her voice. "We freely offer our assistance to the Coalition."

"Then we'll begin," the deep voice replied. "Our indicators tell us she should be right inside."

"She?" Sheimee's voice rang with disbelief. "You don't mean to tell me you're after that child?"

"So she is here?"

"Yes, but I am expected to believe that she is a criminal? Why, I don't think the child has even made it to her seventeenth harvest!"

"Ma'am, the criminals at Misty Summit are clever and manipulative," the female voice countered. "It should not surprise you that she would use her harmless appearance to her advantage."

"Come now," Sheimee scoffed. "Dangerous? A stiff wind would blow her away."

"She managed to kill two inmates before her escape," the male voice retorted impatiently. "We won't ask you again to stop wasting our time."

Heavy boots stomped into the landing, followed by the sound of many bare feet pattering to the door.

"Mama!" Mina cried. "What's going on?"

"Go find your father, Mina. Boys, I need you to go tend to the goats."

One of the boys began complaining. "We were going to do that *later*, Mama!"

"Now, Jorem," Sheimee said firmly. "Go. Quickly."

There was a brief hesitation before the small feet pattered away. "She is only just up the stairs," Sheimee disclosed to the Coalition guards. "Sleeping, in the guest room."

The heavy boots tread loudly through the house, stopping at the base of the stairs. Mouse held her breath as they drew nearer. She could hear whispers – Mouse only assumed they were planning their approach.

A loud thump down the hallway, followed by a great crash, echoed throughout the house. Mouse heard Toma groaning.

"Help!" he shouted.

The guard pounded up the stairs. She heard Sheimee gasping.

"Toma! What happened?"

He groaned a little more before answering. The guards tramped through the bedroom door.

"Boy!" the male voice roared angrily. "What happened here?"

"Unhh…" groaned Toma. "I heard… noises. Sounded like she was in pain. When I came in… she hit me…"

"Where is the fugitive now?" The male voice shouted impatiently.

"Out... side…" Toma replied. He sounded absolutely pathetic.

"She won't get far on foot. She's wounded," the male voice said to his companion. His tone changed as he addressed Toma.

"You! You let her escape. Which direction, boy?"

"I… didn't see. I blacked out when she hit me."

The male guard spouted a litany of curses.

"Idiot!" he barked. "You must have seen us arrive – all you had to do was wait! I'll have the transport take double the tariff next week simply for your incompetence!"

"He had no way of knowing she was a fugitive," Sheimee cut in sharply. "And since you take so much as it is, he had no reason to believe this wasn't just one of your *standard* pick-ups."

For a few long moments, Mouse could only hear the slight creaking of the floorboards. Even she could feel the awful tension in that room.

"Sir," the female broke in. "Permission to search the perimeter."

"Permission granted," he replied, his voice even and cold. "Let's move."

Those heavy boots clomped down the stairs and out the front door. Sheimee breathed a long sigh of relief.

"You stay right there, Berr-Toma Breythorn. I'm going to get your father."

Her footsteps fell lightly on the stairs as she raced down them. It was silent again in the house. Mouse listened for the rumbling sound of the transport, wondering if it was safe to come out of the crawlspace. It occurred to her that even if the transport had left, she would not be able to come down. Toma had not just deceived the guards concerning her alleged escape, but his family as well, and they could not know where she was. There was too must risk—both for her and the Breythorns.

Mouse wiped the sweat from her forehead and tried to get comfortable. There was no telling how long she would be stuffed in the closet crawlspace, waiting until Toma could discreetly let her out.

The front door suddenly slammed open. Another pair of boots, though certainly not as heavy as the ones the guards wore, strode purposefully up the stairs. Toma's groans started anew, and she held her breath. It was a little over the top – she wondered if whoever was coming up the stairs now would be quite as easy to persuade.

The boots stopped at the top of the stairs in front of the guest bedroom. To her surprise, there was no voice asking Toma why he was on the floor. Instead, the boots began to pace – first, into the room, and then out into the hallway. Someone from the transport must have returned to investigate the house after finding the surrounding areas empty. *Oh no. They didn't believe Toma. They're coming back for me.* She clutched at the pocket on her chest. *Did they know about Red's chip card? Are they tracking it even now?* Nothing, it seemed, was beyond the Coalition's power. Her legs felt weak and began to tremble; Mouse clenched them tightly with white knuckles to stop them.

The owner of the boots walked slowly, but the gait was steady and sure. They were coming toward her hiding place with purpose. With every step, her heart raced, and Mouse feared its wild beating would give her away. She resisted the urge to slap her hand over her chest to muffle it. The beating pounded in her ears, cacophonous in the tense silence. Mouse stifled a sharp breath as the boots stopped directly in front of the doorway. They stood quietly, waiting. *He's listening for me.* To her horror, the door handle began to turn. As silently as she could, Mouse slid down to the end of the crawlspace, hoping the action could save her, even if the trap door was opened. As she shifted, the trap door flew open, and the stairs tumbled down below her. Again, silence filled the room. *What now? How do I get out of this one?* Mouse despaired, but remained rooted to the spot, fear of discovery freezing her solid to the back of the crawlspace. Not that she could move, anyway–she was completely plastered to the back of the hole.

"You might as well come down," a male voice said calmly, breaking the false security of the moment's silence. "I know you're up there."

CHAPTER THIRTEEN

Resigned to her end, Mouse turned over and peered down the ladder. She was surprised to find Berr-Teo looking up at her, his arms crossed over his chest.

"Mr. Breythorn – I…" Mouse stammered. *What can I even say?* Berr-Teo simply nodded as she poked her head over the edge and politely gestured for her to come down. His expression was indistinguishable – Mouse could easily read either terrible fury or harmless amusement in his discerning gaze. She hoped against hope that it was the latter, but then again, the Coalition barging into his house on account of her probably did not fuel any friendly sentiments. Afraid of getting it wrong, Mouse made no assumptions and climbed down the ladder obediently.

"Come. They have gone," Berr-Teo said as she lighted on the floor, already striding away from the closet.

Mouse followed behind at a distance as he walked to the guest bedroom door. Before entering, he beckoned Mouse to come in. There was Toma, sitting cross-legged on the floor amidst an array of broken furnishings. A dresser had been toppled, and a mirror lay in shards on the floor beside it. Mouse could also see what looked like the sheets and pillowcase from the guest bed knotted together and hanging out of the open bedroom window. The basin, however, remained intact, and the water in it was still pink with Mouse's blood. As she hid, Toma dismantled the room and staged her attack. She was impressed; it appeared convincing.

Toma peered up in astonishment as Mouse scurried in behind his father.

"What! How did you know?" Toma asked, a little fear entering his voice. "What gave it away?"

"Those sheets are older than your grandfather, Berr-Toma. They couldn't even hold your sister." Berr-Teo let out a low chuckle. "Your mother is going to kill you, by the way."

"Hard to say what's worse – angry Mom or angry Coats. Well, I'm glad they've gone."

He hoisted himself from the floor, smiling at Mouse with pride. Though the room was in shambles, Mouse noticed none of Red's things were among the wreckage. She smiled and nodded in return, Toma's thoroughness immensely appreciated. Swaggering a little with the satisfaction of a job well done, Toma winked and said, "Did you hear how angry the big one was when he thought you outsmarted him? I almost laughed in his face!"

"A practical joke for you, Toma, until they return," Berr-Teo admonished. "And I don't expect they'll find it quite as amusing."

Toma rubbed the back of his neck, carefully avoiding his father's penetrating gaze. "I guess I have some explaining to do then."

"In time. Until then, you can start by putting the room back in order. Mouse, if you would, come with me."

Mouse shot a panicked glance at Toma, but he was already staring glumly at the mess around him. Berr-Teo put his calloused hand on Mouse's shoulder and guided her to the stairs. In heavy silence, she walked with him, dreading what was to come. 135's graceful form sprinting through the marketplace sprang into Mouse's thoughts. Again she saw the glinting barrels of the Enforcement Squad, poised for action. She saw the blue blurs of the Healers, the terror of the taken ones. *And what would they do to me if the Breythorns hand me over?*

Berr-Teo walked stoically on. He was inscrutable, and that made her uneasy. At least, it seemed, he was in no hurry to come to a verdict on her, but that was only a little comforting. He led Mouse to the kitchen, his movements measured as he sat next to his wife, and then gazed at her with that same unreadable expression. Mouse gazed back, curious and cautious, wondering what kind of man Berr-Teo would show himself to be.

Toma had taken to her immediately, but his father was wary. She imagined he wore this same visage at any stranger who came through his front door. Long years of tending to his animals and his crops seemed to thicken and callous more than his hands. His eyes were dark and penetrating, empty of Toma's mischief and humor. Toma resembled his father otherwise. She could only hope that behind those sifting, sober eyes, Berr-Teo was just as kind and understanding. He waved his hand over the wooden bench and extended her a polite smile, indicating she should sit. Despite the events of the afternoon, Sheimee regarded Mouse warmly and offered her a cup of steaming tea.

"My son likes to think he is much cleverer than he really is," Berr-Teo began. He leaned back against the wall behind him and crossed his arms. "I am not saying that he has never deceived me, but I know when my son is not telling the whole truth. He has always been... a bit of a storyteller. So when he comes home later than expected with a stranger, and then spins me some tale only he could come up with, I have to wonder – what is he hiding? And not just any stranger, but a young woman, wandering alone in the Empty Vale. I thought you must have been in trouble, but it was not the time to ask about it."

"We only want to help, of course," Sheimee added. "We've known some children to run away from home. And in the past, we have been able to make sure that they got home safe to their families and loved ones. We thought you might be one of them."

Berr-Teo continued, "So you see, I was surprised when Coalition guards intruded upon the peace of my farm, claiming that I was harboring a criminal who had murdered two men, escaped from a high security prison, and survived a night in the Mistlands. Certainly not the sort of trouble we were expecting.

"Sheimee filled me in on some of the details the guards gave her, after they had left," he clarified, registering Mouse's look of surprise. "And she told me you had knocked Toma out and escaped. That story... hm. Not one of Toma's best."

"And when you came upstairs and found him..." Mouse trailed.

"Yes... rolling around and groaning. One look at him and the room, and I knew you were still in the house. Yes, there was only one place you could be."

Sheimee shook her head. "I can't guess how they even knew you were here, or why we never received a message that they were coming. Everything about it was so... abrupt. They release dictums, you see, whenever there are things we should be on the lookout for. Bandits, rogue creatures, Mistwolf sightings – dangers to us common folk. Nothing came before the hovercraft."

"So I'm curious. How did Toma know they were coming?" Berr-Teo leaned forward, steepling his hands on the table. "The truth, please."

"Oh, and dear, we don't want any harm to come to you," Sheimee said. "I know I let those guards in before, but I had little choice. They can be ruthless."

Berr-Teo and Sheimee watched Mouse expectantly.

"Uh, well..." Mouse started with no small amount of trepidation. "I have a feeling that my story will be the worst one you've heard all day."

"And that was what I was afraid of," Berr-Teo chuckled softly. "Try me."

Mouse hesitated as she looked back into the intent eyes of the Breythorns. *Would you really be so eager to help if you knew the truth?* She squirmed in her seat, determining if she were a good enough liar to get out of this. At that moment, Toma burst into the kitchen.

"She doesn't really remember a whole lot about her past!" he practically shouted. "She told me everything she knew, and it was not much. Mouse was at the prison, but she didn't do anything wrong! It's the Coats! They locked her up because she's an Elmling!"

"Berr-Toma, I thought I had told you I would come get you," an irked Berr-Teo rumbled.

"Yes, uh, you did, but I... thought you ought to hear from me. Before you do your interrogation. Anyway she's told me the truth when I asked, and I believe her!" Toma persisted earnestly.

"I just wanted to hear it from her, *without* you jumping in," his father replied sharply. "And I will be the judge of the merit of her story, not you."

"You don't believe her? Or me?" Toma asked incredulously.

"He's not saying that," Sheimee stepped in. "But, Toma, she was accused of murder. That's no light thing. We only want to know the truth and – well, and what we're risking."

Toma opened his mouth to protest, but Mouse interrupted this time.

"And of course, I understand." She bowed her head humbly as she spoke. "You have every right to that."

Mouse started at the beginning, quickly recounting the events she remembered up until then. Berr-Teo pressed Mouse for details. She offered them, but the secret of Red's chip she kept to herself.

Finally satisfied, Berr-Teo turned to Toma. "And this lines up with what she told you?"

Toma nodded. "It happened just as she said."

Berr-Teo sat with his hands folded, thinking.

A brief silence fell on the conference.

Sheimee gently spoke. "So, what can we do?"

"You've already done enough," Mouse replied, relieved the hard part was over. "You didn't have to do anything... so thanks. But I need to find answers. I can't stay much longer."

Toma frowned. "What do you mean?"

From the moment Mouse laid eyes on the last page of Red's journal, written in the language only she could read, she knew what she needed to do. She only needed to say it.

"I need to get to Elmnas, of course."

Further silence met her. Sheimee and Berr-Teo exchanged dark looks before Berr-Teo finally shook his head.

"I'm afraid that it cannot be done. It is impossible. There are only two ways to enter that land – one is by way of these mountains and through the Mistlands, and the other is through the heart of Gormlaen. You are unlikely to get far by either route. Even if you did get there, Elmnas is far too dangerous. I am sorry, but it would be completely irresponsible to allow you to even entertain any ideas of going."

"But don't you see? It's the only way," Mouse protested. "What if my family is still there? What if they're looking for me? And it doesn't matter where I am, the Coalition will be looking, too. I'm in danger – even if I stay here. Especially, if I stay here."

"I cannot, in good conscience, allow it. It would be a death sentence to send you out." Berr-Teo declared staunchly.

Mouse could not believe her ears. Only minutes ago, they were not entirely convinced that she was not a criminal – and now they wanted to protect her. She looked to Toma for some sort of confirmation, but he simply shrugged and looked away.

"Look, we know we can't stop you," Sheimee said gently. "But you have been through a lot today. It would be wise to rest before you made any decisions. Let us feed you, clothe you, and give you a bed for the night. By morning, you may find your path has changed."

Sheimee placed her hand on Mouse's arm and looked at her pleadingly. "Besides, you cannot go anywhere with your hand in that condition. Please."

Mouse huffed in frustration. They had no claim on her or any right to force her to stay. Her business, in truth, was no concern of theirs. Even still, Sheimee was right. Mouse was exhausted, and a bum hand was no asset. Elmnas had waited this long; it could wait another day.

"Alright, I'll stay for a bit," Mouse agreed begrudgingly.

Sheimee brightened and clapped her hands. "Wonderful! Toma, you cleaned up the guest room, yes? I trust you removed all that you destroyed and replaced the sheets as well?"

"Uh…" Toma said, scratching his head.

Sheimee shot Toma a look of fleeting disappointment before turning to Mouse. "No matter. I'll have you stay in Mina's room. Come on, let's head up there now."

Mouse could not deny Sheimee's kindness as she now suddenly and fully felt the heaviness of her exhaustion.

Without waiting for an answer, Sheimee took Mouse by the arm and led her to Mina's small, cozy bedroom up the stairs. As soon as Mouse's head touched the pillow she was gone, sleeping the deep sleep of those weary both in mind and body.

CHAPTER FOURTEEN

Though her eyes were closed, Mouse sensed she was drifting. No, not drifting – she was being carried, cradled firmly in someone's slender, loving arms. It was warm there, safe; a good place to sleep. But something had roused her. What was it? A smell, thick in the air. It clogged her nostrils, made her cough. The drowsiness was lifting, and sounds came to her. Crackling, breaking, and shouting filled her ears. Her eyes snapped open in fear. Writhing orange flames leapt past her, shadowy objects appeared and then blurred. Where was she? She looked down to see a pair of feet running on broken stone, and they were not hers. She squirmed, but the arms desperately held her tighter. Mouse twisted her head back to see who held her.

A woman looked back at Mouse, her two dark brows knit together with grave concern.

"Sleep," she said breathlessly. "Go back to sleep."

There was a loud pop over the woman's head. She stopped short and gazed up at the crimson sky. Suddenly, a blinding light seared Mouse's vision, and everything blurred as Mouse felt herself hurtling along. Piercing screams and bursts of white and orange light erupted around her, and Mouse cried out until everything went black.

111

Mouse opened her eyes, her body coated in a cold sweat. She was not moving, but lying in Mina's bed, alone in a dark, still room. Her pulse raced wildly and she drew in a shaky breath. It was only a dream. *Or a memory.* Yes, just as Red said it would. The dream expanded. Mouse remained still, terror mingling with excitement. The details were still there; for the first time, they did not fade.

With a yawning stretch, Mouse inspected the room. Long, dark shadows covered the walls and crawled over the floor. Sheimee must have allowed her to sleep through dinner. All was quiet, Mouse noticed, except for a whispered conversation in the room next to her. Low but animated voices echoed through the cracks of the bedroom door. Out of habit, Mouse strained to listen.

"So we still have yet to come to a decision about this," Berr-Teo said.

"I know, I know… But it just doesn't seem right. Maybe she is troubled, but I can't, in good conscience, send her back there," Sheimee asserted.

"But we can't protect her, either, can we? Not like this. You heard that insane conspiracy with your own ears! She's delusional. Possibly dangerous."

"You can't think that she is criminally insane!" an exasperated Sheimee hissed. "She's only a child! What if all she needs is a good home, a family?"

"I don't know what to think," Berr-Teo replied. "But the dictum was clear. If it's the only way to help her, we would be very wrong to do otherwise."

"I just…" Sheimee sighed. "No, I don't want to call them. I can't bear to see them haul her away. She'll be so frightened."

"Sheimee, think about it. We are not Healers. There isn't anything we can do for her."

"We could take her to the Healers in Parin, couldn't we?"

"Come now, my love," Berr-Teo implored tiredly. "That's a three-day journey by horse. And they're looking for her. You know the consequences if we were to be caught. Everything we're doing right now is treason!"

"Don't you lecture me!" Sheimee snarled. "You seem to forget what they have done to us! And I can tell you, whatever is wrong with her, that was their doing, too!"

"I do not forget," Berr-Teo answered stiffly. "And that's why I protect my family at all costs. *At all costs*, Sheimee."

"Fine. Do what you will. I won't be a part of it."

"If it makes any difference, we can wait until morning."

"I don't want the children to see it, either. Toma's really taken with her."

"Alright, alright. I will work something out."

No one spoke. Somewhere, a watch ticked softly, filling the long silence between them.

"I still don't like this," Sheimee contended, breaking the lull. "If she suffers – that is on you."

Berr-Teo let out a heavy sigh. "What do you want from me? I'm just one man, Sheimee. One man. I don't like it either – do not think for a minute I want to do this. I don't have a choice. We don't have a choice."

"I'm going to check on the children."

The door handle of the Breythorns' bedroom clicked and turned. Sheimee's light footsteps fell softly down the hallway. They stopped outside of Mouse's door. She heard the handle jiggle. Mouse lay still, but it never turned. The footsteps pattered away, the sound fading as Sheimee hurried down the hallway. In time, she passed Mouse's door again. Mouse heard Berr-Teo's deep breathing momentarily as Sheimee opened their bedroom door, which was immediately muffled when she closed it.

Now Mouse lay awake, contemplating her next move. Not that there was much to think about. Remaining in the home was clearly out of the question. She would leave tonight, under the cover of the darkness, as always. Strange it was that darkness had proved a more eager ally than all she had encountered yet.

Listening intently for any sound or sign of disturbance, Mouse carefully lifted herself out of Mina's bed. Her bare soles met the cool, wooden floor, reminding Mouse just how comfortable she had made herself in the Breythorn home. There was a sting of regret, but Mouse shook it off as quickly as it had come. With all the near-certain death experiences of the day before, it was a gift to have a place to rest and recover, if only for a brief time. It was her own naïve mistake to expect complete strangers to harbor her, an apparently troubled girl on the run, and hide her at the expense of their family and their livelihood. And no matter how much they resented the Coalition, they were under its control. It was a reality Mouse would not soon forget. She could linger nowhere in this land. Mouse was an enemy here, and any who aided her were sure to become the same.

Exhaling sharply, Mouse searched the room for her things. She regretted her transparency with them, but there had not been any other way. There were too many questions Mouse could not answer, too many loose ends, strange events, and ominous whispers of trouble for her to leave them in the dark. In any case, her stay there had not been completely pointless. For one thing, Sheimee had provided her with clean, soft clothes to wear, food to fill her aching belly, and a bed to rest her tired bones. She had also met Toma, the first person with which she had felt a bond... something like friendship, but something else, something she was not sure how to describe. Well, if there were one thing she would regret, it would be leaving Toma without saying goodbye. She shook the ache of the thought away. After dropping in on the scattered remnants of Red's returning memories, Mouse had a journey to make. Nothing could hinder it now.

At all costs, she needed to reach Elmnas. It was the common denominator for every question, every lead, every mystery that troubled her heart. It was there Red believed their people could make sense of what was really happening at the Summit. Maybe, with Red's chip and her help, even the taken could be saved. As soon as she could get dressed and find all of her things, she would be on her way.

Mouse crouched silently upon the wooden floor and stretched her good hand beneath the bed, searching for the familiar, coarse texture of her coveralls. Before sleeping, she had shed the vestments of the prison and left them piled beside the bed, but after waking, they were nowhere to be found. Mouse stretched a little further and swept her arm in a wide arc on the floor around the bed. Her fingertips grazed the toes of her sturdy, worn-in work boots, which were sitting upright just slightly beneath the foot of the bed. Mouse groped along until she reached the end of the bed. There she found them neatly folded on top of a chest at its foot, along with her other garments – all washed and stacked together. Mouse spotted a few extra garments lying neatly beside them, and mentally thanked Sheimee for her kindness. If anything, the woman cared.

Stripping off her bedclothes, she reached for the coveralls. Though clean for maybe the first time since Mouse owned them, the torn and faded jumpsuit wouldn't do her any favors outside Misty Summit. Casting aside her prison attire, she chose a pair of deerskin trousers, a black cotton tunic, and a light tan field jacket she could button up to her chin instead. The chip, which she had carefully tucked under the pillow, found a home in the jacket's inner pocket. Mouse threw on her boots and shoved the remainder of her items in a light satchel lying next to the chest. She swung the satchel over her shoulder guiltily. Mouse had never enjoyed stealing – especially from those who had been hospitable – but then again, they were planning to hand her over to the Coalition.

And if it was any consolation, she knew she would make good use of it. The satchel hung comfortably at her hip. Its contents rustled lightly as she readjusted the strap. Mouse nodded approvingly, confident she looked enough like a normal traveler to deter any suspicion. How necessary that was, especially if she had to pass through the heart of Gormlaen. This was not a fact Mouse was particularly fond of, but she would rather expose herself to the possibility of capture in the heart of the Coalition stronghold instead of the certainty of a fatal mauling in the Mistlands. Mouse quickly surveyed the room, hoping she might find something useful for her trip. For good measure, she stuffed a few of the sheets and some of Mina's extra pillows under the quilted cover of the bed, beating the lumpy mass into a human likeness. The shape was only mildly convincing, but Mouse doubted anyone would discover the fraud before morning. It also seemed unlikely they would follow her after she had fled, but in the slight chance she misjudged the Breythorns, she needed as much time and distance as she could afford.

Shadows shifted quietly as Mouse creeped to the door. It sighed as she slowly pulled it open. Mouse held her breath and gazed into the hallway, listening for any indication someone had heard. To her relief, nothing stirred. She stepped gingerly into the hall and gently closed the door behind her, grimacing as it clicked into place. Glancing at Sheimee and Berr-Teo's bedroom door warily, Mouse paused to get her bearings. There was a fragile silence in the hallway. Mouse placed a hesitant foot down upon the wooden floorboards, which groaned suddenly with her weight. She drew it back hastily, cursing her heavy boots. With a long last glance toward the main bedroom door, Mouse gathered enough courage to slink forward. She took each step only with the balls of her feet, cringing at the sound of the shifting boards. And still, nothing else stirred.

Moving as briskly as she could stand, Mouse hurried to the mouth of the staircase and made her way down. The further Mouse got from the sleeping family upstairs, the more her confidence grew. As she reached the bottom of the stairs, Mouse half-jogged, half-tip-toed down the hallway toward the front door, her hand already outstretched to grasp the handle.

Then, out of the darkness, Mouse heard the sound of breathing. She stood perfectly still, both too afraid to turn or to open the door only a handbreadth away. Mouse listened intently, holding her own breath, but only silence met her. She relaxed, annoyed her nerves constantly got the best of her. For once Mouse had lived up to her moniker. *It's okay, no one's heard you.* Taking a shaky breath, Mouse reached out and turned the door handle slowly. It swung open softly, letting in a cool night breeze that chilled the sweat beading upon her brow and against matted wisps of damp hair clinging to her face. She drew a bandaged hand across her forehead, suddenly realizing sweat dripped from every pore, drenching her. *That was the easy part.* She was crossing the threshold when she felt the hand gripping her shoulder.

CHAPTER FIFTEEN

Mouse staggered through the door and sprinted before she had the chance to think. The assailant behind was caught by surprise as well, grunting as he tumbled clumsily through the doorway. She ran hard toward the greenhouses, unsure of why or where to go, but not daring to stop or turn. It was not until she heard the footsteps right behind her, easily gaining on her short strides, that fear overwhelmed her. Against every reasonable inclination Mouse tried to scream.

Before she could, however, her pursuer fell upon her, his clammy hand around her mouth. Mouse struggled in his grip, but he drew her tighter to his hard, bony chest, dragging her behind one of the closest greenhouses just off the path.

"Mouse. Shut up. It's me," Toma whispered breathlessly. "What are you running for?"

Surprised, Mouse relaxed in his grip, and Toma promptly released her. She spun around to see him, his chest heaving. Like her, Toma was fully dressed, his black overcoat hiding his wiry frame in the semidarkness around them. He placed his hands upon his knees to gather himself, and adjusted a satchel of his own that hung across his chest. Mouse gazed at him curiously.

"What in the world are you doing?" she asked.

"Trying to catch up to you, of course. I didn't expect you to light out like a mountain cat with its tail on fire!" Toma exclaimed. "See, I would have caught up to you sooner, but in my defense, you are a lot faster than you look."

"You had me scared to death!" Mouse hissed.

"No kidding." Toma chuckled to himself, he leaned back against the shed behind him. "You took off."

Mouse shot him a sour look.

"Sorry," he added, recoiling at her displeasure. "I wasn't trying to frighten you, really. I was waiting for you."

"What? How did you know I was leaving?" Mouse demanded.

"Come on, Mouse. I saw the evidence, heard the truth. Too many people are in trouble, and the way I see it, whatever the Coats are up to isn't good for any of us. You've come this far already. Even I know my parents forbidding you from going wouldn't stop you."

"Fair enough," Mouse conceded. "You must have also guessed that they didn't believe a word of what I said."

Toma nodded. "They don't like the Coalition, but they're not about to grab their pitchforks and storm the palace."

"I'll have to take your word for it," Mouse remarked shortly.

"What do you mean by that?" Toma asked, tilting his head quizzically.

Mouse hesitated, not so sure she should tell Toma of his parents' intentions. And yet, the bitter sting of their betrayal was still fresh in her mind. *Why shouldn't I tell him? He ought to know.* She opened her mouth to speak, but again, hesitated. What would she gain from it?

Just the smug satisfaction of giving this perfect little family something to argue about.

"Nothing," she finally said.

"Okay." He did not press, but his eyes searched hers.

Mouse shuffled awkwardly, feeling far too exposed under his gaze. Though never predatory like the hungry stares of men at the Summit, it was too curious, too personal, too intimate. It was the kind of look that touched too deeply, bringing out in her an unfamiliar and peculiar feeling she could not place. What was it? She was not sure she wanted to know. Breaking his gaze, she glanced up at the sky, and sighed.

"I better get out of here. I've got a feeling those Coats will be circling back. I'm glad to see you, but I really should go."

Mouse hiked up her satchel and placed her hands on her hips, wondering which way to go.

"Aren't you forgetting something?" Toma asked slyly.

"Red's things," Mouse said. "Of course. You have them?"

Toma reached into the breast pocket of his coat and pulled out the tattered leather casing, grinning knowingly. "It's all right here."

"Great. Thank you," Mouse said gratefully as he handed it to her. She smiled at him, the slight twinge of sadness catching in her throat. "I guess this is goodbye."

Toma snorted. "Think I got all dressed up with nowhere to go? I'm coming!"

She waited for the joke to come, but he just stood there with his arms crossed, wearing a serious expression that reminded her of his father. Mouse gawked at him. He had his family, his farm, a warm bed, a guaranteed meal every single day – a good, simple kind of life – one that Mouse could only dream of. *You're just going to walk away from all this?*

"You aren't serious," Mouse said flatly.

"And you really are insane if you think I'm going to let you walk across Reidara without a proper guide," Toma contended.

"What? No way." She shook her head vehemently. He couldn't come. Mouse had troubled an already volatile relationship with the Coalition. *And if they knew what he was doing now…helping me…it's treason, isn't it? What would the Coalition do to him? Or…his family?*

"Don't worry," she insisted. "I'll be fine. I've made it this far."

"Oh, of course." Toma nodded, a smile playing at the corner of his mouth. "So, uh, which way are you headed?"

"Um…" Mouse stalled. She was still working on that one. Berr-Teo had only mentioned two routes: the path through the Mistlands or the one that lead through Gormlaen. Neither path sounded agreeable. Maybe there was another way. She pointed to a direction parallel to the

Mistlands. Something less traveled would probably be her best bet, anyway.

"Oh, you could do that," Toma said. "You'll only hit the Slate Snake River, where the biggest Coalition outpost this side of the Jagged Jaw Mountains sits. There they've been known to check every man, woman, and child for papers, and send them packing when they don't have them. But, I'm confident you'll get to the ferry without, you know, being immediately sent back to prison on the first transport out of there."

"Fine," Mouse ground her teeth in annoyance. "I'll just have to go another way."

"Great! The long way 'round. Good decision. I hope you brought enough food for the journey as well, or at least a little gold to buy it as you go along."

"Hmmm." She looked at her hand, remembering any wages she had accrued no longer existed – another glaring lack of foresight on Mouse's part.

Toma wore a self-satisfied smirk, which seemed to grow the longer Mouse considered her dwindling options. As much as she would like to wipe that smirk off his face, she knew, unfortunately, that he was right. There was no way she was going to be able to cross Dominion borders without arousing suspicion, walk who knows how long without food or money, or get to where she was going without a map or guide. Mouse sighed, accepting defeat.

"Alright, *guide*," she said with a sardonic simper. "What do we do now?"

Excited, Toma opened his satchel. Pulling out an old roll of yellowed parchment, he unfurled and held it open in front of her. In the darkness, Mouse could make out shapes, lines, and words.

"Okay, so you probably can't really see it now, but this is a map of the United Dominions." Toma pointed to the bottom right corner part of the map. "We're down here, so, in order to get into Elmnas without being interrogated to death by a Coalition outpost, we'll need to head this way, through the Pilgrim's Pass, into Gormlaen."

Mouse did not really like the idea of passing directly into the Coalition's midst, but it seemed like everywhere she went, they were there anyway. She squinted at the lines on the map, most of it concealed in the darkness.

"There won't be any outposts to cross this border?"

Toma shook his head. "No. Where we are in Maiendell is right across from Gormlaen territory. It's a common trade route. Tons of people pass back and forth every day. Travel isn't so watched here like it might be up in other places. Anyway, it should be pretty easy to get into Gormlaen, we just have to pay a little toll."

"And you've got the money?" Mouse asked.

"That I do." Toma pulled a small, burlap coin purse from his pocket and shook it with delight. "Here it is. All my earnings from working on the farm and with the locals. To be honest, it isn't that much, but we'll be able to get supplies, get where we are going, and maybe stay in a nice, warm tavern along the way."

"You've put a lot of thought into this, haven't you?" Mouse said, impressed.

"Truth is I've always felt like I had something I was supposed to do. Something other than this. I couldn't say what before you came, but now... Well, it didn't take me long to decide I was going with you after we first opened up those letters, anyway." He put the map back in his bag and winked at her. "And we can't go unprepared now, can we?"

"I guess not." Mouse smiled. "If we can help it, anyway."

Heaving her satchel up once more, she turned toward the path that led through the farm.

"Since I can't shake you, let's get going," she teased, waving him over.

"Right," Toma said. He cast a long glance back at his home. But the boy turned, striding to meet her with renewed determination. And before he fell in step beside her, she thought she heard him say:

"I'll come back. I promise."

CHAPTER SIXTEEN

Morning arrived with a titian haze upon the two lone travelers as they walked briskly down the winding, dusty road that led to Pilgrim's Pass. The whipping winds of the night before had settled into a cool breeze that pushed the lower clouds lazily across the sky. Breythorn farm was well behind them now, the open road forlorn and quiet ahead. Toma carefully watched the ditches and rocky outcropping as they went along, searching for any sign of trouble that often befell the unwitting. But nothing stirred, and the uneventful night turned into a still, comfortable morning.

They plodded silently along the wide, dirt road that rose and fell with the rolling hills it lay upon. The brightening of the dawn revealed a wild country, where thorny fields and spiky grasses choked the ground. Enormous boulders broke up the desolate landscape and sat in haphazard piles all around. Satisfied by their progress, Toma picked a collection of rocks where they could eat and rest. He wedged himself in a crevice and swung his satchel around to open it.

"Here." He tossed Mouse a few biscuits. "This should keep you going."

"Thanks." Mouse snagged them eagerly and slaked the hunger she had felt since they left. Even so, it was not unbearable; not like the constant companion of emptiness at the Summit which she had learned to ignore. In contrast, Toma seemed to pale on an empty stomach in just these few short hours. She watched with amusement as he produced several more morsels from various pockets within his jacket. Crumbs spilled from his mouth as he addressed her between bites.

"So, do you think the Coalition guards will recognize you if they see you? When they came yesterday, they just knew the chip was there. Now they do have your description to go off of, but that doesn't have to be a problem." Toma bit off another large chunk and chewed thoughtfully. "They'll be expecting you to travel alone, off the road. It's risky, but I think going out the main road is our best option.

"Once we reach the border, there should be a group of travelers that you can hide in, but that might not be enough. What are you going to do about your hand? That will give you away."

"Hmm, you're probably right." Mouse examined her bandaged hand. Dressed with clean linen, the wound no longer hurt, and Mouse hardly noticed it. Yet, as she flexed her fingers, the pain returned. It would not matter if she took the bandage off – the wound was still raw enough to draw attention. She placed her hand in her pocket.

"I'll keep it in here. It's cold enough out, I think it wouldn't look too strange."

"Yeah, that should work," Toma said, wolfing down his last mouthful. As soon as his hands were free, he reached back into his satchel and pulled out two dark brown hoods.

"Here, put this on. It should solve our other problem."

He threw one of the hoods at Mouse who caught it with her good hand.

"How?" Mouse studied it skeptically. "Won't we look even more suspicious in these?"

"Nah, the winds can get pretty bitter in the valley. It's a traveling necessity." Toma positioned the hood low over his eyes, leaving only his grinning mouth uncovered. "See? Practical and fashionable! Now, ready to get moving?"

Mouse let out a mock groan, but smiled nonetheless as she pulled the hood over her head and tucked it into the collar of her jacket. "Yeah, okay, let's go."

The pair hopped down from their crevasse and were ambling back to the road when Toma stuck his arm out in front of Mouse.

"Wait," he whispered, looking cautiously into the distance. "Just stand here for a minute."

Mouse nodded and hunched down into the low ditch on the roadside. Curious, she peered over the edge, and soon, a familiar light rumbling echoed in the distance. As the rumbling grew louder, Toma trudged down the road beyond her. Presently, a small hovercraft appeared on the horizon. It flew rapidly toward them, the glint of the black metal plates and the shape of its sleek, smooth body catching her eye as it zoomed by, not even slowing to avoid Toma. Rocks, dirt, and debris rattled and jumped from the road in its wake. Toma stopped walking and watched it as it passed, waiting until it disappeared before returning to the ditch.

He lent her a hand and pulled her up onto the road. "Just a speeder. Nothing to worry about."

Mouse dusted herself off and followed Toma as he turned to head to Pilgrim's Pass.

"It is only the Coalition who uses the hovercrafts?" she asked, trotting to walk beside him.

"I don't suppose so," Toma replied. "But you have to be pretty wealthy to own one. Lots of manpower and time to make, and the power cells – Byndithine crystals – are very expensive. Only Gormlaeans seem to have that kind of coin. As for us, we take our horses, hitch a ride, or walk."

"I see," Mouse said. "You know, we never worked with the materials that you keep mentioning up on the Summit. We have all sorts of stones and metals, but nothing known as Byndithine or Kyrthite. Are they rare?"

"Well… I guess Kyrthite you can get most places, but it's expensive." Toma clicked his tongue. "It sure cost us a good bit a coin to get ours."

"Now, Byndithine crystals are mined from the deepest parts of the mountains, and the supply is not so plentiful. But if you're lucky enough to have one, it'll last you awhile. It's the only thing that holds a candle to Cardanthium. And of course all that's regulated by the Coalition. You'd have to be natural-born Gormlaean with a lot of gold to get your hands on any of that."

"Cardanthium?"

"Oh, it's this really rare ore," Toma explained. "Very powerful and unique. Harder than every rock and metal known to man, I've been told, and basically indestructible, too. I've even heard it could repel an energy blast if it was shot at, heal sicknesses, and bring good fortune. The tales old folks pass down say it was almost magical. Unlike anything ever seen in Reidara. But, here's the real reason everyone wanted it—when used for energy, it was ten times more powerful than a Byndithine crystal."

Mouse shot Toma a puzzled look. "You keep saying, 'was.' What happened to the Cardanthium?"

"I've never seen it," Toma admitted. "It got all used up when people started using it for fuel."

"They weren't conserved?"

"That's the thing," Toma said. "No one knew it would happen. They lasted so long that people could live their whole lives before the power cut out. And then, of course, by that time, people were using Cardanthium to power everything. When the Cardanthium ingots started to die, people tried to melt them down to use like they did before, for weapons and buildings and things, but they just crumbled. My father says many tried to save the ones they had – take them out before they lost all power, but it didn't matter. The damage was done, and they crumbled, too."

"Whoa," Mouse remarked. "What happened after that?"

"Nothing good," Toma replied. "Cardanthium used to be everywhere in the United Dominions, actually. You could find it in the rocks everywhere. But as soon as everyone found out it could be destroyed, it was mined out of existence. And then came the hard times. Cities went dark, life halted everywhere, and people started to starve – the Great Power Crisis. Of course, that's when the Coalition swooped in to 'save' us."

Here Toma scoffed loudly. "Anyway, another legend from a lost time."

Mouse fell quiet, chewing her fingernail contemplatively. How strange it was that Toma talked so vividly of things he had never seen but had only heard. His world was a foreign one to his ancestors. She wondered what life must have been like in the days before the war–the days of the sun, of abundant energy, of an era full of hope and potential. Indeed, her own world never greeted her in such a way, from its lost beginnings to the present. Even the scenery surrounding her was cold, desolate, and broken. Mouse jammed her hands into her pockets, speculating if anything would ever change. Would Reidara look just as bleak and dull in another mile as it did where she walked now? And what of the many miles ahead? Was there any hope?

She sighed, unable to muster any optimism. Instead, she turned her head slightly to look at Toma, whose hooded profile only revealed the pointed tip of his nose. She thought it hid him quite well, but she would not have minded seeing his disheveled hair, bronze skin, and his ever-ready smile.

An unruly wind began to blow roughly along their way, kicking up torrents of dirt and debris around them. The morning was shifting into the afternoon, and already Mouse could not ignore the stiffness in her joints and muscles lingering from the perils of the day before. She hoped they would not have to run – at this point, she was not sure if she could. Toma, however, walked purposefully on, hurrying despite the constant and unpleasant spray of pebbles and dirt pelting them as they went.

"There." Toma pointed through the dusty haze. "Pilgrim's Pass is just beyond this hill."

Mouse squinted into the distance, unable to discern anything but the silhouette of some hills rising beyond them. "I can't see it."

"You'll see it as soon as the winds die down," Toma assured her, attempting to shield his eyes from the dirt now blowing into them. "Ah, that's better."

The wind changed as they made their way over a particularly steep hill and came down the other side. Ahead of them, Mouse could see the path, which wound down the hillside and into a small gap between two high ridges. It rose sharply with the ridge and snaked along it, but the ground at the mouth of the gap was low and flat. Groups of travelers as well as several speeders lined the road in front of them, forming a large queue in front of the narrow pass. Toma drew closer to Mouse.

"When we get there," he said, keeping his voice low. "Don't say anything or look at anybody. Keep your hands in your pockets, too. I don't know if there will be any Coats around, but if there are, remember that they should be looking for you on your own. Just don't panic, and don't stick out. I think we'll be able to manage. Okay?"

Mouse nodded vigorously in response.

"Okay." Toma smoothed his coat and tugged his hood over his cheeks. He exhaled sharply. "Don't panic."

"Toma?" Mouse interjected before he stepped forward.

"Yeah?" he replied shakily, turning toward her. The shadow of his hood cloaked his face down to the bridge of his lips, but his amber eyes gleamed from beneath it.

"Stay close?" Mouse asked.

Toma's lips curled into a brief smile.

"Obviously."

Gathering their courage, they walked down the path and joined the straggling groups of travelers beyond the entrance to the pass. Conversation and commotion immediately surrounded the two as they slipped into throng's midst. Toma had been right – there were far too many people here for her to stand out. Like her, many of the travelers wore heavy hoods over their heads. Quite a few were completely cloaked. Feeling his gentle touch against her arm, Mouse sidled closer to Toma and laced her arm through his. The last thing she wanted to do was lose him in the milling mass.

Toma elbowed Mouse and pointed through the crowd. "There will be a toll up ahead. I've come up with my father once before, and it is pretty simple. You just pay the man and go."

The clustering pack thinned out beyond them and formed a short, messy line. As they inched forward, Mouse could see the path disappearing into the ridge, winding along until it came down into

Gormlaen. Transports and speeders passed impatiently by on their left side, slowing just enough to avoid running anyone over.

"Don't they have to stop?" Mouse wondered.

"There's a checkpoint a little way ahead for hovercrafts, on the other side of the pass. I doubt they check them, though. Not much of a reason to, since they're mostly Coats anyway."

Despite the large group, the line moved quickly. Trading caravans and carts with goods seemed to take the longest. Here the toll man would come out and check the contents before waving them along. As they drew closer, apprehension washed over her. She hated the thought of being scrutinized, even if it was the only way to cross the border. Doubt overtook her as a host of unanswered questions entered her worried mind. *What if the toll man grows suspicious? What if a transport stops to question the travelers? And even if we get past the toll, what will happen when we walk by the checkpoint through the pass?* Surely, there would be Coalition guards crawling all over the place.

Tingling with unease, Mouse threw a covert glance at Toma and squeezed his arm. He appeared entirely unconcerned, flashing a reassuring smile her way before idly whistling as they waited. If he was nervous, Toma did not betray it. Mouse hoped the man was not as discerning as Toma's father. Unable to mirror his nonchalant attitude, Mouse stared at the ground, trying to control the leaping of her heart at each step.

"Names and papers," a voice in front of them rasped.

Mouse peeked up to see a miserable man standing there, skewering Toma with frigid, blue eyes. The man may not have been that old, but the deep lines in his face and the great curvature of his bent back gave him an ancient appearance. His thinning, wispy gray hair sprouted and pointed in odd directions on his wrinkled, leathery head. Shoots of those gray hairs bristled on his jutting chin and around his thin, taut mouth.

He stood in front of a little shack, which Mouse assumed he operated his collections from and stayed in when it became too cold. Her heart jumped to her throat as she saw a younger man standing beyond him, his back partially turned as he mindlessly smoked a long pipe. His coat bore a red insignia of two four-legged, maned creatures facing each other, baring fangs with their front paws meeting. The coat fell to his waist, pulled back on the side facing her to reveal a sleek, short-barreled weapon hanging there. She pulled the hood lower over her eyes and tried not to sway nervously.

Without missing a beat, Toma granted the toll man's request. "Bren Grey and Tilia Stone," he offered, rather convincingly. "We have no papers. They were never required in the past."

The toll man raised an eyebrow as he looked at the two of them. "The dictum came through yesterday. Missed it, did you?"

He turned to stare suspiciously at Mouse, blue eyes probing her. Mouse remained motionless, pursing her lips to keep from whimpering. She distracted herself from his piercing gaze by looking straight ahead, watching the Coalition guard. It was terrifying enough to have the gate man interrogate Toma, but if the guard were paying any attention, they would not stand a chance. He was distracted, for now, but at the rate they were going, he would be over to them soon enough.

Behind them, the waiting travelers were growing restless. They stood a few feet away, far enough to keep from hearing their discussion, but close enough to be annoyed at the hold up. An angry grumbling was already starting. Mouse only hoped their grumbles did not turn into anything worse. She chanced an inconspicuous glance at the queue to gauge the situation, and met the startling gaze of a shadowy figure instead.

The figure, a man, wore a long, dark cloak clasped at the neck. He stood a head taller than most of the travelers, and as such, had no trouble observing them at the mouth of the pass. Mouse could not see his face, but there were two sharp eyes glowering defiantly from behind the shade of his hood into hers.

Breath catching in her throat, she diverted her gaze to the ground. Still, she could feel the eyes upon her, causing prickles of panic to dance up her spine.

"State your business," the toll man demanded.

Toma looked a little taken aback, as if offended he would ask such a question. He puffed out his chest and glared back, annoyed.

"That's never been required in the past!"

Mouse bit her lip at Toma's response. *This isn't helping!*

Casting a quick glance over his shoulder at the Coalition guard, the toll man frowned. The guard, though still preoccupied with his smoke, appeared to be finishing up. His return to his post would be momentary.

"You'll need to be telling me, boy."

Toma scratched the back of his head, doing his best to look unconcerned. Out of the corner of her eye, she watched the stranger behind them. He stood silently by, still watching.

Toma leaned in toward the old man, his tone confidential. "What will it take to get you to look the other way?"

The toll man cackled.

"What have you got to offer, peasant?" He jeered, nodded at Mouse. "This one'll fetch a nice price, sure, but I ain't in the trade."

Toma rolled his eyes. "I have gold."

"Sure you do," the toll man said, wiping a tear from his eye. He cast another glance at the Coalition Guard, who had finished his smoke, but was lethargically twiddling his pipe in his hand. The toll man raised a hand to his chin, debating his options.

"I'm suppose t' stop any young women comin' through here, get your papers, and have this here gentleman give 'em a check." The man jabbed his thumb in the air, aiming at the guard behind him. "And since you don't have no papers, that would be a bit of a problem."

"We've been traveling for a while," Toma replied, visibly irritated. "From the other side of Maiendell. Most folk there have no use for papers – why would they have them?"

He glowered, unconvinced. Wearied of the conversation, again his gaze drifted behind him. As the Coalition guard returned the pipe to his coat and meandered lazily toward them, Mouse knew it would be over soon. As she gritted her teeth, a sudden great commotion broke out behind them. Mouse, Toma, and the toll man looked on curiously as travelers shouted and roiled around each other. One particularly enraged bellow came from the middle of the group. Fists flew everywhere. Standing in the thick of it was the dark cloaked stranger, throwing men off of him like ragdolls.

"Hey!" the Coalition guard roared, ripping his weapon from its holster and brandishing it toward the crowd. "What's going on over there?"

There were shrieks of pain, fear, and anger as the guard bowled through the horde, whacking heads with the butt of his gun. Mouse looked on intently, but the shrouded stranger was suddenly missing. Shrugging, the toll man turned back toward Toma.

"Like I said, I should be getting papers," he repeated. "But seeing as my friend there is a bit preoccupied, I might just look the other way. If you give me a reason, of course."

"Of course," Toma answered, relieved. "How much?"

"40 pieces," he grinned.

Toma's jaw dropped. "Are you serious?"

His smug grin quickly twisted into a snarl. "What are your options otherwise?"

Taking the hint, Toma dug into his pocket and pulled out the coin purse, dumping the gold into his hand, contempt curling his lips. Only a few loose coins rattled around in the small bag, which Toma stuffed hastily into his pocket. Delighted, the toll man greedily counted his haul. He waved them off distractedly.

"Move along then!"

Needing no other incentive to leave, Mouse dragged Toma into the pass at a near trot. Toma, however, seemed little affected by the encounter, save for the look of disgust he wore as they hurried away. Only until after they had gone a good distance into the pass did Mouse release Toma's arm.

"What was that all about?" she cried, bewildered.

"That man thoroughly robbed us," Toma said angrily. "I mean, it worked, but—"

"Worked?" Mouse interrupted, hissing. "You call that working? Your friendly little chat back there nearly had us killed! Lucky for you that the guard had his hands full!"

The contempt on Toma's face melted into a grin. "Oh come on, Mouse, haven't you heard of bargaining before? That was just small talk."

"Small talk?" Mouse groaned. "Is that what you call bribery?"

"Hey, those types are all the same! They don't care about anything except an extra lining for their pockets. You didn't need to worry. Although I did underestimate his patience a little."

"He was about to hand us over!" Mouse exclaimed.

"Eh... I probably should have been hastier to flash the gold," Toma admitted apologetically. "But the man was being unreasonable. That whole papers thing? Ridiculous. No one carries papers. We've been crossing the borders without papers since I was a kid."

"Well, I don't want to have to do that again." Mouse rubbed her temples. "That was way too close."

"Yeah," Toma agreed. "But we were lucky. Had that Coat not been putting down a riot, we might have been in a little trouble."

Mouse shuddered to think of what would have happened otherwise, but it was no coincidence. She remembered the cloaked stranger, standing ominously in the midst of the crowd.

"Toma," she whispered. "There is something I need to tell you. Something I saw."

"What is it?" He twisted his neck to look back over his shoulder. "That guard isn't coming after us, is he?"

"No, no it's not that. I saw... someone. Watching us. A tall man, wearing a dark cloak. I couldn't see his face." Mouse lowered her voice further. "I think... I think he may have started the riot, trying to get in front of people at the pass. He was in the middle of it, and he looked right at me. I don't know how, but I got the feeling he knew exactly who I was."

"Oh," Toma said, shaking his head. "That can't be good."

"Do you know who it was?" Mouse asked. "He definitely wasn't Coalition. He hid from the guard."

"I'm afraid he's something worse."

"What could be worse than the Coalition?" Mouse said, surprised.

"A bounty hunter," Toma replied darkly.

"Uh... a what?"

"A hired human hunter. To find fugitives, like you. A good bounty hunter is an expert tracker and a skilled fighter, and they stop at nothing to get their payout. They're very good at what they do."

"But why would the Coalition hire someone to catch me if they've got just as good of a chance to find me themselves?"

"Maybe they need to keep the search quiet," Toma considered. "The secrets you're carrying... people get curious. Can't imagine the Coats want anyone to get a whiff of that. Bounty hunters, on the other hand, don't ask questions. All they see when they look at you is a bag of gold."

Mouse looked fearfully over her shoulder, sure she would see the cloaked stranger tailing them. To her relief, all she saw were the walls of the pass, rising and falling around her. As it snaked along the ridge, sharply turning with the contours of the mountain, the path left the mouth of the pass far behind them. A few travelers had been let into it and had come around the corner, but no shrouded figure walked among them. She breathed easy, for once, and turned back to Toma.

"How long does it take to get through the pass?"

"Not long," Toma answered. "Maybe the rest of the day. The city of Lilien is right on the other side. We should get there in the late afternoon."

"And you're not worried we'll be stopped on the other side of the pass?"

"Nah." Toma waved his hand dismissively. "Lilien gets a lot of traffic – it's a big trade city. My father used to go there all the time to sell produce before the Coalition started visiting the farm every week. Once we get there, you'll see. It'll be a lot easier to disappear."

"What about the bounty hunter?" Mouse wondered.

"I don't know, but our best bet is to surround ourselves with people. They don't really operate under the rule of the law, if you catch my meaning, so taking us on publicly would be pretty stupid. Even if the Coalition uses bounty hunters, Coats don't like them. I'm sure they will take a prisoner from them if they can. No bounty that way, you see."

"Makes sense," Mouse replied. The two rounded a sharp turn in the pass, coming upon a body of travelers in front of them.

"This looks like as good of a chance as any to get lost," she whispered.

"It sure does," Toma agreed, and once more, they slipped into the crowd unnoticed and unhindered on the way to Gormlaen.

CHAPTER SEVENTEEN

T he rest of their trek through the pass was relatively uneventful, despite the brief excitement that got them there. Joining the large herd of commuters had easily been their wisest decision. Noise and dust kicked up by the laden carts, large horses, and braying livestock hid them in plain sight. Hovercrafts occasionally zoomed by, which was of no concern to both the group of travelers and the animals with them. Mouse observed all these things with fascination, barraging Toma with questions every time something new caught her attention. Amused by the novelty of her wonder, Toma indulged her as they made their way into Gormlaen.

It was the first time since Red's disappearance that Mouse enjoyed contentment. Indeed, Mouse knew it could not last, but within the confines of the ridge, the world was small and comforting. She set aside the plans they had laid and all that may come on the other side of the pass. As for now, she smiled, basking in the warmth of an unexpected moment.

Of course, it was hard not to do so with Toma. His natural disposition was humorously impish, and she found herself smiling at his antics more than she might have ever smiled in her life. Toma, for his part, relished having an audience. And, at every punch line, his eyes lit up, and he grinned all the broader to see Mouse crack a smile or offer a rare but sincere chuckle.

Presently, Toma grew serious, and lowered his voice.

"Look," he said, pointing. "The opening of the pass is just ahead. We'll be in Lilien in no time."

Indeed, the ridge peeled away from the path in front of them, dumping them into a valley just on the other side. The ground, which had been sloping downward for the last part of their journey through the pass, gradually leveled as they walked. Ahead there was a small Coalition outpost, where the guards who constantly watched the pass could rest and wait for their shifts. Two speeders idled in front of the outpost. The Coalition guards who drove them stood by, chatting with the guards as they indifferently waved on the crafts that came down the ridge.

"I told you," Toma whispered. "They never check the hovercrafts."

"Let's just hope they don't decide to check on us," Mouse muttered in reply. Instinctively, she pulled her hood over her eyes and kept her head down, the imaginary hedge of protection fading as they approached. Falling silent, Toma laid his hand between Mouse's shoulders and drove her closer to the center of the group. The guards, however, only paused their conversation long enough to eye the crowd contemptuously as it passed. Toma breathed a sigh of relief and smiled at her weakly.

"Well, we've made it. Welcome to Gormlaen."

Cautiously, Mouse lifted her head to peer out from the midst of the crowd, stunned by what she saw. Greeting her on the opposite side of Pilgrim's Pass was an entirely different world. Unlike Maiendell, the dominion Mouse had stepped into had been completely tamed by its residents. The unruly dirt was plowed over and covered with an intricate network of cobbled roads and infrastructure, aligned in perfect grids that webbed over the countryside and stretched to clusters of homes far off in the hills. A sprawling city rose up before her, dotted with buildings that grew denser the further on it went.

Mouse gaped at the meticulous and perfect order of Lilien. The mud and rock studded path had transformed into a paved stone road, which branched away from a broader highway clearly meant for hovercraft traffic. Instead, their path followed the contour of a murky canal on the right. Tall, black lamps lined the walking path, giving way only to the occasional holograstone. Smiling images of Coalition Party Representatives shone from the holograstones and repeated a warm welcome to Gormlaen. As the travelers drew closer, great buildings of stone and metal rose up and loomed over them, crowding the sky with spires and pitched roofs.

The path broke off from the canal and turned toward the heart of the city, where it ultimately emptied out into a gridded market square. Mouse looked on with wonder as they wandered in, the square barely containing its bedlam. Booths, carts, and tables haphazardly marked the square, situated to avoid the intricate fountains and statues erected strategically throughout the grid. Shouting out from their booths and tables, peddlers proudly displayed colorful baubles, ripe produce, or exotic creatures to any who lingered. Myriads of people milled around the market, shifting around and filing past each other in a chaotic dance that threatened to erupt in entropy at any moment. Though their group of travelers had dispersed throughout the market, some even setting up booths and carts of their own, Toma and Mouse were by no means alone. It was unlike anything she had ever seen.

"This… this is Lilien?" Mouse whispered in awe.

"Yes." Toma grinned. "Would you believe me if I told you this is a small city for Gormlaen?"

Mouse shook her head slowly, her mouth hanging open at the sight. Toma chuckled.

"Yeah, I felt like that on my first trip, too. Come on then, before someone tries to sell us something."

Taking Mouse by the arm, Toma promptly pulled her around the square to the city's streets. Though it was not nearly as chaotic in the channels between the buildings, there was still a great deal of activity. Horses, people, and one-man hovercrafts moved down the street in both directions. Bricked-in shops and houses lined the street, looking strangely archaic as metal structures protruded behind them. As they came to the street's corner, Toma halted, swinging his head indecisively in each direction.

"Now, if I remember correctly, there is a tavern somewhere... up this street."

He pointed toward a cluster of aged buildings.

"Are you sure?" Mouse asked doubtfully.

Toma squinted up and down the street. Finally, he offered a confident nod.

"Yeah, I'm sure." He motioned at a group of rectangular, metal-sided structures with cylindrical shafts shooting out from them, towering over the street crossing ahead and down to the canal. "See, over to the right, that's the industrial district. We don't want to go there. But if you keep taking this road to the left, you'll hit the business district, where all the new Coalition buildings are. Probably want to avoid that as well. But up ahead, that's all part of the old city, and that's where we'll stay."

"Think we'll be safe?" Mouse questioned, gazing in awe at the city around her.

"From the Coats? Absolutely. They steer clear of the old city district at night," Toma said.

"Oh?" Mouse's eyes narrowed. "Why is that?"

"It's... kind of a seedy area – but don't worry," Toma quickly supplied. "As long as we stay inside the tavern for the night, we should be left alone."

"Hm," Mouse said, frowning. She had known her share of seedy places and people, and she was not anxious to spend time around either. Besides, how could Toma be sure they would be safe? She pressed her hands in her pockets, shaking her head.

"I don't like it."

"Listen, Mouse – we got to stay somewhere. Honestly, anywhere else that's not crawling with Coats is going to have the same problem. Also"–he lowered his voice–"there's still that bounty hunter to think of. The sooner we get inside, the better."

"Yes, I suppose you're right," Mouse conceded, albeit reluctantly. "I'm with you."

Long shadows cast by the ancient buildings enveloped the streets as the two passed into the old city district, hastening the transition of late afternoon to dusk. Though Toma had led them in the right direction, the walk to the inn had taken longer than he had expected. They hurried along without words, perilously exposed as the foot traffic diminished with the lengthening shadows. The pair halted before passing beneath a wooden sign jutting just over the street corner.

"Twin Lions Inn and Tavern," Mouse read as the sign swung noisily in the stirring wind. "Is this the place?"

A remnant of days long ago, the building attached to the sign was cobbled together with large, irregular stones and crumbling, black pitch. An awning that sagged wearily with neglect and age hung over two large, dingy windows, and a heavy black door. Through them, Mouse could see the weak glow of dimmed lights on the tavern tables.

"This is it," Toma confirmed. "Come on, let's go inside."

Toma yanked on the wooden door, releasing the scent of simmering food and the din of laughter and conversation trapped inside. Mouse stepped into the doorway behind Toma, careful to keep her face covered as she peered around. She was surprised to see the room rather full, with patrons cloaked in muted tones that made them seem to melt into the framework. There was a noticeable hush as they entered. Mouse winced and nervously stuffed her hands further into her pockets. As inconspicuously as she could, she surveyed the room, hoping they had not drawn any real attention to themselves.

Groups crowded the crude tables, eating and drinking voraciously. Some paused to eye Mouse disinterestedly as she clacked over the rickety wooden floors, but to her relief, most simply ignored her. The clamor of conversation rose once more as they crossed the room. Mouse exhaled shakily. Though satisfied with the general response of apathy, she still got the feeling someone was watching. She glanced briefly toward those huddled in the shadowy corners, but the low light and the tendrils of pipe smoke curling in the air obscured them.

Not daring to let her gaze linger, she followed Toma. He approached the bar at the back of the room, where several men sat hunched over the counter with pints in hand. There was no innkeeper in sight, so Toma waited, drumming his fingers on the counter's surface. Mouse stood awkwardly behind him, impatiently searching for anyone who looked capable of helping them. A portly middle-aged man soon appeared from a doorway in the back. Mouse breathed an easy sigh as he approached them, smiling.

"Welcome to the Twin Lions," he hailed, compensating for the din of the room. "I'm Dresher. What can I do for you this evening?"

"We're looking for a place to stay. Do you have room?" Toma asked.

"Sure, sure," Dresher replied, grabbing an empty mug from one of his patrons to refill it. "Got at least one left yet, up yonder stairs."

He wagged his head toward the doorway he came from. Mouse could glimpse a staircase winding up just beyond it.

"How much?" Toma pressed.

"Ten piece a' night," Dresher answered. "Per person, that is."

"Good, we'll take it," Toma said, handing him a few coins. "Oh, and any chance we can get what's cooking? It's been a long day."

"Yessir. Have a seat. I'll bring it on over," Dresher said, sweeping his hand toward one of the corner tables.

Mouse plopped into the seat, exhausted. Toma slid in across from her, no hint of weariness betrayed in his broad smile. Instead, he rubbed his hands together excitedly.

"What a day, huh? Ran away from home, crossed dominion borders, and slipped right under the Coats' noses. I'm going to go ahead and thank myself for a job well done."

"I wouldn't do that just yet," Mouse replied. "You did almost get us caught, and now there's a bounty hunter after us."

"Don't sully my victory!" Toma pouted, jesting. "Even if it was… poorly executed."

"Okay, okay, I'll give you that," Mouse granted. "But I do have to ask you. What do we do now? Getting into Gormlaen is going to feel pretty lousy if we can't find a way out."

Toma nodded solemnly, the grin fading from his face. "Yeah. There are still a few things I haven't quite got figured out yet."

"We're going to have to know soon," Mouse whispered. "We can't stay here."

"I know, I know," Toma said, running his hand through his hair. "I had most of it planned out, I really did, but there are just some things I can't get around. First thing – I'm not exactly sure what the best way is to get into Elmnas. If you remember, on the map I showed you, there is a mountain range between Elmnas and Gormlaen. Sure, there are multiple passes, but I know for a fact all should be heavily guarded. We just can't count on the fortune we had getting in."

"But you've thought of something?" Mouse asked.

"Yes…" Toma spoke hesitantly. "There is only one other way I can think of getting through. I once heard of a place, way up north, where no one goes. A river that cuts through the mountains, called Thunder Run."

"And what's the catch?"

"It's uh, pretty dangerous."

"How dangerous?"

"Well," Toma replied, taking a deep breath. "The kind of dangerous two non-river folk like you and me probably wouldn't survive."

"What do we do?"

Toma leaned back and rubbed his chin. "Maybe we could hire a guide? Hmm, I don't see how I'll have enough gold to pay for a decent one. And I guess… you're gonna need it if you want someone who'll break half of the Coalition's laws for a few strangers."

"All I had to give you was the truth." Mouse raised an eyebrow. "And for everyone else, money talks."

Toma squinted suspiciously. "What are you implying?"

"You learn to get things you need if you want to survive at Misty Summit," she said, lowering her voice. "I can get you the gold."

"Mouse…"

"Last resort, okay?" she compromised. "What else do we need to worry about?"

"Okay, the other thing is this – neither of us know what we're going to need to do or where we need to go once, if we get to Elmnas."

"What do you mean?"

"It's a big country, Mouse. Bigger than Gormlaen, Maiendell, and Heibeiath combined." Toma frowned as he considered it. "And once we're there, we can't exactly go up to people and ask them to point us in the right direction. It's Coats country now. And the Elmling tribes… well, we've all heard the stories. Not your friendliest group of natives. We're walking in there blind."

"I guess you're right about that," Mouse sighed. "Even if Red had anything to do with the raids or rebellion or whatever happened there, I don't know anything about who he was in the past. At least I can speak the language, though. That's got to be worth something."

"Yeah," Toma held up a finger hopefully. "And we might have something else, and we just haven't tapped into yet."

"What could that be?" she asked, frowning. There were no other clues to follow. All they had was in Red's things, and nothing more could be gleaned from those letters or her fleeting dreams.

Toma crossed his arms and nodded. "You."

Mouse scoffed. "Me? I doubt it."

"Think about it though. If you really were an Elmling before you came to Misty Summit, you'll start to remember things about being there."

"Oh, Toma, I don't know…" Mouse exhaled sharply. "It's been a long time. Those dreams – memories – whatever, they don't make sense. What if I can't remember anything useful?"

"You will, I'm sure of it. All you need to do is go back – retrace your steps. Sometimes, forgotten things come back that way," Toma answered emphatically. "Maybe that's just what you need. Maybe something will be familiar."

"So that's the plan." Mouse commented, a touch of cynicism in her tone. "Go back, and hope I remember something helpful?"

At this, Toma shrugged helplessly, a rakish grin tugging at the corners of his mouth. "Yep, that's what I got."

She had to admire his playfulness, even now – completely unfazed, as it were, by her sober, steely demeanor. He was disarming, calming, a sliver of light in a dark room. Once again, Mouse felt exposed, laid bare beneath Toma's gaze, but this time it didn't frighten her. It was as if he had searched and found some part of her still childlike, wondrous, and innocently mischievous. Something she never dreamed was there – at least, not until she met him. Had she ever met anyone like him before?

Mouse shook these new thoughts of her head and continued their conversation.

She raised her hands in mock resignation. "Well, Toma Breythorn, you just might be in luck. I had my dream again, just last night."

She waited as Dresher brought drinks and bowls of thick, saucy stew to their table. He nodded before hurrying off to attend to the needs of the other patrons. She took a few bites hungrily before continuing.

"But there was more to it, as Red had predicted."

Toma's bright amber eyes lit up with hopeful excitement. "Tell me what happened."

"I was asleep in my dream," Mouse began. "Someone was carrying me. I opened my eyes. We were moving. There was so much noise, and it seemed like everything around me was on fire. When I looked up, it was the woman – the face I have been seeing night after night at Misty Summit. She told me to go back to sleep. I heard something pop, and then the sky just… exploded. I was so scared. It was awful. Then, I woke up."

Toma stared wide-eyed at Mouse, listening raptly.

"Do you think it's a real memory?"

"I don't know," Mouse replied honestly. It seemed so real even as she dreamed it, but how could she be sure it was not the product of a mind crowded with the terrors of the previous day? "I still can't remember anything else."

"That's it. It has to be," Toma said confidently, pounding a fist on the table. "You remembered."

"Maybe," she shrugged. "But that still does not get us any closer to Elmnas."

"It may," Toma speculated as he dug into his bowl of stew. "You're already remembering more. If you keep doing that… well, we just might have the answer to at least one of our problems."

"So what do we do now?" Mouse asked, distractedly pushing the remaining meat mixture around her bowl with her spoon. Yes, they had accomplished getting this far, but that anxious desperation was returning with a vengeance. There was no telling what would come next, and though Toma had proved capable, here he was just as clueless as she.

"Well?" she asked again when Toma did not answer.

Instead of bedding her fears, Toma simply shrugged and continued devouring his stew. "Get some sleep, hope you have another dream, and plot our course in the morning," he said between bites. "Don't worry so much. I'm a plans kind of guy, but I work best under pressure. I'll come up with something soon."

"Uh huh," Mouse eyed Toma doubtfully as he buried three rolls in his mouth with gusto. Too worn out to press the point further, Mouse sighed and said nothing. It was becoming clear that like her own spontaneous life-or-death decisions, Toma's schemes were sometimes just as half-baked. Of course, Mouse had to give him credit – Toma got them this far. Even the incident at the toll seemed miniscule in retrospect. Still, the fear of discovery continued to fester. Though she did not want to admit it, Mouse knew that it was only a matter of time before their luck ran out.

"I think I'm going to find Dresher," Mouse finally decided, pushing herself away from the table. "I'd like to get some rest."

"Oh, go ahead," Toma grunted. "I'll be up shortly."

Mouse made her way to the bar area, but Dresher was nowhere to be found. Hoping he was preparing her room, she slipped behind the open doorway in the back. Like the rest of the tavern, the rustic room sagged with age. It stretched back into a hallway, where Mouse could see a few open doors full of dusty bottles and cleaning supplies. Dim lights hung in sconces along the walls where low, wooden beams joined and braced the ceiling. She stopped at the rough, wooden staircase that lay directly in front of her. It climbed into a hole in the rafters, as if the rest of the building had been an afterthought.

The din of the tavern continued in muffled tones behind her as she walked further into the room. Back here, it was oddly quiet, except for the creaking of the building as the outside winds blew tirelessly against it. Glimpsing the glide of a shadow in the hallway behind the stairway, Mouse hastened toward it.

"Dresher?" she said softly as she approached. Curiously, the hallway seemed empty when she reached it. The only thing that appeared to move was the flickering light in the hallway sconce.

"Hello?" she called again, a bit louder. No one answered. The narrow hall had dead-ended into a small, cobweb infested closet. Mouse sighed as the light in the sconce behind her suddenly died. She flicked off the dust beginning to settle on her shoulders. Clearly, no one had been back here for a while. Shrugging, Mouse turned around, wishing she were already in bed and sleeping off the heavy stew sitting in her stomach.

Instead, she found the cloaked stranger from the pass standing directly in her way.

CHAPTER EIGHTEEN

His tall silhouette filled the frame of the narrow hallway, blocking the feeble light streaming in from the room behind him. Mouse shrank back into the darkness, realizing with mounting panic there would be no escape. He approached with singular purpose, his calculated steps thudding against the creaking, wooden floor. She thought of stunning him with a surprise offensive, but as he approached, he drew back the inside of his cloak, revealing the hilts of two blades glowing a faint green in the darkness. Mouse whimpered as the cloaked stranger towered over her. He had her hopelessly cornered. She opened her mouth to scream, but with almost inhuman speed his hand wrapped around her face to stifle it. He was close enough for Mouse to see the whites of his eyes gleaming out from beneath his hood.

"Don't cry out," he said. "Your friend will come along shortly."

Mouse struggled desperately, but the stranger's grip was strong. He waited motionlessly for her stop, holding her there as one would hold a child throwing a tantrum. After a few moments of fruitless twisting, Mouse settled onto the floor and glared at him angrily.

"Out of your system now?" he asked impatiently. Mouse continued to glare at the indistinguishable face inside the hood. "I don't have time for it."

He grabbed her by the nape of her coat collar and yanked her to her feet. Her pride hurt more than anything, Mouse stood and brushed herself off gingerly. He simply stood in front of her, waiting. Mouse did not know much about bounty hunters, but this certainly did not seem conventional.

Mouse eyed him quizzically. "What do you want with me?"

"Come," he answered.

The stranger placed a firm hand on her shoulder and pushed her in front of him. She could hear the muffled noise of the tavern beyond the staircase, but the cloaked stranger swiftly guided her to a door across from the hall. Before Mouse had the chance to think, she was behind the door and inside a darkened room. The bounty hunter pushed her onto the floor and bound her hands and feet to a post behind her with professional efficiency. After looping and tightening a gag about her mouth, he turned on his heel and exited the room, shutting the door with a soft click.

Mouse struggled against the restraints, but it was no use. She was completely immobilized – unable to either move or shout for help. Squinting into the inky room, she searched for something that could aid her escape. Large, opaque shapes emerged around her. She pulled against the post she was bound to, and it creaked with her effort. Encouraged, Mouse tried to stand up, only to be pushed down by a joint low on the post. *It's a bed.* The bounty hunter must have rented a room at the inn and thrown her into it. She shifted down on the floor and attempted to pull her bonds from beneath the post, but ceased when she heard the familiar click of the door.

It swung open, flooding the room with light. Toma stood in the doorway, the cloaked stranger at his back. She could see the glint of metal in the stranger's hand as he shoved Toma inside and shut the door. In the darkness, Mouse could hear Toma tumble to her side and land clumsily on the wooden floor. Suddenly, the light flicked on, revealing the stranger decisively holding a short dagger. Purposefully ignoring the man's presence, Toma leaned in toward Mouse.

"Are you okay?" Toma asked breathlessly. His hands, she could now see, were also bound behind his back. He looked at her expectantly, the corner of his mouth betraying a slight tremor. Unable to answer, Mouse nodded. She appreciated Toma's concern, but her eyes were now on the stranger, who moved silently about the room, the edge of his cloak floating about him like a shadow. Toma glared at him, seething.

"What do you want?" he demanded.

The stranger simply held a finger to the mouth of his hood and stood in the middle of the room, listening. He twirled the dagger in his hand dangerously, effectively silencing both Toma and Mouse's objections. Instead, Toma stared hard at the floor, avoiding the man's piercing gaze. The stranger watched them for a long moment, waiting for Mouse to stop struggling. Finally satisfied, he crouched in front of them.

"Do not move," he said, cutting loose the bonds on both Mouse and Toma. Registering Toma's look of surprise, the stranger again made the dagger dance upon his fingers.

"I do this with the expectation you will behave. Do not test me." He stood up and pointed to two chairs behind him. "Sit."

They did as they were told. The stranger strode the room in agitation, still brandishing the dagger. A familiar blade.

"Is that your dagger?" Mouse whispered to Toma, her eyes glued to the pacing man.

"Nicked it from before I even saw him," Toma's sullen reply came.

"Now," the bounty hunter said, stopping mid-pace to look at them. "I have hunted many different kinds of intelligent creatures, all in a variety of desperate situations. Sometimes, in their desperation, they will make mistakes, and it is in that moment of miscalculation, I strike. But I have never, in all of my years, witnessed a move so incredibly half-witted that I almost missed the moment myself, because I was too stunned to believe that it had actually happened."

Taken aback, the two stared at the stranger, open-mouthed.

"What?" Toma bristled, finally recovering from his own shock. "Are you crazy? What are you talking about?"

"Do you have any idea why I prevented you from going upstairs? Or of what is awaiting you there?"

"I couldn't say, bounty hunter," Toma spat sarcastically. "Seeing as how we're down here."

The stranger shook his head. "I am no bounty hunter, and I am the least of your concerns."

"You were at the pass," Mouse spoke up. "I saw you. You tried to capture us there."

"I am glad to hear you're not nearly as unobservant as I first suspected." He sighed. "Yes, I was there, but not to capture you. Traveling, if you can believe it, just like yourselves. As fate would have it, the only reason you made it through that pass is because of me."

"Yeah, that must be it," Toma sneered dismissively. "Or, we got through because that Coat was stopping you from cutting ahead, and I had the sense to bribe the toll man."

"Do not think for a moment it was your cunning that got you through," the stranger said sharply. "If I had not started that disturbance, the two of you would be on a transport headed directly for Misty Summit, or in more dire straits."

"How do you know all this?" Mouse said, astonished.

"Tell us," Toma demanded, squinting at the stranger. "Who are you?"

Mouse flinched as the stranger approached, anxious that Toma's smart mouth might have merited him more than an answer. Instead of retaliating, however, the stranger stood still in front of them, calmly considering the question.

"That would take a long time to explain," he said finally, lowering his hood. A gaunt and pale face with thin lips, a long, straight nose, and two stormy gray eyes emerged from beneath the cowl's shadow. Black hair hung over the man's ears and a short, shaggy beard grew thickly around his face and neck, rugged as if he had been living wildly for many days. His steeled, worn demeanor hinted at sobriety, but not malice as Mouse expected. He took a seat on the bed opposite of them before speaking again.

"Some of these things must wait. But for now, you may call me Blade. In this life, I am a hunter of sorts. Beasts, not people. Many call upon my services when the need arises. Two days ago, I was contracted to track and kill a pack of Mistwolves in the shadow of the Jagged Jaw

Mountains, only to find that they had already been slaughtered. Completely gutted and wantonly blasted apart by energy rifles. The curious work of the Coalition, no doubt. Then came the reports of an escaped prisoner – a murderously mad girl whose insanity had driven her out of the safety of Misty Summit's Healing Ward.

"I suspected something was amiss when the reports had suddenly been hushed. Holograstones briefly claiming the patient had been returned, everything put back in order by the Coalition's estimation. The Coats, however, remained restless, still stopping and questioning every lone girl they came upon in Maiendell. I thought little of it until I came to the pass, and that is when I saw you."

"How did you know it was me?" Mouse whispered.

Blade pointed to her hand. "You never took your hands out of your pockets. The dictum said you would have a wound on one of them. But you were wise about it, and you kept your face covered as well. That was also my first indication that you were not insane."

"And what was your second?"

"Fear," he replied simply. "The mad do not know it. You were petrified."

"Oh," Mouse said, embarrassed. "I had hoped I had hid that better."

"So, why kidnap us and tie us up? What does that have to with anything?" Toma interrupted impatiently.

"Everything," Blade asserted. "I followed you through the pass and then, here. You must know I was not the only one to do so."

"How?" Toma asked incredulously. "We didn't see a single Coat once we got to Lilien."

"There were two men who followed you from the square to the Twin Lions. Dressed as travelers. Energy rifles, military grade, hidden beneath their cloaks. I know, because I was following them." Blade raised a hand to his jaw thoughtfully and stroked his beard. "Like me, they sat in an unassuming corner of the tavern after you arrived, and they watched. While you two were busy enjoying yourselves, they 'asked' old Dresher where you were staying and made their way up to your room. That is where they wait now. What I have done, I did to stop you from wandering into a trap."

"Let me get this straight," Toma started skeptically. "Just a minute ago, you had Mouse completely bound and gagged, you ambush and bind me, and you tell us you've been stalking us all day. But you're 'helping' us – what, out of the goodness of your heart? How did you expect us to believe you, again?"

Blade contemplated the question. "I suppose I can't. I readily admit it is an unbelievable story. But then again, so is yours." He nodded toward Mouse. "Tell me then, how does a child, frightened, but certainly not criminally insane, wind up in a place like Misty Summit Prison? And then, how does that same child survive the hungry hunt of both the Mistwolf and the Coalition?"

"That would take a long time to explain," she quipped.

"Indeed it would," Blade said, raising an eyebrow. "Fair enough. I will save my questions. But maybe I should indulge yours."

"Yeah, thanks buddy," Toma derided.

Blade shot Toma an annoyed look before continuing. "There were many within the Four Dominions, before your time, who suffered greatly at the hands of the Coalition. Not all so willingly fell into rank as they would have you believe. It was through cunning manipulation and limitless cruelty that they prevailed."

The man closed his eyes, and suddenly, years of weariness etched the lines of his face.

"The days of justice are long past, and we are powerless to usher them in once more. Nothing truly heals the wounds, but frustrating the efforts of the Coalition by protecting those who cannot salves those of us who remember – a small victory, yes, but a justice nonetheless."

"Oh sure, the stranger who attacked us and tied us up wants to be our noble protector," Toma mumbled.

"Have I harmed you?" Blade replied earnestly. "Have I not provided reasonable explanations for my actions? On good faith, I have unbound you. Does that not display my true intentions?"

Toma opened his mouth to protest, but Mouse cut him off.

"How are you going to help us?"

"I've concluded you are going to Elmnas," Blade said. "Surely, that is the only reason you would place yourselves so close to danger by coming this way. I do not know what drives you to that wretched country, but on your own, it would be impossible."

"Yes," Mouse concurred. "You're right, and it is very important we get there."

"What are you doing?" Toma muttered under his breath furiously. "You want to give him a better reason to turn us over?"

"If he was going to turn us in, don't you think he would have done it already?" Mouse turned back to Blade. "We need a guide, if you are willing."

Toma shook his head adamantly. "No, Mouse! Just because he hasn't yet does not mean he won't!"

"We don't have a plan, Toma. You said it yourself. There's no way we'll get through Gormlaen on our own. And if he's telling the truth… we're in trouble."

"And what if he's not?" Toma said fiercely.

"I will not stop you, whatever you decide," Blade interrupted calmly. "But if you choose not to believe me, know that you most likely will not leave here alive."

Toma took a deep breath and glanced back at Mouse.

"You're sure about this?"

"Yes," Mouse said, nodding resolutely, "I am."

Toma gave Blade a long, stern look before answering.

"Fine. We'll go with you," he conceded. "As long as you give me back my dagger."

"Of course," Blade said. Solemnly, he stood and placed the dagger in Toma's palm. "If this goes the way I suspect it might, you will need it."

CHAPTER NINETEEN

As Mouse and Toma gathered up their things, Blade briefly outlined his plan to leave the Twin Lions. It was decided they would escape through the back entrance at the end of the hallway to avoid attracting any attention. Heavy shadows shrouded the streets beyond the tavern's walls, which Blade determined would provide them with needed cover. From there, he would lead them back toward the canal, where they could escape into the wild.

All Toma and Mouse would need to do was keep as close to Blade as possible. He crouched by the door with one hand on the handle and the other poised strategically on a black hilt jutting from his cloak. His hood fell over his eyes like a pall, once more concealing him ominously.

"It's almost time," he said, nodding toward them.

Tension mounted in Mouse's chest, but Blade waited calmly, coiled and almost eager for action. She took a deep, cleansing, breath, but it did not help.

He gestured above him. "If we wait any longer, those waiting upstairs will grow wise to our intentions. Mouse, you will follow directly behind me, and Toma, you behind her. Keep your dagger at the ready. We cannot be sure of what awaits us beyond the doors."

"You're still sure about this, right?" Toma murmured into her ear.

Again, Mouse nodded firmly, falling in step behind Blade. Toma's suspicions were understandable, but a plan, she decided, was better than none at all. Even if Toma did not want to admit it, he surely realized having Blade as their guide would give them a much better chance of surviving. She could not quite explain it, but she believed she could trust Blade, just as she believed she could trust Red. At any rate, Mouse hoped she was a better judge of character than Toma was, who continued to glance doubtfully at Blade whenever he turned his back.

"Quietly, now," Blade whispered. "Stay with me."

He flicked out the light and slowly twisted the handle, pulling the door slightly ajar to look outside. The few dim lights in the hallway sconces did little to illuminate their path, and one flickered and died as they stole into the passage. Blade prowled stealthily along the joints of the wall, his dark cloak melting into the flickering shadows.

Mouse followed along closely, afraid she would lose him if she dared to blink. Muffled sounds of merriment and dining floated toward them. How surreal it was, to be hiding in the dark as life went on all around them. And all this life, this busyness – none of it had existed until several days ago. She remembered the drudgery and concreteness of her days on Misty Summit, and she wanted to laugh. None of it made sense. And yet, Toma's anxious, measured breaths behind her struck her as all too terribly real, and the strange spell was broken. If Blade was right, they could very well die this night.

Blade continued to cut a covert path through the tavern's inn, weaving expertly through the maze of doors and halls that Mouse could not have guessed existed. The Twin Lions had looked so small from the outside, but it was turning into a veritable labyrinth that Blade inexplicably knew how to navigate. She began to wonder if the place would ever end when Blade came to a sudden halt in front of her. He threw his arm back to steady her as she and Toma nearly toppled into him.

Blade pointed to the indistinguishable rectangular frame before them. "This door will take us to an alley beside the Twin Lions. Remember, stay close."

Gently turning the knob, Blade opened the door only slightly to slip through it. Mouse and Toma followed at his heels, stepping into the empty, cobbled alley beside the tavern. They had come out at the right side of the building beside a deserted side street, where refuse lay in piles along the tavern's wall. The darkness overhead and the claustrophobic closeness of the adjacent buildings sheltered their alley from the main street ahead of them, where Mouse could discern a silhouette floating unknowingly by. Toma breathed a sigh of relief beside her.

"Good, he hasn't killed us yet."

"Quiet," Blade ordered tersely. He tightly gripped the hilt beneath his cloak as he intently watched the opening in front of them.

"What is it?" Mouse breathed fearfully.

They seemed to be alone in the gloom of the alley, and even the occasional figures wandering by on the street ahead were oblivious to their sudden presence. Blade gave no answer, but held up his free hand, signaling for them to listen. Surely enough, the sound of heavily shod feet echoed from the street to the alley toward them. Motioning for them to crouch, Blade crept along the wall, his hand poised within his cloak. He stopped immediately and shrunk toward the ground, disappearing into the shadows as barely audible voices drifted toward them.

"...if a fight breaks out... doubtful... already captured."

The feminine voice reverberated softly along the stone walls. A lower voice grunted in response, but Mouse did not catch the reply. The sound of clanking and leaden footfalls grew louder as they reached the mouth of the alley. Mouse held her breath as two Coalition guards plodded past, their weapons and armor gleaming beneath a glowing orb resting on a staff that one of the soldiers carried. Blade waited behind a heap of refuse for them to pass. Unaware of their presence, the Coalition guards did not turn aside. The echoes of their boots thudded down the street. Blade crept swiftly back to Mouse and Toma, the grip on his hilt relaxed.

"Sentinels," he said softly. "They do not suspect trouble, as of yet. Let us hope it stays that way. Now come, this way."

Blade hurried toward the back of the alley, where it connected with a dark, narrow side street. Mouse and Toma ran to catch up with him. Just as they were about to round the corner, the side door of the tavern burst open. Mouse swiveled to see two nondescriptly cloaked men brandishing short barreled handguns spilling out into the alley. She froze as they leveled their weapons at her and Toma.

"You're under arrest by order of the Coalition Council. Come quietly," one of the men demanded.

"That's not a possibility," Blade replied. With amazing speed, he leapt in front of Mouse and Toma, shielding them. There he stood resolutely, his towering frame the only thing between Mouse and Toma and the two men. Surprised, they stumble backward a step before they regained their composure.

"We have no quarrel yet, citizen," the other man stated. "Turn over the fugitives, and the Coalition may see fit to reward you."

"Surely," Blade said with an easy cool. "Just as you rewarded my brothers and sisters, yes? Accept this as a token of their gratitude."

In one fluid motion, Blade unsheathed two slender swords from beneath his cloak and swung them with deadly precision. A strange, emerald glow hovered in the air as the glinting twin blades wound gracefully through it, effortlessly slicing the weapons of the Coalition operatives into pieces. They illuminated the shock on the men's faces in a ghoulish green light as Blade set them upon the spies' throats.

"A living Guardian?" one sputtered. "It can't be!"

"He is nothing but a traitor and enemy to the Coalition," the other spat. "You'll die for your crimes, Elmling! I'll see to it personally!"

Without a word, Blade sprung up and surged forward, bashing his hilts onto the top of their heads. They crumpled senselessly to the ground. He then spun around to face Mouse and Toma, who stood with their mouths hanging wide open behind him.

"There is no time to explain. We must move!"

The heavy footfalls of the sentinels who had passed earlier echoed down the street, quickening and growing louder until they stood at the mouth of the alley.

"Run!" Blade hissed, pushing them toward the side street behind them. "That way! Go!"

Mouse whirled and rounded the corner of the adjacent building.

Toma sprinted alongside her, his long legs carrying him easily down the unevenly paved road. Her satchel jostled noisily against her as she fled. She could hear Blade darting behind her, his swords slicing the air as he ran.

"Halt there!" A voice shouted at their backs. Mouse glanced over her shoulder to see the sentinels charging after them. They were gaining, despite their heavy armor. She faced forward, only to find a large, brick wall rearing up in front of her. Skidding to a stop, Mouse spun in a panic. Blade's back was already turned to Mouse and Toma as his blades flashed dangerously in the darkness. The sentinels responded, unslinging long, black rifles from their backs. One sentinel aimed for Blade's heart, and the other, toward Mouse and Toma.

"To the ground!" Blade roared.

Before Mouse could react, Toma roughly grabbed her by her coat and yanked her to the wet, dirty stones below. There was a loud hiss, like steam escaping from a suddenly twisted valve, and she soon felt a blazing heat jet past her. The air around her crackled with energy, pulling at the hairs on her head as light sped by. White streaks crashed into the walls. Blade stood in the midst of it, green and white flashes exploding around him as he parried away the blasts. With another angry hiss, the sentinels' rifles screamed anew, but Blade was not deterred. He let out a ferocious growl as the volley continued.

"Come on!" Toma shouted amidst the madness. "This way!"

Half-pulling, half-dragging Mouse with him, Toma brought her round a corner into another alley. She gained her footing, only to narrowly miss being struck by a white jet hurtling in front of her. The smell of singed hair filled her nostrils as she ran.

"Where are we going?" she asked breathlessly.

"Toward the canal." Toma panted. "I hope."

They ran desperately on, putting as much distance between them and the raging battle as possible. The sound of exploding brick and stone ceased suddenly as they raced forward, deadening the air with an unnatural silence. Mouse's puffing and panting immediately replaced it as she and Toma found themselves running senselessly along a small, brick corridor. Without Blade as their guide, Mouse realized it would be impossible to navigate the endless rows of alleys and side streets.

Toma slowed to a jog before stopping altogether, his expression indicating the same understanding. He breathed heavily as he looked about in confusion. Mouse doubled over in exhaustion and pain, her breath catching in her throat like needles.

Toma laced his fingers behind his head and let out an exasperated sigh. "None of this looks familiar," he rasped. "I have no idea where we are."

Catching her breath, Mouse took in their surroundings. They had wound up in a deserted back alley that lay in the darkness between rows of houses and other smaller buildings. Trash heaps sat in piles against the tall, wooden fences separating the homes from the alley. A rat skittered in front of her and darted into the closest mass of garbage. Mouse choked on the distinct, repugnant stench emanating from it.

"The canal has to be back this way somewhere, doesn't it?" Mouse asked hopefully. "We came from this direction earlier today… I think."

"Maybe," Toma equivocated. He cast a long, dark look at Mouse. "Do you think he made it?"

It was a thought Mouse had no time to dwell on as they fled, but as they stood in the abandoned alleyway, at a loss for what to do next, she began to dread the worst. She had never seen anyone fight the way Blade had, sure, but who could stand against such a firestorm? Even at Misty Summit, she had never seen that kind of force displayed. It was something conceived only for destruction, and she knew to survive the blow of a weapon intended to obliterate everything it touched would be a miracle.

"I don't know." Mouse sighed. "That was horrible."

"That was a sight, wasn't it?" Toma agreed. "Those energy rifles… man! We have one at home – a much lower caliber. I've never seen that kind before. That was just unreal."

He paused, somberly considering his statement. Mouse nodded in agreement as she adjusted her coat. The evidence of one energy blast smoldered on her coat's shoulder, which she extinguished with a frantic slap.

"But did you see Blade holding them off with just his swords?" Toma interjected hopefully. "I wouldn't have believed it if I hadn't seen it myself."

"Never take the blade for granted," a voice said from the shadows. "Nor those who wield it."

Blade emerged, his light steps making no sound on the cobbled stone. The sheathed hilts poked out from beneath his cloak, casting a soft, green glow around him. Blade approached, mostly intact, with one seared gash across his forearm that betrayed the intensity of the battle. His singed, battered cloak appeared to get the worst of it.

"You're alive!" Mouse exclaimed, relieved. "How did you escape?"

"I was the more able warrior," Blade answered simply. "They won't be following us, but others will be. The racket of those energy rifles will have alerted every sentinel in the city. I am glad to have found you before they did."

"But how did you find us?" Toma interjected. "We ran for a while before we heard the blasts stop."

"A beast hunter must be an able tracker," Blade answered. "Tricks of the trade, which, if we live tonight, I might yet teach you some day. Follow me."

Blade cast a cautious glance around the alley before gesturing for them to follow. He took off down the street at a run, Mouse and Toma sprinting to keep up. They passed down the twisted, uneven streets, and wheeled sharply around shadowy corners. Then, echoing along the corridors, a loud wailing pierced the night air. Blade stopped abruptly, motioning for Mouse and Toma to stay completely still. He crouched and crept to the mouth of the alley, peering out around the corner. After a long moment, he waved for them to join him.

"What is that sound?" Mouse whispered as they crept toward him.

"Sirens," Blade replied. "The alarm has been raised, as if the entire city were under attack. Someone wants you two in Coalition hands, and desperately."

"So what does this mean?" Toma asked.

"It means we will need a new plan," Blade said, pointing to the street in front of them. Mouse recognized it as the road she and Toma had walked along only hours before. Bright light flooded the street, interrupting the deep shadows that would have served to conceal them. Sentinels, lining themselves up in groups of four, amassed at the spot, their number growing larger by the minute.

"What do we do now?" Toma wondered nervously. "Once they start the search… there's no way we'll get away."

"I had hoped we would not have to do this," Blade whispered. "But we have no choice."

He crept over to a large grate in the middle of the alley and pulled out one of his swords. A sharp crack echoed around them as he slashed the metal bars holding the grate in place. It collapsed inward with a slight groan. Placing his foot against the bars, Blade leaned onto the grate, forcing the opening to widen. He motioned to Mouse and Toma.

"Get in," he said, pointing as they joined him. "Toma, you first."

Frowning, Toma gazed into the hole. "Uh, are you sure?"

"There's no time!" Blade urged. "Or would you rather me throw you down?"

Casting Blade a disdainful glare, Toma climbed into the hole, grasping the edge of the drain before releasing his grip to drop. Mouse heard the sound of sloshing water as he landed in the bottom. Blade nodded approvingly and held out his hand to Mouse.

"Your turn," he said. "The drop is only a few feet. I will be right behind you."

Mouse leaned over to look into the drain. Glittering points of light amidst the deep shadows greeted her.

Toma's voice drifted up through the hole. "It's alright. It's just wet. Oh, and disgusting."

Mouse followed Toma's lead and lowered herself into the opening, careful to grasp the edge before letting herself down. Blade motioned for her to hurry, and so she let go, her feet almost instantaneously hitting the slippery bottom. Mouse stumbled as she landed ankle-deep in a foul-smelling liquid, reaching out blindly to steady herself in the dank darkness. She found Toma instead, who took hold of her arm to keep her from falling.

As soon as Mouse had steadied herself, Blade dropped gracefully into the hole after her. She shielded her face to avoid the spray of the fetid water, but Blade's descent had hardly created a ripple. Shafts of light fell sporadically through the opening of the drain, casting Blade in and out of shadow.

"They're on the move," Blade whispered as the sudden sound of quickening footsteps echoed above them. He reached up to forcefully push the bent bars back into place, and then hid himself in the shadows beside Toma and Mouse. They waited in heavy silence as a detachment pounded down the alleyway overhead. Mouse watched the opening of the drain fearfully, anticipating with dread the sentinel's footstep on the weakened bars that would reveal them. To her great relief, it never came. She let herself breathe as the sound of pounding above died away. Even Blade, she could sense, relaxed slightly. He unsheathed his blades, which cast an eerie, green glow on the walls of the sewer.

"Another close call for the night," Blade said, exhaling sharply. He gestured toward them, grinning beneath his hood. "I think it's safe to let her go, for now."

Mouse looked to her wrist, which Toma had been holding onto rather tightly. He let out an embarrassed chuckle as he briskly released it and sidled away.

"Right then," Blade continued. "If we head this way, we should eventually arrive at the drain that empties into the canal. Follow me."

"Won't there be sentinels at the canal?" Mouse asked. "It looked as if it was just within city limits when we first got here earlier today. Wouldn't they check there?"

Blade shook his head. "The sewer doesn't empty into the canal by the city. Its opening is about a mile south, right where the canal meets with the river."

"Wait a second," Toma interjected, confused. "If we could have avoided the sentinels all along, why didn't we just come down here in the first place?"

"The sentinels are not our only problem," Blade said darkly.

"What do you mean?" Mouse asked.

"These tunnels belong to Myergo – the most ruthless crime lord in Gormlaen. Our end at the hands of Lilien's Coalition Guard would be much more merciful than from his."

"Oh, that's... not comforting." Toma glanced over his shoulder anxiously. "So what do we do?"

Blade nodded toward the end of the tunnel. "The sewer system is very large. It runs beneath the whole city, in fact. There is a possibility we could pass through undetected. If we are quiet enough."

"Not that we have any other choice," Mouse chimed in. "I guess we have to try."

"Precisely," Blade replied. "We should move on. Quietly, now."

Without another word, Mouse and Toma sloshed behind Blade as he carefully lead the way through the sewer. The dull light coming from the grate above them soon faded as they went along, leaving nothing but the other-worldly gleam of Blade's twin swords. Mouse walked in silence, listening intently for any sign of trouble, but she could only distinguish the sound of their feet mucking through the dirty water.

The quiet left Mouse alone with her thoughts, which were crowding her mind with hundreds of questions. For one, she desperately wanted to ask Blade about Myergo. Blade had been absolutely fearless up against the Guard, but his apprehension at an encounter with Myergo was as intriguing as it was terrifying. She wondered what manner of man he must be – and then shuddered. Maybe she didn't want to know.

Right now, there was but one man's identity Mouse was sure she wanted to know: the stranger now guiding her through a dark and dangerous subterranean labyrinth. *Who is he, this Blade?* His astonishing skill in close combat made it clear he was more than a beast hunter. Hope rose within her. *Is he truly from Elmnas? And even, maybe, a Guardian? Is it possible?* The Coalition operatives seemed to think so. Their fear and hatred seemed genuine enough. Still, she wondered in disbelief. *Why would a Guardian be here, in Gormlaen, of all places?*

The answers, she knew, would have to wait. Blade, suddenly and intensely alert, slinked along the passage, his sodden feet hardly stirring the water. Even Toma fell unusually quiet. She glanced into his face, hoping to read the same exhaustion and frustration in his expression that she herself felt. His countenance, however, was stony and set – determined, as it were, to get out of the sewer alive. She turned her head just in time to avoid an impending collision with Blade, alert and rigid ahead of her.

"What is it?" she whispered timidly, her voice surprisingly loud within the stillness of the tunnel.

Blade gave no answer, but raised his swords defensively. Mouse peered around him, dreading attackers in the ghostly haze hastening to strike, but the low light exposed no one. The tunnel simply went on, fading into abysmal obscurity. They waited nervously, a tense hush stretching on until at last, Blade lowered his swords.

"I did not mean to frighten you," Blade said apologetically, turning to face the two youths shivering behind him. "I thought I heard something."

It was the last thing Mouse remembered before she lost consciousness.

CHAPTER TWENTY

The woman's slender arms were around Mouse again, tightly wound as she ran on in desperation.

"Sleep," the woman said breathlessly as Mouse stared up at her. "Go back to sleep."

The sky spun above her as she heard the distant pop. Mouse cringed, bracing herself for the world to dissolve in flames, but it didn't. It simply wheeled on, spinning faster until it threatened to launch her off the ground. Suddenly, it stopped. She was alone now, floating in darkness. One by one, pinpoints of brilliant light revealed themselves, twinkling and dancing around her. She reached out to touch them, but even now, they were too far. To her delight, one light descended, falling slowly out of the night. It grew and grew, flashing orange and red as it approached. The lustrous point began to separate, and tongues of fire swirled out of it. They spread, and something was rising from it. She squinted and tried to shield her eyes, the light almost too bright and too hot for her to bear. Her arms and legs useless, Mouse continued to float, absorbed in the blaze.

Two enormous wings, gilded in copper, rubescent, and golden flames, unfolded from the light. They rustled majestically, shaking off the wisps of effulgence that obscured them. A creature rose from the aurulent dust. It lifted its great, feathered head and body, which shone brightly in the vast darkness, filling Mouse's vision completely until she could see nothing but splendid radiance.

Mouse blinked. It was dark now. White bursts scattered behind her closed eyelids, but faded as she rubbed them. Mouse opened one eye slightly, only to see a staffed orb like the ones the sentinels carried floating in front of her. It was harsh and bright, causing her head to spin when she looked at it. In fact, it felt as if her head was about to split open. Mouse closed the eye completely and considered going back to sleep, but the aching in her temples only grew worse.

"Turn that out," she groaned, putting out a hand to push the staff away.

"She's awake!" a familiar voice shouted, the light thankfully falling out of her vision.

Mouse winced. The shouting was not helping, either. She opened her eyes fully now, only to see Toma leaning over her, wearing his broad, mischievous grin. It faded as she let out another groan and rubbed her face.

"Sorry about that," he apologized sincerely. "The headache will go away soon, but I had to wake you up for that to happen."

"Uh huh," Mouse grunted. At the moment, she preferred endless sleep over the pounding in her skull. Nonetheless, she mumbled a half-hearted word of thanks. She was supposed to be awake, she vaguely remembered, but the reason as to why eluded her. It was important, wasn't it? Something had happened, something only moments before. She searched Toma's eyes as she tried to recall it. He smiled encouragingly. Yes, it was coming back to her now. The dark sewers, the glowing of Blade's swords, the danger. The danger... panic filled her as she remembered. They had never escaped the sewers. They had been captured.

With great effort, Mouse propped herself up on her elbows and surveyed her surroundings. Fully expecting to find herself and Toma locked in a dingy dungeon, Mouse gasped in surprise at the sight of the room. There were no bars in front of her, but simply a rough, wooden door. A writing desk, covered in scrolls and dictums, sat meagerly in the corner. The walls were made of the same stones that built the sewer tunnels, but they appeared to have been cleaned, and someone had even taken the time to decorate it with various wall hangings and old, frayed tapestries. Even the mat beneath her was surprisingly comfortable, carefully stuffed with soft furs and loaded with warm blankets. Though rustic and plain, it was no prison cell.

"Um, Toma?" she started, confused. "Where are we?"

"It's okay," he cooed, attempting a soothing tone. "We're in the tunnels. We're safe."

"What?" Mouse nearly shouted, despite the searing pain of the effort. "The tunnels? Where's Blade?"

Immediately, she tried to lift herself from the mat, but the strain was too much. Her vision blurred as agony surged behind her eyes and spread to every one of her aching limbs. For a moment, Mouse was sure her head would explode.

"Calm down!" Toma exclaimed, catching her as she collapsed. "Everything is fine! Just relax, alright?"

"What's going on?" Mouse demanded, weakly fighting Toma's grasp.

Just then, a sharp knock rapped on the door. Toma sighed, betraying his exasperation.

"Come in, Blade. She's up."

The door scraped open, revealing Blade's tall, sinewy frame in the doorway. To Mouse's surprise, he was not wearing the shadowy cloak she had been accustomed to seeing, but he had instead donned a brown, leather cuirass, exposing the glowing blades dangling from his hips. His stony, gray eyes were full of concern, but softened as they rested on Mouse.

"You are awake," he said. "Good. How do you feel?"

"Like I fell off Misty Summit and hit every rock on the way down."

Blade chuckled. "Ah, yes, the wonderful effects of Sleepers' Poison. It will wear off in time, as I am sure Toma has told you."

"Oh! He didn't tell me I was poisoned," Mouse replied, more puzzled than ever. "What's going on?"

"It's alright," Blade assured her. "Sleepers' Poison is only a paralysis compound, meant to render you unconscious, not to kill you. Granted, it appears to have hit you harder than the two of us."

"You've been out for a while," Toma offered sympathetically. "Blade's been up for two days now. I only came to last night."

"And to set your mind at ease, we have not fallen into the hands of Myergo, or anyone worse," Blade supplied. "I will explain in detail shortly, but I don't want to overwhelm you. Until the effects of the poison wear off, it will be difficult to sustain conversation for long. But, as you can see, we are unharmed and... relatively safe."

"That's surprising." Mouse was glad to be put to ease in that respect, at the very least. However, Blade's vague response did little to satisfy her curiosity. Despite the aching in every muscle of her body, Mouse pulled herself up into a sitting position, pressing her back against the cold, brick wall behind her.

"Now," she said, her head swimming from the effort. "Can you tell me where we are?"

"I s'pose I could answer that one for you," an unfamiliar voice interrupted.

Mouse looked up, quite startled to see a grinning stranger leaning leisurely on the doorframe. Though a head shorter than Blade, he appeared stronger, his muscles bulging from beneath rolled sleeves. He had glowing, olive-colored skin and long, thick, black hair pulled back into messy, frayed braids. The unkempt hair contrasted with his clean-shaven face, both no doubt styled so to accentuate the perfect definition of his jaw and complementarily defined neck. He wore a cuirass similar to Blade's, but it had seen better days. By all accounts, the man was roguishly handsome, and his self-assured, easy smile told Mouse he knew it. He stepped into the room with a swagger.

"Welcome to the Den, Miss," he proclaimed grandiosely, stooping into an overly elaborate bow. "Home of the Jackal Syndicate."

Mouse stared at him in confusion, unsure of how she missed his initial arrival. She had only looked away from the door for a moment, and somehow, he had come with enough leisure to place a tray with food, a bowl of water, and a steaming kettle on the desk by the doorway without anyone noticing. He stood from his bow and waited politely for her response. When she offered none, his brow wrinkled at her lack of comprehension.

"I said, home of the *Jackal Syndicate*." He crossed his arms importantly. "I'm sure you've heard of us."

Baffled, she shook her head no.

"Now really!" the man exclaimed, astonished. "You're pulling m'leg!"

"Come now, Woldyff," Blade gibed. "You're a company of thieves, not the Coalition Assembly."

The man called Woldyff snorted indignantly, but Blade ignored this as he turned to address Mouse.

"Mouse, this is Woldyff, leader of the Jackal Syndicate. You may not want to meet him on the streets above, but down here, he's a welcome host."

"Aw, my friend, you injure me!" Woldyff covered his heart. "I swear I've never harmed a lady. Not even the ones I robbed."

Blade raised an eyebrow. "That senator's daughter might not agree."

"Aye, so lovely she was," Woldyff reflected, rubbing his chin. "And so very rich."

He continued to rub his chin, lost in thought as he gazed at the ceiling. Toma cleared his throat awkwardly, rousing Woldyff from his reverie.

"Anyway," he said, appearing surprised that he still had an audience before him, "I s'pose that's a story for another time. Where were we?"

Mouse narrowed her eyes. "You were the one who poisoned us?"

"Oh, that!" Woldyff laughed. He coughed as he caught sight of Mouse's glare. "Ah- yes. But, before you go getting upset, we had good reason for it."

"Not sure robbery counts as a good reason. Sorry to disappoint – we travel lightly." The thought occurred to Mouse it might not be wise to test the kindness of a self-proclaimed criminal, but she held her resolute stare all the same. With the aching in her head growing, she had no patience for his careless amusement.

Woldyff, however, simply smiled wider and looked over at Blade.

"Got quite the firebrand here, don't you?" He jerked his thumb toward her.

Blade did not give an inclination of what he thought one way or the other, but simply dipped his head, encouraging Woldyff to continue.

"I understand." Woldyff shrugged. "Our line of work is not for everyone, but we've all got to make ends meet somehow. Sure, sure, some can get by on an honest living in Gormlaen – if you can carry on scrapping about like a dog at the feet of the Coats, that is – but me, I see it this way: Those who have a lot don't get that way through honest means, no matter what they say. I just give 'em what's been a long time coming. Even the odds, you see."

He puffed his chest up in mock pomp. "I'm really quite the gentleman, if you ask me."

"No one is asking, Woldyff," Blade said tiredly. "Now continue, before she wearies of your constant babbling."

Woldyff smirked. "Right, right. Well, as you might've guessed, our little outfit has been having a little problem with the management. Sure, the Syndicate has always had its occasional run-ins with the Coats, but lately, it's been... more than coincidence. Easy jobs ain't so easy anymore, and wherever we go, the Coats somehow get there first. Well, when I heard the commotion goin' on up above, I thought they'd be after us. So I came up with a quick plan. We were just goin' to teach them a lesson, you see, shake 'em up a bit. Send 'em out with their tails b'tween their legs – remind them who owns Gormlaen's shadows. Well, here I was, thinking I was ambushing a lost lot of dirty Coats, and who do I find instead? It was none other than my old partner and good friend, Mr. Blade, King o' the Shadows himself!"

With this statement, Woldyff roared heartily and slapped a heavy hand across Blade's back, nearly knocking him over. Blade steadied himself and cast Mouse an apologetic look.

"King of the Shadows," Mouse repeated flatly. "What does that mean?"

"What, he never told you?" Woldyff replied, looking quite taken aback. "M'friend here is only one of the greatest thieves this country's never seen! Well, back before he retired, that is. Used to live and eat like the kings o' old, he did! And my, my"–he patted Blade's gut–"feels like he could use one o' them kingly meals now, couldn't he?"

Mouse turned to Blade, open-mouthed.

"Is this true?" she asked, astonished.

Blade opened his mouth slowly to answer, but Woldyff interrupted him before he could make any defense.

"O' course it is!" he exclaimed. "I'm a thief, not a liar! But, that was years ago. The mighty King o' the Shadows is as much a legend as the moons and the stars."

Mouse made no reply, but crossed her arms and stared at the floor. As far as she was concerned, their conversation was over.

"Right," Woldyff said, taking the hint. "Well, I just wanted to let you know that any friend of Blade's is a friend o' mine, and you are welcome to stay as long as you need. Even though we got off on the wrong foot, I'll do right by you and help you get clear of Lilien whenever you're ready. In the meantime, feel free to explore our, ah, headquarters. Just let one of the Syndicate members know and we'll be happy to give you the grand tour."

Mouse nodded in understanding. Woldyff grinned, stood, and turned to leave the room.

"Just so you know," Woldyff said, pausing as he reached the door. "I've never met a lady I couldn't make like me. You just wait."

With a quick wink and a flash of his charming smile, Woldyff exited the doorway and robustly began a rowdy and rather crude tune about a sailor, which echoed loudly about the sewer walls. Several other garbled voices joined in as he went along. Mouse shook her head and sighed. She might be able to get used to Woldyff's being a thief; his arrogance, however, was another matter. Beside her, Blade chuckled.

"Ah, Woldyff," he said, also shaking his head. "Ever the charmer."

"I think I've had enough of his charm to last me awhile," Mouse huffed.

Blade allowed a small smile, despite her clear annoyance. He patted her gently on the arm before standing.

"You take your rest now. Regain your strength. I have some business I need to set in order, but I will return in time."

He quickly strode from the room, leaving Toma alone with her. Toma flashed an awkward smile and rocked on his heels. He worked his mouth, attempting to form words, but nothing came out. Whatever he wanted to say, it would have to wait.

"I'm surprised you're okay with this," Mouse interjected. "Considering all the trouble with bandits you've had in the past."

Toma shook his head emphatically, relieved she took the lead. "The Jackal Syndicate isn't a group of marauders that steals from and murders the poor. They only operate in Gormlaen, and they only rob the wealthy – which is more often than not Coalition Party members and leaders. They take from the Coats, and I'm not going to pretend like I'm unhappy with that."

"I've known plenty of thieves, Toma. I've been one myself. None of them were decent."

"I know, and I understand," Toma replied. "But these ones basically saved our lives. If Myergo or the Coats had found us first, we wouldn't even be having this conversation."

Mouse had not thought about that. Certainly, a warlord would have done away with them for simply being a nuisance, and the Coalition had shown little intention of taking them alive. She wondered if Blade's presence had actually saved them, but then again, she got the feeling Woldyff was not exactly a cold-blooded killer. A charlatan and a womanizer, sure, but probably not a murderer.

Toma reached over to pat her arm, accidentally placing his hand on hers. Mouse could feel the flush rising in her cheeks as he withdrew it embarrassedly, but strangely, that short moment set her at ease.

"I know it's a weird situation," he spoke quickly, changing the subject. "It's better than the one I had gotten us in, though. Honestly, when Blade first found us, I didn't think we'd get through the night. As it turns out, all of this seems to be a good thing."

"I guess that's true," she agreed. "And I'm sure I'll be more up to talking to Woldyff when I can think straight."

"You'll feel better about it when your head clears. I promise." Toma reached out to offer another reassuring pat, but withdrew his hand and let it fall to his side. "I can let you rest, but I'll be back later. Maybe if you're up to it, I'll show you around – I mean, if you didn't want to get the tour from Woldyff, that is."

"Um…" Mouse started. She considered asking him to stay with her. That would be okay, wouldn't it? And maybe this time, he'd leave his hand wherever it fell. He waited expectantly, unaware that he had begun to lean closer to her.

"That would be great," Mouse mumbled instead. She sensed a brief shadow of disappointment as Toma nodded and quickly stood to leave. Upon standing, however, he grinned down at her knavishly. Had she fabricated the entire moment?

"Hey, I'm glad we're still alive," he said as he crossed the threshold of the door. "This is kind of fun."

"Yeah, all kinds of fun." She laughed. "Now get out of here so I can sleep."

It was not long before the aching in Mouse's limbs began to subside. Over the next few days her strength steadily returned, and she felt more and more like herself with each passing minute. Even her sleep had been dreamless, and her last dream faded as the poison drained from her body. Toma wasted no time introducing her to some of the Syndicate members, who were, to her surprise, rather good-natured and very welcoming. It was an infectious sort of mirth they shared, and soon Mouse felt a tenuous but sure affection for them growing within her. The sewer, though damp as it may have been, did little to dampen their spirits. That was a welcome respite, even as it reminded her of Red's propensity for cheerfulness in cheerless places. She just wished she could share some of that cheer with him now.

Of course, it did no good to dwell on the events of the past few days. To distract herself, she took to exploring the home of the Jackal Syndicate. The Den, as Woldyff had so affectionately referred to it, was a fascinating place. Beyond her room was a vast and intricate sewer system, and the Syndicate's operations sprawled out within in every direction beneath Lilien. Shafts leading up to the surface gave the thieves easy and discreet access to the city above.

Mouse wandered along the concrete gangways, finding that along with the shafts there were halls, armories, and even markets carved into the tunnels. Those passing Mouse as she walked nodded in friendly acknowledgement. The tunnels here were wide and deep, and the Syndicate had built wooden paths along them where the concrete walkways ended. Peering over her own walkway, she could see another level of rooms, sealed off with heavy wooden doors. Further below was the canal, full of murky water that moved along lazily. Several skiffs rocked in the current, tugging on the ropes that tethered them to an old dock beneath.

Presently, Mouse ducked into a small service tunnel. It widened after she entered, but there was no canal or water within this one. Instead, there was a damp, dimly lit walkway that disappeared into the darkness. Out of the shadow, Mouse could hear voices.

"No, no, no!" a woman said in exasperation. "That's not right, that can't be right at all!"

A man responded. "Why don't you let me give it a try? You aren't getting anywhere."

"Come off it, Raim! I was doing just fine before you showed up!" the female voice barked.

Curious, Mouse made her way toward the argument. As she drew closer, a large, strange machine resolved from the shadow. It was spherical and made of rough metal plates, bolted together all around. The machine was suspended by four spindle-like structures, outfitted with wheels that lay in grooved, metal rails attached to the tunnel walls. The top half of the sphere was an open metal cage, and Mouse could discern two seats and a steering mechanism. She looked on with interest – this machine was unlike any she had seen before.

Beside it stooped a stocky, young man, presumably the one called Raim. Short, brown hair ending in a long, thin braid on his neck poked out from beneath a dusty gray cap. His clothes were covered in grease stains, and his high gray boots were worn almost through at the knees. He frowned and looked down the end of his sharp nose as he studied the machine.

"Careful Maren!" he said nervously. "Whatever you're doing, stop. I think something's sprung a leak."

"Just hand me that tightener," the woman growled in reply. Two strong legs poked out from beneath the thing's iron belly. She shimmied out enough to hold a work-worn hand open expectantly. Raim sighed and slapped a tool into her palm. She slid back underneath, and Mouse could hear the sound of metal on metal as Maren got to work.

There was a pop and a loud hiss, followed by a string of curses from below.

"What did I tell you?" Raim clamored angrily.

Maren shot out from beneath the machine, fire in her eyes. She was a thick, strong woman, bearing a striking resemblance to Raim. Her shortish black hair, held out of her eyes by a heavy, braided cord around her head, was tangled and messy. Glaring, she took a swing at Raim, who narrowly avoided a nasty hook to his jaw. Unsatisfied, she threw her tool against the tunnel wall, which bounced hard into Raim's calf. He yelped in pain and surprise, but Maren took little notice as she stomped over to the machine and began to kick at it.

"Worthless – awful – outdated – piece of junk!" she yelled, punctuating each word with a kick.

It was not until then that Raim, vigorously rubbing his sore calf, noticed Mouse standing in the tunnel.

"Oh!" he said, tapping Maren on her shoulder.

"What now?" she hollered as she turned. Her scowl quickly faded as she caught sight of Mouse standing timidly before them.

"Ah-um-well, hello!" Maren said embarrassedly. "You're that girl who came with Woldyff's friend, that shadowy one, aren't you?"

Mouse nodded.

"You saw all that, too, didn't you?" Maren said, shuffling guiltily.

"Yes," Mouse admitted, but she waved her hand dismissively. "Don't worry about it. I've been there, especially with old machines like that one."

"You?" Raim interjected. "You're a little, well, small, to be a mechanic."

"Not where I'm from," Mouse shrugged. "Anyway, I've never seen one of these before – what is it?"

"It's called a locosphere," Maren answered. "And you're right, it's ancient. They used to get around down here in these for repairs. Through the maintenance shafts, they connect the whole sewer. Problem is, it doesn't budge if the engine's not running. Nothing here is working."

"And it will never work!" Raim chimed in. "I say scrap it and build another."

"Oh sure, great idea, Raim," Maren derided sarcastically. "Go ahead and find me the parts for it and I'll get right on it."

"At least I've got an idea! You know, just because you're 5 minutes older –"

"Mind if I take a look?" Mouse interrupted as politely as she could.

Maren shrugged. "Be my guest."

The pair watched quietly as Mouse got down and pulled herself underneath the locosphere. There was a small lantern waiting for her, illuminating the undercarriage. The engine was still hissing as Mouse observed the damage. Coincidentally, the locosphere was not entirely unlike the machines she had worked on at Misty Summit. She recognized its different parts easily, noting in her mind what would need to be replaced or repaired.

Raim stooped down toward her. "Need anything?"

"Something to work with?" Mouse replied, and soon a box of tools materialized beside her.

She set to work immediately, isolating leaks, loose parts, and corroded piping. After some time, the hissing from the engine stopped. Finally satisfied, she scooted out.

"Try it now," she said.

Raim crossed his arms, scoffing. "Right, we've been working on this for two weeks now and you've gone ahead and fixed it in seconds."

Mouse shrugged. "Doesn't hurt to try."

"That's good enough for me!" Maren exclaimed, and she jogged over to the locosphere. Hopping inside, she threw the ignition switch. There was a click and a short, high-pitched grind, and then the locosphere whirred to life.

"How did you-" Raim stuttered, his mouth dropping open.

Immediately, he ran to the locosphere and jumped in beside Maren. He had to hold his hat down as he hopped back out to look beneath it.

"I can't believe it!" he cried as a small, satisfied grin spread across Mouse's face.

"Give the girl some credit, Raim!" Maren laughed as she turned to Mouse. "But seriously, how did you do that? I don't mean to brag, but my brother and I are the best mechanics the Syndicate's ever seen."

"I grew up learning the trade, where I'm from," Mouse replied.

"Ah, and where's that?" Raim asked. "Out west? The industry sector's booming out there."

"Sure," Mouse lied, but Raim did not notice. He and Maren were back at the locosphere, excitedly looking it over.

"You've saved me days of work, girl," Maren said. "How can I thank you?"

"Oh, uh, don't mention it..." Mouse trailed. It was the first time anyone had ever complimented her on a job well done.

"You'd make a fine addition to the Syndicate, you know." Raim added. "We sure could use someone like you. Lots of things to tinker with, and you got a gift for it."

Mouse smiled sadly. It was an appealing offer. How many days at Misty Summit had she longed to spend her time problem-solving, building, creating? Maren was nodding in agreement, going on about how she could put in a good word with Woldyff. Eventually, Mouse shook her head.

"I can't," she replied. "But thank you."

Maren reached out and grasped Mouse's hand firmly.

"Don't write us off just yet." She winked. "And let me know if you want a ride some time – I'm doing a test run now, but come back later and we'll have a go."

Mouse nodded and smiled, stuffed her hands in her pocket and turned to leave the twins to their work. She glanced back as the two crammed into the idling locosphere. Maren pushed a few buttons and the iron sphere guttered and then shot forward into the darkness.

"Someday, maybe," Mouse said long after they were gone.

Mouse returned to her quarters to find Toma with Woldyff, deep in conversation.

"There you are!" he said, slightly exasperated. "We've been looking all over for you!"

Woldyff breathed a visible sigh of relief, but smiled, wiping his brow with feigned distress.

"I should have told you, you shouldn't go wandering off all alone like that," Woldyff said.

"Oh, aren't we safe here?" she asked.

"Well, mostly," Woldyff answered. "As long as you're with a Syndicate member. I just wouldn't want you to cross into Myergo's turf. They're not exactly the friendly neighbor types."

"I was wondering about that. Why do you share the tunnels with him?"

"Not much of a choice." Woldyff explained, his lips curling into a distasteful sneer. "We've an arrangement, and we do alright when he deals with us fair. But know this, Myergo isn't known for his honesty."

Woldyff patted his energy pistols and smiled grimly. "But that's what these are for, if need be."

Mouse nodded. "Understood."

It had been nearly a week since the night she, Toma, and Blade escaped into the tunnels. During this time Blade and Woldyff frequently disappeared, leaving Toma and Mouse to their own devices. Again, Mouse ruminated on the unanswered questions of their shadowy guide, the mystery gnawing at her.

"Who do you think he is?" Toma wondered, echoing her silent sentiments. "What's he up to?"

She didn't know, but maybe she could find out.

Mouse set herself to lingering in the hub of the Den, asking questions of anyone who was willing to answer.

No one, it seemed, knew much about Blade. His work with the Syndicate was more akin to a private contractor than anything, and why he ever left remained something of a mystery as well. He kept his time among the members brief and professional, and his stoic demeanor deterred attempts at the frivolous camaraderie of which Woldyff was so fond. What could be said for certain, however, was the King of the Shadows lived up to his moniker. No one had made the Syndicate as rich as Blade did – either before his time or after. His reign, they said, would go down in history.

Mouse got to know many of the Syndicate members this way, finding that each was eager to share their own stories. Particularly, Mouse enjoyed the company of Raim and Maren. The twin siblings, hailing from a small town named Dunaidos, joined the Syndicate only a few years prior. They were adventurous, roaming types with a propensity for thrill-seeking – a trait common among many of the Syndicate. Mouse listened to story upon story, more than she could count as her new friends recounted tales filled with danger, cunning, and a bit of exaggerated bravado.

Over the days, Mouse's initial perception of these thieves softened. Yes, they were an organized crime ring, but their end goal was never craven gain. Often conversations were abuzz with political discontent, and discussed targets for their jobs were almost always Coalition Party members or their sycophants. It betrayed what they really were – an underground movement, sneakily rebelling against the Coalition.

Strangely, the Coalition seemed like a distant danger here. Mouse's thoughts often drifted to Myergo and his company, lurking just beyond the Syndicate boundaries. Even so, all was quiet here below and on the streets above. *But how long will this calm last?* Mouse wondered. *When will the Coalition come for us?* The questions unsettled her, and she brought her fears to her hosts.

"Don't worry about that," Maren said dismissively. "Word is that Woldyff set the Coats on a wild goose chase. They're looking for your lot west of the city."

"Do you know what they're saying your little run in was?" Raim added. "An emergency drill! Ha! They really do think we're all idiots, don't they?"

With the city calm and Mouse's wits and strength returned, she sensed their time with the Syndicate was drawing to a close. Twilight fell on the streets above as Mouse made her way to the mess hall. The smell of simmering stew overcame the stench of the sewer, reminding her all at once of her brief encounter with home at the Breythorn farm.

She shook the thought away as she entered the tight dining quarters. There she found Blade and Woldyff, huddled with Toma in the corner of the room. A long piece of parchment lay open on the table as they ate.

"It's time, isn't it?" she said as soon as she had reached them.

Blade nodded. "Woldyff has kindly offered to lead us to the canal, whenever you are ready."

"I am," Mouse said with a deep breath. "I'm ready."

"Good," Blade replied. "I have taken the liberty of mapping out a route through Gormlaen, one that should help us to avoid detection entirely. Here."

He handed her the parchment which, as Mouse studied it closely, turned out to be a detailed sketch of a map. A dotted line, snaking north from Lilien, wound through a rough drawing of the country's wilderness. Mouse traced it lightly with her finger, following it as it made its way to the border of Elmnas. The dotted line stopped at the border, hindered, it seemed, by the unbroken mountain range that separated the two countries.

"So how do we get in?" Mouse asked. "It doesn't look like there's any way to cross here."

"I believe he had mentioned this pass to you before." Blade nodded to Toma. "Thunder Run. There's a gorge, and though it will be difficult, we might yet be able to reach it and navigate it with a proper guide."

"You can't navigate it?" Mouse asked, her hopes falling. Toma's plan had also depended on finding a guide – a plan that was doomed to fail now that they were at large. As a traveler and a hunter, Blade was the obvious answer, but if he could not brave it, Mouse did not see who could.

"Don't you worry your pretty head," Woldyff cut in. "I can take care o' that one for you. See, I know a smuggler up north, owes me a favor. He'll be waiting for you by the river."

"Thanks to Woldyff's arrangements, we should be able to enter Elmnas without incident." Blade gave both Mouse and Toma a hard stare. "Be warned, it is a route that even the most determined hunters have difficulty navigating. It is a wild country."

"It's the only way, right?" Toma shrugged. "This is the best plan we've got."

"It's settled then." Blade rolled up the parchment. "We will leave shortly. I suggest you eat something."

Mouse grabbed a few rolls sitting on the table and hurried back to her room. Hastily, she began to pack her things, stuffing them down to the bottom of her satchel to make them fit. The bag bulged awkwardly, so she beat it into shape before slinging it over her shoulder. Satisfied, she sat in the creaky chair by the door, waiting.

Only a few moments had passed, but Mouse grew more anxious by the second. Though she had enjoyed the brief detour from the dangers of the outside world, she could not help but feel guilty about her stay. If Red could be helped, she was the only one who could do so now. But as the journey stretched on, hope for him dwindled. He had trusted her, too – given her the responsibility for exposing the truth. Was she wasting too much time? Would her efforts even matter—not just for him, but for Elmnas?

No, Mouse did not want to think on that. The hopelessness of that thought crushed her. *We'll get there. And maybe we'll all be saved.* Even as she thought it, the doubts crept in. She needed proof she could save him, something to hold to keep her sane. Her hand wandered to her chest, to the pocket of her field jacket where she had kept Red's notes and the chip ever since they set out from Breythorn Farm. Gently, she reached into the breast-pocket and extracted the wad of old, cracked leather. With the distance and days quickly mounting between her and the complex, it was strange to think this was the only connection she now had to Red. She stared at the delicate bundle, careful to cradle it in her hands. There were so many questions she could not answer, so many things she could not know or control. Many of them were raised by the journal and the evidence itself, but still, other things were that much closer because of it. All she could do now was press on.

A short rap on the doorframe shook her from her thoughts. She looked up to see Toma, leaning against it, dressed in his travel gear and wearing a smile.

"Wow, you're ready?" he asked, surprised.

"Yeah, I've been waiting," Mouse replied. She carefully slid the journal back into her pocket before hopping from the chair. "Are we good to go?"

"Should be. Blade and Woldyff said to meet them out by the mess hall."

"Alright," she said soberly, pulling her hood up over her hair. "This is it."

After a few goodbyes, a quick packing of provisions, and short run-through of their course upon leaving the tunnels, the trio followed Woldyff out of the Den and into the darkness of the sewer. He led them silently through its twists and turns, and in little time, they had reached the straightaway at the mouth of the tunnel leading to a large, circular grate at its end. Woldyff stopped them there and pointed to the grate.

"You'll find that there's a hinge on the right side here, so with a little push, it'll swing open for you. You can follow the canal up yonder a ways, oh, say about one or two miles, and that'll take you far enough from Lilien that you won't be seen when you climb up the bank. Oh, and before I forget"—Woldyff pulled two energy pistols from the back of his trousers and handed one to each of the youths—"they're older models, but they're in workin' order. Better t'be prepared than… well, dead!"

He smiled at this, his white teeth gleaming in the low light of the tunnel. Mouse nodded in thanks before hanging it carefully on one of her belt loops. It amazed her how incredibly light the weapon was, but was terrified all the same to be strapped to one. She did her best not to cringe as she remembered the smell of burning hair and singed clothing. Toma, however, looked rather comfortable with his, coolly placing it in an empty holster.

Wasting no time, Woldyff reached his hand out to Mouse, who

held it firmly. "It's been a pleasure t' meet you. Maybe we'll see each other again one day, and if we do, I hope you'll have decided to like me better by then."

Mouse offered a smile in return. "I guess first impressions aren't everything."

"Ha! S'pose not." Woldyff shook Toma's hand before thumping Blade on the back.

"It's been good t' see you, my friend," he said. "You best be off now."

Blade gave a firm shake in response, nodding in agreement. Woldyff waited and observed as they made their way to the grate. As they reached it, Mouse turned to see him waving.

"*A lak krataman wan mim bil'hhab!*" Woldyff shouted after them.

"*A lak tikkh nan shi sulnye,*" Blade replied. "Good fortunes to you, for now and forever."

Woldyff nodded before disappearing into the shadows. Mouse watched the darkness in silence. It was strange to see him go, she thought, but she also had the feeling it would not be the last time they met.

By the time she turned, Blade was pushing against the grate, which groaned as it yielded. After a few feet, its rusty hinges ground to a halt, leaving just enough space for the three of them to squeeze through. He waved her and Toma over.

"What was that all about?" Toma asked when he reached Blade.

"Ah, that is an old Syndicate farewell, in the nomad tongue of the Heibeithans," Blade explained. "It means, 'May the gold flow like wedding wine.' The polite response is, of course, 'And may the bottle never be stoppered'."

"Nice," Toma said. "You'll have to teach me that one."

"Maybe one day," Blade replied. "But not now. As soon as we step into the open, we must be alert for any sign of danger. Keep to the shadows, and be as silent as one. Now follow me."

Blade stepped nimbly out from the mouth of the tunnel, pausing briefly to check his surroundings. Again, he waved to them, indicating that they follow. Mouse slipped out from behind the grate, amazed at the lack of change in the darkness. She glanced up into the night, hoping to find the seam between earth and sky, but there was none. It had melted together, and Mouse had the peculiar feeling she had stepped into a void. She took a deep breath, gripped the cold butt of her pistol, and moved forward resolutely. The next step of their journey had begun.

CHAPTER TWENTY-ONE

In the late afternoon, beneath the roiling clouds of the blood-tinged sky, a hooded traveler steadily made her way through a dusty, lifeless vale in the southwestern corner of Gormlaen. She had come from a job in Gilba, the central region of Heibeiath – a sandy, barren place where water was scarce and people were scarcer. For some folk, it was a sure refuge from those who would hunt for them – creditors, crime lords, even the Coalition would steer clear of that wasteland. The risk of being forever lost in Gilba's unforgiving sands was enough incentive to keep them at bay. There existed, however, a certain brand of people who feared neither the risk nor the consequences. There were those who reveled in the hunt, whose fear, pity and weakness were driven away by the ever-present thirst for blood and gold. If the prize were great enough, they were the few who would do anything to retrieve it.

With half the gold up front, the reward had certainly been enticing enough for the traveler. Her target, it seemed, owed a great deal to the wrong people, and they intended to make him pay for it. Like many of her contracts, this job was a search and capture. Her contractors had made her sure of this. No, blood alone would not do, though she did have a special flare for kill jobs. He would be called to account for his debt with more than his flesh, and if she did the job as asked, she would reap the benefit of his miserable labor.

The desert had not dismayed her, for like the rest of her kind, she had no use for pain or fear. Despite the scorching heat, sudden dust devils, and constant threat of wild beasts, she pursued him, and had successfully tracked him to the meager dwellings of his nomadic companions. She was close, so much closer than any of the other bounty hunters had dared to come. Nothing, therefore, could compare to the enraging disappointment of failure when she had found him two days dead on the dusty floor of a desert hovel. It was unclear exactly what had transpired, or whom else the dead man had happened to cross, but it was certain someone else had gotten there first. For the first time in many years, she had to return empty-handed. The unfortunate sandstorm that claimed the life of her horse and had forced her to make the rest of the trip on foot only fed her rage. She had wasted precious time and resources on a fruitless job, and not even half the gold could placate her anger.

The hunter climbed the path to the Borderland Brig House, her temper growing shorter with each step, and flung aside the door. A small pub sitting on the crest of the vale she had just crossed awaited her. Voices hushed and laughter ceased as the traveler stepped inside, and for good reason. Imposingly tall for a woman, sinewy, and mysteriously shrouded by a red cowl covering her head, she was an intimidating sight. Daggers and energy pistols winked wickedly on the holster about her waist in the dim light. She shook the dust from her dark jacket. Her most impressive weaponry, the set of crossed blades strapped to her back, shimmered faintly within their sheaths as she brushed the remaining sand from her shoulders. All eyes followed her as she strode solemnly across the room to the bar, her grit-splattered boots making surprisingly little sound. The bartender eyed her warily over a glass as she approached.

"Yeah, what d'ya want then?" the bartender said, his voice suddenly hoarse. The bounty hunter stood poised in front of him, boring through him with fiery eyes. Involuntarily, he flinched as she reached up and pulled the cowl from her head. Thick, raven-black hair tumbled out in loose curls from beneath the hood.

"Fire mead and whatever's cooking," she said evenly, tossing a few gold pieces onto the counter.

"Yes, ma'am," the bartender replied, the relief plain on his face. As quickly as his old fingers would allow, he poured her a frothy cup of rosy liquid and promptly handed it to her.

With a curt nod, she strode from the counter and made herself comfortable in the corner of the room, facing the door. The other patrons, who had been watching the exchange, turned back to their tables and continued their conversations in hushed tones. Satisfied, she drank deeply from the cup, not quitting until she reached the dregs. It would not quell her frustration, but a good mead could dull it for a while. She propped her tired feet on the chair next to her and lazily drummed long fingers on the wooden table, silently surveying the tavern. Though her masked cowl had not readily revealed it, she was, by all accounts, rather beautiful. Her long hair shimmered red in the low light, cascaded down her shoulders, and framed her oval-shaped face. The orbs of her eyes were a dark brown rimmed in a blazing yellow ring, which she cast fiercely at any who dared to look in her direction. She had flawless olive skin save for three deep, identical scars that ran diagonally from her eyebrow to her jaw.

In no time, the barkeep dropped a large, steaming plate and another pint in front of his newest patron. He made no eye contact, but mumbled something about having a nice night before hurrying away. The traveler nodded, her haunting gaze following him as he made his way back to the bar. Though famished from her long journey, she ate with unusual decorum, pausing politely between bites. There she sat, and from the corner of her eye, observed the man watching her from the other side of the room.

It had not taken her long to discover him. He had picked an inconspicuous place to sit–in the corner, to the right of the main door. Smart. Most guests would not take notice of him there, especially those just arriving. Unlike the other customers however, he looked out of place. His cloak was too clean, too manicured for the average traveler. He wore a pair of polished snakeskin gloves which, as she quickly ascertained, matched his equally polished boots. Expensive gear. Nothing a walking man would wear. His eyes shifted back and forth shrewdly as she entered the pub, his posture a dead giveaway – he waited for someone. When the man nearly stood up to approach her as she made her way to the bar, her suspicions were confirmed. He was waiting for her. It would have been short work to dispatch him, but fortunately for the man, the pair of large men sitting at his table had reached up and pulled him back into his seat before he made his move.

She saw right through them, as well. The woman eyed them up, taking in their charcoal coats and high, black boots. Though they were not marked, she could tell it was Coalition-issued apparel. Interesting. Now, as she ate her meal, they whispered amongst themselves, stealing glances at her whenever they thought she might not be looking.

At any rate, this game was beginning to bore her. In one swift motion, she pulled a large dagger from her hip and hurled it toward the three men in the corner. A deathly pall fell over the room as it whizzed by and, with a loud thunk, stuck in the wall between the polished man and one of the guards. He gaped, astonished, as she smirked at him. The two Coalition guards jumped to their feet hastily, their hands already reaching for their pistols, but with a quick glare and a shake of his head, their ward waved them off.

"A wise decision," she spoke, her voice the only sound breaking the stillness. "Now, would you be so kind as to bring me my knife? I'm rather fond of it."

The man nodded to his guard, who then, with a grunt, ripped the dagger from the wall. After the group had approached her, he tossed it on the table with a look of disgust. Satisfied, she nodded and waved her hand over the table, indicating they should have a seat. As they obliged, the din of conversation started anew in the tavern, breaking the awful tension that had been building there.

She leaned back in her chair easily. "So, what chaos brings a Coalition page to the Borderlands Brig House?"

Doing his best not to look surprised, he leveled a composed stare at her. "I'm not sure what made you arrive at that conclusion, but –"

"No?" she interrupted. "You didn't think your oafs here would give you away?"

She ignored the growls of the two guards. "Or those boots that clearly have not seen a day on the road? A word of advice – try stomping about in the dirt after you step out of your hovercraft. It might have been harder to spot you."

"Indeed," the page conceded, after a moment. He turned to his guards. "We will be fine here. Stand down."

The guards glared at the bounty hunter before leaving the table. They returned to their corner of the tavern, eyes alert and hands ready to draw their weapons.

The Coalition page's mouth widened into a frigid simper. "If I may say so, your attitude certainly betrays you, as well, Arctura."

"I am known as Fox and that alone," she snarled, her eyes flashing dangerously.

"As you wish," the page sighed indifferently. "Have we covered our formalities? If so, I would appreciate getting down to business. I did not travel to this dreadful, worthless corner of the world for no reason."

The huntress named Fox relaxed, smirking at the page. "Yes, I see that. So what is it that you seek, then?"

"There is a need for your… services."

"Go on."

The page glanced from side to side covertly. "Not too long ago there was an unfortunate incident at our prison facility in Maiendell. Two prisoners died – messy business. It happens often enough, but we soon discovered that it was more than a prisoner scuffle. Two of the prisoners managed to escape the facility, and one made it safely across the Mistlands and out of our reach. At any rate, she is currently at large. During her time in the facility, she had close contact with a key rebel leader. We were able to discover that she now carries sensitive information, but the nature of it is still in question. Reports placed her in Gormlaen not more than a week ago. We believe she intends to contact the remaining rebellion in Elmnas. This is our target."

Discreetly, the page pulled a small tablet from his cloak and slid it across the table. Fox browsed through it, stopping as she read the description of the target and studied the image that accompanied it. A girl with short, light brown hair, and inquisitive, gray eyes stared back at her.

Fox raised an eyebrow. "You want me to hunt a child? Forgive me if I'm mistaken, but I did not think your people had become quite that incompetent."

The page leveled an angry glare at her. "I would appreciate your cooperation, without the condescension. It is within my power to make life very difficult for you, if I so choose. Do not give me a reason."

Fox bristled but studied the page instead. Taking this as an act of cooperation, the page continued. "The girl does not travel alone. She has two companions. One, a farm boy, of little consequence, but the other…"

He set a small file in front of Fox, who could not help but raise another eyebrow.

"A surviving Guardian?"

"It appears so. He goes by the alias Blade. Even the locals do not seem to know very much about him, except that he is a wandering beast hunter, taking contracts here and there. His identity as a Guardian however, was confirmed after that disaster in Lilien."

"Ah," said Fox, taking a sip of her mead as she perused the file. It was considerably smaller than the one compiled for Mouse. The image for Blade consisted of a mere crude sketch of his cloaked persona, darkness filling the hood of the cloak instead of Blade's face. Fox looked back at the page, smiling smugly.

"And this is why you have come to me."

"So it would seem." The page granted. "He is a master of stealth and hand-to-hand combat. Our efforts to find him have been… unsuccessful, and he wields the ancient blades of his people with great skill."

The page pulled a pipe from his pocket. With some satisfaction, he lit it and puffed ponderously, thinking.

"Eliminate him," he said. "I do not care what you do with the boy, but it may be best to dispatch him as well. The fewer witnesses, the better. The girl, however, must remain alive for questioning. The job will be considered complete once you return her to the old outpost below Filk. If you would assist the Coalition, we will surely reward your efforts. Every resource at our disposal will be yours to use, if you deem it necessary."

Fox leaned back from the table and crossed her arms. "And if I do not?"

His lips curled into a wicked sneer. "Are you still so proud, Fox? I think even you would feel foolish to turn down such handsome compensation."

The page reached into his cloak once more, producing a small, black box. He set it on the table and unclasped the hinges gently. "Go on," he said. "Open it."

Fox delicately lifted the edges of the lid. A bright green glow emitted from the box, casting a pale reflection across her face.

"Pure Cardanthium." She let out a low whistle. "How did you come by that?"

"This is not your concern, is it?" The page replied, snapping the box closed. He returned it to his cloak with a wicked sneer. "Don't worry. You will receive it, if the job is done. In the meantime, whatever you may need, I can provide. I understand that this life your type lead can be... hmm, challenging in that aspect?"

Fox shrugged. "I seem to manage."

"Of course," the page said, bowing politely. "Do you accept the contract?"

Fox sat silently for a moment, thinking.

"Alright," she finally agreed. "But I have conditions."

"As I had expected. What are your terms?"

"I'll have gold up front. I will not work on good faith as I have none in the Coalition."

The page waved his hand nonchalantly, like he was swatting lazily at a gnat.

"Fine, fine," he sighed. "It can be arranged."

"You will also give me a horse."

"A horse?" the page snorted. "Really."

"They won't be on the roads," she scoffed. "Not to mention, any idiot could hear a hovercraft coming from over a mile away. Get me a horse, and you'll have your dead Guardian."

"Then these things shall all be arranged. We want this done before they reach Elmnas. And of course, I needn't remind you – this contract requires the utmost discretion."

He stood, extending his arm toward Fox. "We have an agreement?"

Fox also stood from the table and shook his outstretched hand. He winced a little as she grasped it tightly.

"I honor this contract, page, but that changes nothing. Be sure to remind your superior of that."

"Do not flatter yourself," the page spat back, pulling his hand from her hold and wiping it on his cloak. "The Supreme Chancellor is ever above these backward dealings. I would not even trouble him with the news of your death, you marauding filth."

"Pray you do not meet me again, page," Fox threatened fiercely. The man, however, had already waved her off, turning pompously to walk out of the Brig House's door. His guards surrounded him, gripping the hilts of their pistols aggressively as they eyed her with disdain. She picked up the dagger still lying on the table and slammed it into its surface in response.

Another tense silence filled the pub as the Coalition guards and representative exited the bar. Fox watched them angrily as they left, the page showing as much regard for her wrath as he would an agitating wasp. The heavy door slammed closed in their wake, and after a moment, Fox could hear the rumbling of their hovercraft as it sped away from the Brig House. She sat back down, once more relieving the terrified tension of the room. Fox sighed. Dealings with the Coalition were never pleasant, but she could not avoid them if they sought her. She settled back in at her table, intent on enjoying the rest of her meal, only to see a large coin purse tucked neatly beside her plate. It rattled and clinked as she removed it, laden with gold. Fox smirked and tucked it away.

The bartender re-entered the Brig House from the back door, puffing a little with exertion. He made his way over to her table and slipped her a note, stamped with the Coalition insignia.

"Your horse is tied up in the back. Been fed and rested well, so she's good to ride when you're ready."

He offered a timid nod before rushing away.

Surprised, Fox nodded to the barkeep and read the note. *For services to be rendered*, the note read.

CHAPTER TWENTY-TWO

E vening fell over the wilds of Gormlaen by the time Blade decided
to make camp for the night. The trio had distanced themselves
from Lilien by several days, daily traveling from the early morning to
the late dusk. Even so, the hurried trek through wood and vale seemed
to stretch time itself. Mouse wondered if months had gone and she
had somehow missed it. Blade's goading pace was her only reference in
this forbidding and strange land.

Despite its immense difficulty, they had avoided Gormlaen's many
roads early on in their journey. It was, of course, at a cost. Blade
pushed them to keep going through the night, and by now Toma and
Mouse were exhausted. His desire, as he expressed often, was to keep
moving, but now they haunted Gormlaen's wilds, and this seemed to
satisfy Blade well enough. He picked a small clearing on the edge of an
enormous forest, and in no time, they set up camp. With a grateful
sigh, Mouse settled down in the field's long, matted grass. Toma
inelegantly collapsed next to her, sighing heavily himself as he
proceeded to tear off his shoes and rub his feet.

"You need to eat." Blade tossed a few hard biscuits to them before
perching himself on a dry tree stump nearby. "Then rest. I expect we
will need to cover just as much ground tomorrow."

Toma groaned and stuffed the entire biscuit into his mouth. "We've got to be miles away from the closest road by now. Do we really have to leave as early as yesterday?"

"No, not as early, but we need to keep moving. Woldyff's contact is on a non-negotiable schedule, and we want to reach him when he is there."

Blade leaned thoughtfully on his elbow and gazed into the forest beside them. "Besides, it is not wise to linger in any one place for too long."

Mouse followed his gaze into the forest. It was an impressive sight: tangles of thick, towering trees lined the clearing, their branches so broad and intertwined that she could hardly see beyond the first row. They stretched on and on for as far as Mouse could see, all growing taller than any tree she had ever seen before. Their green boughs allowed no light to escape, and in the gathering dusk, the already black shadows of the dense wood deepened menacingly. Even sound seemed to disappear within it – a strangely stark contrast to fields buzzing with insect life around them. Mouse shuddered, unable to shake the feeling that the forest was gazing back.

"Where are we?" she asked with a low voice, the stillness in the air only adding to her unease.

"We are at the very edge of Brizbane Forest. An ancient wood that even the Coalition could not manage to tame." Blade let out a low chuckle. "Though I am certain they have tried."

"Why not just cut it down?" Toma interrupted, his mouth full. "They've taken out plenty of forests like this back home."

"To appease the locals, most likely," Blade replied. "I have heard it said that there is old power in these woods. Ancient gods, they say, or demons maybe. Superstition runs deep, even here in Gormlaen."

"Well, maybe they're right," Toma speculated. "This place gives me an odd feeling… can't really place it…"

"Like you're being watched," Mouse added quietly. "That's what it feels like."

Toma grimaced in response. "Ugh, kinda wish you hadn't said that."

"We will be fine," Blade assured them. "There is no need to create fears when we have enough true ones as it is. You are tired. Rest."

Exhausted as she was, Mouse did not need to be told twice. Even the depths of Brizbane Forest could not keep her from drifting off. She curled up on the ground, the rhythmic chirping in the fields around her offering a humble, peaceful symphony in an otherwise rugged and forlorn place. It was then that Toma joined in, adding to the chorus with a haunting tune of his own. In a strong and clear voice, he sang:

I looked for my love in the vale and the hills
In forests and caves, o'er the brook and the dells
I came by a great river, ancient and strong
Whispering in secret of days now bygone

There she did stand, her feet in the flow
"It is time, love," she said. "On I will go
The boatman has come, and so ends the day
Cool are the waters that must speed me away…"

Toma's voice echoed on, and though Mouse tried to catch the words, she slipped away with them into sleep.

It was always the same. The woman carried her desperately, the worry knit on her face as she urged Mouse to sleep. Faces and shadows faded in and out around her. Mouse braced herself as she heard the familiar popping sound, watching as the sky overhead dissolved into crimson. Her entire world shook violently, and the woman cried out as some unseen force tore Mouse right from her arms. Lines, colors, and voices blurred as Mouse flew through the air. She flailed about, trying to steady herself before she slammed into the ground, but before she did, darkness overtook her.

Mouse rubbed her eyes, the tumble startling her from sleep. She gazed out into the darkness, waiting for her eyes to adjust as she lay still on her side. Trees began to take shape in front of her, and she was suddenly aware she had awakened facing the forest. It was strange – though she still could not quite see it, she felt its presence, ever looming in the unsettling silence. The night was quiet in the fields as well, and it looked as if even Blade had dozed off. He sat, neatly slumped against the tree stump, his head drooping onto his chest.

She lay there, debating whether or not she should wake Blade or resume the night watch for him. It was not like him to sleep while on watch. Whereas Mouse had startled awake many times to find she had drifted off during her shift, Blade never seemed to sleep. He always insisted on staying up for a good portion of the night, only waking Toma or her for a few hours while he rested. And even as he rested, Mouse noticed he never slept lightly, waking at even the smallest sound.

He must be exhausted. It would be best not to wake him. As Mouse tried to get up, something strange happened. She found, though as hard as she tried, that she could not move. Mouse wriggled furiously, but to no avail. Panicking, she tried to call out to Blade, but her voice made no sound. Even Toma, asleep soundly next to her, did not wake at her struggle. She was trapped, and Blade and Toma were both completely unaware. As she fought fruitlessly to move, Mouse noticed a dim glow weaving through the forest. It was far away, but sure enough, it was there.

The forest vibrated and the air crackled with energy as it approached. Mouse struggled violently against her invisible shackles, but there was nothing she could do. It drew closer. Helpless, she tried to scream, but her voice caught mysteriously in her throat. Then, beams of shimmering light poured through the tree line. Her heart pounded as the blaze faded in and out of the shadows, growing brighter with each pass. It breached the edge of the forest, slowly but surely coming through the thinning trees to reveal its source. Terror filled her as she waited for whatever horror steadily closed in on them. No horror, however, greeted her. The tree line yielded to the glaring sheen, momentarily blinding Mouse. Her eyes adjusted in time to see the shape of a familiar creature, crested in gold, yellow, red, and blue flame. Mouse's eyes opened wide with awe.

It was that unfamiliar bird, the one she had so easily forgotten about, from her dream many nights before. It stepped lightly into the clearing, only paces behind the spot where Blade slept. Mouse could not see Blade. She could only see the bird, burning splendidly. It stretched out its enormous wings, multicolored flames flickering from each feather. The beast drew itself up to its full height, greater than any creature Mouse had ever seen. Fire and light cast about in all directions, dispersing even the crushing darkness of the forest from which it came. Mouse could feel the heat from the tongues of flames surrounding it, just as if she were feeding the furnaces on Misty Summit, but oddly, nothing around the creature caught fire. Not even the ground on which it walked was scorched. Each movement was fluid and graceful as the bird came forward. It stopped just outside the forest and turned to look at her.

The creature seemed to gaze expectantly, as if waiting. Mouse stared right back, unsure of whether she was too frightened or too entranced to look away. The heat emanating from the creature continued to grow, hitting Mouse like a hot gust of desert air on a dry, summer day. It was too much. she closed her eyes, suddenly finding herself able to brace herself and cover her face with her arms. A hand gripped the arm she had thrown over her face and yanked her backward.

"Careful," Blade whispered as he pulled her away from the heat. Mouse opened her eyes slowly, the searing light before her replaced by inky darkness. The night swallowed everything in shadow, but she made out the fuzzy outline of Blade before her. He held onto her arm as she lay on the ground.

She sat up and looked about wildly, hoping to catch a glimpse of where the creature had gone, but the forest was quiet, still, and black. Blade released his grip and sat down across from her, next to the still sleeping Toma.

"Did you see that?" Mouse exclaimed, continuing to stare into the forest.

"Yes, I did. You nearly rolled headfirst into the fire." Blade pointed to the ground beside her, where a small pit of embers burned dimly. "That would have been very unpleasant had I not caught you. I suppose that is a lesson learned. Next time, I will not make the fire so close."

"No, that's not what I meant." Mouse frowned. "Did you see the creature? The one that came out of the forest?"

Blade shook his head. "I have been on watch this whole night and I saw nothing come out of the forest."

"But you were asleep," Mouse replied, confused. "I saw you. And then I saw the bird…"

"I believe you were dreaming," Blade said, raising an eyebrow.

Mouse shook her head emphatically. "There was no way this was a dream. I could see everything clearly… I could feel everything…"

She glanced over at the embers next to her. "Okay, well that might explain why I could feel the heat, but I could've sworn that bird on fire was… real."

Blade looked at her intently. "You saw a bird on fire?"

Mouse nodded, embarrassed. "Well, now that I think about it, I guess there were some things that weren't quite… real. But it seemed… I just thought… well, I don't know. I'm sorry, that's ridiculous, isn't it?"

To her surprise, Blade shook his head seriously. "No, it is not ridiculous. Peculiar, yes, but not ridiculous. Hmm. Very peculiar."

"What do you mean? Was what I saw real?"

"I doubt that it was real in the sense that you mean, but powerful visions often feel that way. The creature you described is called a phoenix," Blade explained. "I cannot say it was ever thought to be anything more than mythology, but it has been an important symbol for the people of Elmnas, since the very oldest days."

"What kind of symbol?" Mouse asked.

"One of renewal. Of a new age." Blade sat back, his eyes searching the sky. "In the old lore, the phoenix was a creature of immortality. When it died, it would be reborn from the ashes, blazing more gloriously than before and continuing to live forever. It conquered the final failure of all mortal things – death."

"So what are you saying?"

"You seeing this in a dream is… interesting. Some Elmlings might say you saw an omen. An oracle of something to come. As they once sang in the hymns of old – *Come, thou Phoenix, and with your wings bring Elmnas' new dawn.*"

"So something's going to happen because I saw this thing?" Mouse probed hesitantly.

"I was not saying that. It is just lore," Blade replied shortly. Mouse fell silent as he stared somberly into the dying embers of the fire.

"It may be important that you did, however. You are a daughter of Elmnas, indeed. If there is more to it, I cannot say, but I know what you carry may yet save many."

"I see," Mouse eyed him curiously. "You know, for someone from Gormlaen, you sure do know a lot about Elmnas."

Blade offered a small smile, a knowing look on his face. "That is because I am not from Gormlaen. But you knew that."

"You're a Guardian, aren't you? Like the guards said!" Mouse said. "That's why you helped us in the first place!"

"I *was* a Guardian," Blade corrected.

"Sure, I get that you can't openly be one, but you still use the swords! That's how Toma knew, anyway. You exist! I almost can't believe it!"

"Toma knows less than he thinks about the Guardians," Blade said. "But yes, the Guardians existed. And it was more than just swinging a pair of swords. It was a way of existence. A life dedicated to service of the Unseen and to sacrifice for the good of Elmnas. Now that life is as much past as the Order it once served."

"I don't understand," Mouse said. "If you're still around, how can it be gone?"

"You must understand this, Mouse. A Guardian lives by a special code, inaugurated from ancient times. One not meant to be bent or broken."

Blade shook his head wearily. "I have not lived by that code for a long time, and so I cannot be a Guardian."

"Oh," Mouse said, sobered by his heaviness. "I guess that explains the Jackal Syndicate then."

Blade nodded. Again they sat listening to the sound of Toma snoring and embers crackling beside them.

"So, why did you do it?" Mouse pried after a while. "Why did you leave your order?"

Blade cast a disconsolate look at the ground and shook his head. "Because, in the end, there was no justice. Even when I had tried, nothing stopped the slaughter of my brothers and sisters, my people. It may be that some survived, but I will never be sure. It is likely I will never look upon them again. My country is torn, end from end, and no amount of trying will restore it. So I took vengeance into my own hands. I took what I could from those who took everything from me."

Mouse pondered these words, questions brimming as the quiet stretched between them. There was a certain isolation in Blade's silence – an untouchable quality to the matter that halted satisfaction of even her deepest curiosity. He grieved, it seemed, in sacred solitude, and Mouse knew grief. She was not eager to desecrate it. On the other hand, his memories would no doubt give her a clue about her own past. If she truly was a child of Elmnas, was his history not also her own?

Uncomfortable, Mouse delved anyway. "If I'm going to find out what happened to me, I think I need to know what happened to you. To the Guardians... To Elmnas. Would you tell me?"

Blade did not readily answer her, but slowly, he nodded in agreement. He spoke softly, his eyes already betraying the burden he carried. His story began this way:

"Many years ago, in the ancient times, the Guardians were the protectors and leaders of Elmnas. There were three Orders–the Keepers, the Masters, and the Warriors. Each was tasked to protect a specific facet of our people's way of life. Warriors protected our borders, keeping the violence of the warring nations at bay. Masters protected the Law, and taught virtue to the people. The Keepers protected the Oracles, the knowledge of things seen and unseen, past and present, things that were and things that will be, upholding sacred truth. The Orders were meant to be equal and just, and as it was revealed to the Keepers, ordained by the Unseen One from the oldest days.

"I was chosen as a child, as all the Guardians are chosen, by the Guardian Trivium. They deemed me capable to serve in the Warrior

Order, and so, my training commenced immediately. I was sent to the Silver Sea Sanctum, that is, the ancient home of the Guardians and the seat of our rule, tradition, and worship. There I grew learning the customs of my people, and more immediately, the way of the twin blades. This was the sacred tradition of my Order, and it became as much a part of me as my very body and soul. Our people flourished in that time, and even the threats that Gormlaen and the nations across the seas posed were of little concern. We were strong, and we were proud of our strength. Arrogant, as it were, and the arrogance grew with each passing age.

"I was not much older than you when the Keepers brought forth the first Oracles of warning. They spoke of the present, of our arrogance, of the Guardians' failure to protect. We could not accept it. The Guardians had done nothing but protect – how could the Oracles be true? And yet, they continued to come. I became a man under these warnings, and like most of the Guardians, did not see or believe in their significance. All that changed when I was sent out to serve my office. Then, I saw it. The truth. Many days of travel beyond the Sanctum, in the great city of Horn, I walked into a world of suffering. I witnessed the abuse and corruption of power, the lack of concern for the poor and the helpless, the crime running rampant and devouring the weak. I did what I could – I fought the wars raging in the streets – but it had little effect. By that time, many of the people had lost faith in the old ways, and they cared neither for truth or justice, only survival. I was certain the Masters would come, would see what I saw, but their interests were instead the rhetoric of politics and power. Maybe it was our aloofness that made it worse. I am not sure. But we had failed to protect, and our people were reaping the consequences.

"It was then that the Coalition Ambassadors of Gormlaen came to us with their gifts and offerings of peace treaties. Under the pretense of friendship, they extended into our borders, their advances of trade, industry, and technology welcomed by our poor and suffering people. In no time, the Coalition was everywhere. Even the Guardian Trivium had embraced them, foolishly believing, I suppose, that Gormlaen would be a powerful ally. Who can say? No one knew their true intentions, or had understood that the alliances with Maiendell and

Heibeiath were shams. And when we refused to dissolve our leadership and join the Coalition alliance..."

Blade lifted his head once more, searching the barren sky. His face was masked in shadow behind his hood, and only the whites of his eyes shone in the darkness as he gazed upward. Mouse leaned forward in rapt silence, not daring to interrupt the air between them. She felt her intrusion simply being there, even as he spoke aloud. Mouse shifted, suppressed the urge to clear her throat, and stared at the fire as the silence stretched on. It had been painful enough to listen to – she could not imagine how painful it was for him to live through it all over again for her sake. However, to her surprise, he continued.

"I was traveling during the first onslaught. I had left my quarters in Horn to follow a group of bandits to what I guessed was their hideout, far off in the wilderness. Hoping to catch them unawares, I stole away swiftly in the night, alerting only one other Guardian of my journey. This decision, this whim, it seems, preserved my life.

"Two days later, after I had successfully uncovered the location of the hideout, I began my return journey. I was only three or four miles from Horn when a boy met me, half dead with exhaustion. He was a courier for our headquarters, sent by the only Guardian who had known where I was. He had run long and hard to find me. To tell me... what had happened."

Blade took a deep breath. He stirred the embers with a stick distractedly before continuing. "He did not truly understand what had happened himself. The boy woke up to the city on fire, energy rifles blasting in the streets. By that time, most of the Guardians were dead. Ambushed in their sleep, possibly. Only a handful was left to defend the city. They fought valiantly, he told me, but they could not hold off the Coalition swarm. He had watched Theana fall moments after she charged him to find me. The Guardian who knew where I was," Blade clarified, registering Mouse's confusion. "An excellent warrior. An even better friend."

Blade leaned back as he sat on the dewy grass, his hood sliding from his head as he shifted. New life stirred in the embers of the fire, and the resulting flare revealed a curious tenderness on his face. It was an uncharacteristic softness intermingled with deep pain, which started at the corners of his mouth and spread to even the weathered lines around his eyes. Mouse looked away, startled and slightly ashamed she had witnessed it. She had never seen anguish so deep, so loving, so very personal. It dredged up the only comparable situation – that of her own desolation when Red was taken. Mouse snuck a quick glance in his direction, hoping he had recovered. His face fell in and out of shadow, obscuring any expression, but his silence told Mouse he was thinking.

"So, what did you do then?" Mouse asked, hoping it was safe to continue.

"I did what any of my kind ought to," Blade answered slowly, roused from his reverie. "I made my way to the Sanctum."

"Why did you go there?"

"As the seat of our government, the Sanctum would be our best hope for any kind of counterattack. From there, our greatest force could be mobilized and defeat the enemy threat. Elmnas is a large country. The Coalition could not strike everywhere at once, and certainly they could not overtake our capitol. If I could get there, many deaths could be avenged.

"I traveled many long and dangerous nights. I saw that Horn was not the only place that had fallen. Each city and town I passed was either on fire or overrun with Coalition guard. Nothing was safe. I took to the shadows of the forests instead, picking my way carefully over the countryside until I could safely reach the Sanctum. Hope of refuge sustained me, but the journey was tedious. Days became weeks, and weeks, and months. So much time wasted – but there was little I could do. The Coats were everywhere, and strange mists blowing over the land made travel painfully slow."

"Mists," Mouse repeated.

"Yes," Blade confirmed darkly. "They began there, not long after the first attacks. I did not encounter a Mistwolf, however, until I had finally reached the Sanctum."

"Oh no," Mouse whispered. "They were there?"

Blade nodded soberly. "It was chaos when I arrived. The city was on fire, bodies littered the streets… the air was so thick with cinder I could hardly see or breathe. I climbed my way up through the city, fighting shadow and smoke up to the cliffs, where the temple overlooks the sea. I could count a few blades flashing in the chaos alongside me, but we were no doubt outnumbered.

"I hoped desperately that things were faring better within the Sanctum. Maybe, I thought, a remnant was barricaded inside, waiting for an opportunity to strike out. I could provide some distraction, some relief, being on the outside. It was, of course, a fool's fancy. The smoke cleared about the Sanctum, and I could see her walls had been breached. Desecrated, gutted, laid bare to the plundering hands of the Coats. Some of my kin were yet fighting in the courtyard, and I hastened to join them. We took out as many as we could, but our defeat was already assured. There were just too many.

"Yes, I expected to die there. No amount of skill with the sword or quickness of the hand could deflect every blast and blow of those energy rifles. We were falling one by one, and I was among the last. It was then that the Mistwolves came, as day turned to dusk. The mists… rolling in like the tide, shrouding our minds and our eyes and poisoning us with rabid fear. As it closed in, carrying the sound of a corrupted language not one of us could bear to hear, our hearts melted. Even our enemies desisted their charge to listen – just long enough to hear them panting around us, smell their foul stench burning in our nostrils.

"When they attacked, they did so indiscriminately. Everyone, Coat and Elmling alike, was prey. I will be honest with you, I don't know how I survived. These unholy creatures… I had never seen their like, nor have I since. To our horror, the blasts of the Coats glanced off their unnatural hides, and they devoured half of us all as we struck out with sword or rifle. And when our weapons met a mark, we seemed to be fighting only shadows that weaved in and out among us, materializing just long enough to snatch men and women between their jaws. I may have maimed a few of them, but I cannot be sure. You are one of the few who would understand, having lived through a Mistwolf attack yourself."

Mouse offered a curt nod of affirmation. Her own encounter was not something she would soon forget.

"I was just in the right place at the right time," she said softly. "I shouldn't be alive."

"It was much the same for me," Blade replied. "I had never encountered such a creature before, let alone a pack of them coordinating an ambush."

"What did you do? How did you get out?"

Blade sighed and kicked a rogue ember back into the flames. "With the city and Sanctum fallen, there was nothing else I could hope to do there but die. So, in the confusion, I ran. I'm not proud of this. A Guardian never runs from a battle, nor leaves his brothers and sisters behind. It was there, running blindly down the cliffs in selfish, primal fear, that I knew I could never call myself by that name again."

Blade stood abruptly, his sudden movement disturbing Toma enough to reposition and let out a guttered groan. Mouse thought he might wake, but instead, he rolled away from the fire and continued snoring loudly. She caught sight of the edge of Blade's cloak as he melted into the darkness. Mouse sat alone in that heavy night, taking in the tale with terrible understanding. There had been so much loss, such irreparable damage, that Mouse could not even begin to fathom how her little knowledge, how Red's stolen chip, might help at all. *This nation, my home, is so broken. Will what I bring do any good at all? Is there any hope?* It did not seem so. All she carried was more sorrow, more truth of the Coalition's treachery and their hatred for her people. *And how many loved ones have I lost? How much suffering before merciful oblivion carried it away?* Mouse wondered. Fear and doubt crept into her mind. *Maybe it would be better to never know my own story at all.*

She shook off the thought as quickly as it had come. Yes, the truth was difficult, and her own past might be too painful to bear, but she had to know. There would be no healing, no freedom, without it. She owed it to herself, to Toma and Blade, to seek the truth. She owed it to the dead, the dying, the psychologically mutilated of Misty Summit, to the minds that would be enslaved for the Coalition's purposes. To Red, for sacrificing everything, to those resisting from the shadows, to the world, aching for freedom. For herself.

Yes, she would complete this journey, and now, she was ready for it. Though her mind raced with questions, fears, and awful realities,

Mouse forced herself to lie down. There would be no point to lying awake, or waiting for Blade to return to the fireside. She felt his presence a short distance off, diligently taking up his post at the stump. Briefly, Mouse considered offering to relieve him, but as she nestled into the warm grass by the crackling fire, sleep overtook her, and questions of past or present nightmares faded into a dreamless, lightless night.

CHAPTER TWENTY-THREE

Sprawling forests grew thicker with every footstep the party made northward. The combed and civilized Gormlaen of the Coalition yielded to a mysterious and untamed wild, where even the sounds of their voices were swallowed by its increasing presence. It was the closest thing to beauty Mouse had ever seen, even in the dreary haze of the ever-lightless sky. Blade had remarked these wilds were much like the woodlands of Elmnas before the war, and Toma walked along with wide-eyed wonder at its unaided and unusual fertility.

Though Blade seemed satisfied with their progress, movement had become an unavoidable slog. The darkness fell heavier here, the terrain rougher, and the narrow paths they had forged for themselves were becoming increasingly unwieldy. As the elements forced them to make camp each day well before the shadows covered the forest floor, Blade urged them to move faster to compensate. It was harder going, but it came with the small mercy of a longer rest, which Mouse and Toma graciously appreciated. They walked along doggedly, Blade leading the two until they foundered each day.

"You have done well," Blade remarked after they made camp. With their captured feast of rabbit still roasting over the fire, he stood abruptly. "I think it's time for another lesson."

"Guess we've aced trapping, huh?" Toma smirked, nodding to their much anticipated dinner.

"You mean *I* aced it," Mouse corrected. "Your trap couldn't hold a breeze."

"And your aim is still abysmal!" Toma quipped. "That deer would have been long gone if not for me. You're welcome, by the way."

"Now, now, I'm confident the both of you would survive the wilds of Gormlaen quite comfortably after all you've learned," Blade interjected with a smile.

"So what's next?" Mouse asked eagerly.

Blade unsheathed his swords, which glowed, it seemed, in mysterious anticipation. Mouse looked at her hands in shock as he placed one sword in hers and the other with Toma. They looked at each other, open mouths extending into broad, delighted grins.

"I have studied and practiced sword craft since I was a boy," Blade began. "Younger than you are now, actually. Being a master of the sword, especially of the way of the twin blades, means little in this time. Still, it is knowledge I would hate to see pass away. Who can say? One day, maybe, it may save your life. Now, get a feel for your weapon with a practice swing or two."

The two stood at once. Mouse rooted herself as she grasped the sword's heavy hilt, lifting it with concerted effort as she stared quizzically into its illuminated and intricately carved surface. She knew her way around her machinery and her tools, she had even understood her new energy pistol enough to take apart and put back together. This sword, however, was an entirely different matter. Her arms burned as she steadied it, and with all the effort she could muster, attempted an inelegant swing. It was, by all accounts, embarrassingly feeble. She glanced over at Toma who wasn't faring much better. He swung his more like a hatchet, the movements oafish and uncouth for such a graceful relic.

Blade clucked his tongue. "That will not do. My mistake. Bring them to me before you hurt yourselves."

He grinned as the pair surrendered the swords in sullen silence.

"Don't worry, the lesson is far from over," he assured them. "Go enjoy your meal and we'll continue in a moment."

"Where do you think he's going?" Mouse wondered as Blade trudged off purposefully into the woods.

"To laugh at us without hurting our feelings," Toma replied with a self-deprecating smile. "Joke's on him. We get to eat."

Presently Blade returned, carrying two sturdy branches with him. As they ate, he set to work fashioning them. In time, they resembled crude but wieldable sparring swords.

"The balance will be off, unfortunately," Blade lamented after he finished. "But if you must learn with these, so be it. Up on your feet."

Soon Blade set the two opposite the other, correcting their stances and guiding their motions. They were graceless, awkward, and out of their element, but they were having the time of their lives. Twilight darkened the forest beyond the campfire's circle, deepening the shadows of the forms that battled clumsily and gleefully in its light. It was well after dark when Blade drew the lesson to a close.

"You won't be masters any time soon," he chuckled. "But you listen well. Keep this up, and you will be able to hold your own. Now, time to rest."

Nights afterward often ended this way as the dueling partners learned new skills and attempted to perfect old ones. It was, for Mouse, the only real entertainment she had ever experienced. And, though she could not think of an occasion when she would actually use such training, she was stronger, more agile, and more able now than ever before to continue their harrowing journey into Elmnas.

It seemed a welcome distraction for Blade as well. Their faux battles and antics had a way of softening his steeled exterior, bringing out a fondness Mouse recalled only in his mentioning of Theana many nights before. His story did not come too often to her mind now, as other things always seemed to crowd it, but she had not neglected to share it with Toma in hushed whispers as they journeyed along. The pair followed Blade at a distance as they discussed the fate of Elmnas.

"I'm surprised you didn't know any of this, Toma," Mouse said after a time.

"Elmlings don't just drop by for lunch in Maiendell, you know," Toma muttered. "You're the first one I'd ever met, and you didn't even know it at the time."

"I guess you're right," Mouse conceded the point. It was not as if Elmlings were allowed free rein like those of Maiendell or Heibeiath. Even Toma's travel had been limited when it came down to it. Indeed, the Coalition had meticulously squelched the knowledge of Elmnas, so much so that no one thought of those who lived there as anything but myth or cautionary tales. *And why would anyone think of them in any other way?* Mouse had to scoff at that. Guardians, rebels, and Cardanthium – all were lost behind the borders of an impenetrable land or, to Mouse's unending frustration, an impenetrable memory. All she had for now was Blade, her dreams, and the jumbled jottings of the old man she loved like a father.

"I wish we had more to go on. Blade's the only one who can help now."

"Hey!" Toma exclaimed, grinning. "What about your witty, quick-thinking guide?"

He jerked his thumbs proudly to his chest and drew himself up to his full height. Mouse laughed gratefully and kept walking, shyly avoiding his gaze.

How could she express how glad she was he accompanied her, and just how guilty she felt about it? As much as he would deny it, she put Toma in this position – to choose between his family and a foolhardy journey into dangers unknown. Yes, he had come willingly, but it was more than once they could have easily lost their lives. How could she forgive herself if anything happened to him on her account? Could a dream, a memory, a pile of papers – even a mysterious chip – be more important than that?

Her thoughts often drifted back to the Breythorn farm, where his family toiled anxiously, waiting, she imagined, for Toma to return. *Does the Coalition know that missing Breythorn boy is doing the unthinkable – helping me, a fugitive? And if they do know... what will happen to the rest of them?* Mouse's heart jumped to her throat as she thought of the possibilities. Little Mina came to her mind first, and she shuddered.

Mouse glanced over at Toma, who smiled wide. Panting as they walked, he pointed to Blade and gave a sarcastic thumbs-up. She wondered if, behind his heroic humor, Toma truly understood what he had left, and what was at stake. She hoped it was worth it.

Instinctively, she rubbed the back of her right hand. Nothing but a scar remained, the raised pink flesh ostensibly less noticeable than the dark, crude ink branding her shoulder. Still, a shoulder was easier to hide than a hand, and she felt in the occasional tingling of her fingers the chip's phantom presence. In a way, that seemed worse.

By this time, they had walked a long way, and again the terrain was beginning to change. Springy, dense forest floor gave way to dirt, brambles, and short grass. Mouse no longer had to watch her every step for large rocks and fallen trees. She glanced behind her, surprised to realize they left the tangled gloom of a crowded wood as the trees thinned considerably.

"I think we've stopped going uphill," Toma said, wiping sweat off his brow.

"We have," Blade confirmed. "We're close."

He motioned for them to wait as he investigated the sparse forest ahead. After a moment, he returned with an armful of broken branches.

"The rendezvous point should only be about a mile ahead, but we will not be expected until early tomorrow morning. It would be best to camp here, where the forest can yet hide us."

"Alright," Toma said, dropping his pack on the ground. "So what's the plan for tomorrow?"

"We leave while it is still dark and make our way through the clearing and into the valley just beyond it."

Blade pointed out past the trees. Mouse squinted in that direction, unable to make out any evidence of a clearing.

"There we will see the mountains ahead of us. We will follow them until we find a small shack in the ridge," he continued. "There, the boatman should be waiting, ready to take us to where Thunder Run begins. And, if all goes well, we will be in Elmnas by mid-morning."

"You say that like there's a good chance that it won't," Mouse suggested forebodingly.

"These are dangerous waters," Blade replied. "And, there is no telling what we will encounter on either side. We have many risks to account for. But we knew this, and I would not have tried if I did not think it was possible."

"Come on, it'll be fine, Mouse," Toma insisted, playfully punching her arm. "We'll get there."

"I hope so," Mouse muttered, placing her gear on the ground. "I really do."

Mouse lay on her back and stared fixedly at the treetops swaying gently above her. This was the only comforting part of the forest. Often on their travels, she watched them creak back and forth by firelight until she drifted off. Anxiety, however, now kept her from her usual drifting, her mind too full of the next day's plans to fall asleep. Wondering how the rest of her party was faring, Mouse propped herself up and looked around. As usual, Blade sat a distance away from the smoldering embers, perched on a small boulder, and attentively watched the tree line ahead of their camp. To no one's surprise, Toma slept soundly on the other side of the fire, his solid frame rising and falling with each of his long, loud breaths. Mouse shook her head with a smile as she watched him. She could use some conversational distraction, sure, but anyone who could sleep at a time like this deserved his rest. Instead, she rose and made her way over to Blade.

"You should be asleep, Mouse," Blade stated as she drew closer. "I need you to have your wits about you tomorrow."

Mouse tilted her head in consternation. With his back to her, Blade hadn't seen her approaching, but he always seemed to know when she or anyone else was coming.

"I can't sleep," she said, sighing. "Can I do my watch now? If you really want, I will wake you later."

His silhouette was hardly recognizable in the darkness, but she perceived he turned to look down at her from his perch.

"Alright," he said after a time, and she heard his soft landing on the pine needles below. He materialized in front of her.

"Once you start to feel weary, you can get me or Toma to take your place. You understand?"

Mouse nodded, sensing his concern despite twilight obscuring his features.

"I know you are nervous." Blade placed a hand on her shoulder. "I cannot set you at ease, but know this – I will do all that it takes to get you into Elmnas."

"Aren't you worried?" Mouse asked. "You've been gone a long time, and there's no telling how people will react to you, and me, and Toma, even if they are rebels."

Blade brought his hand to his chin in consideration.

"Yes. It has been a long time. Longer than you know," he responded. "No doubt, it will not be easy. Still, if there is good to be done, I hope now to do it."

Mouse laughed, in spite of herself. "I'm not so sure if there is anything we can do."

"Listen to me," Blade urged, crouching a bit so that they were eye-level. "I would not have come all this way, back to the place of my greatest suffering, if I did not believe you had something worth coming for. And I cannot explain it, but I feel something else draws us there, and in my bones I sense the echoes of greater things to come. I don't know who you are, Mouse, but I think you can bring a flicker of hope, of truth, to a hopeless people. It may be you are meant to do something, even if you only see that something dimly now."

"I think you're starting to sound like a Guardian again."

A small but sure smile broke from beneath Blade's hood. "I suppose there are some things we can never entirely abandon, though we try."

"I guess not," Mouse observed thoughtfully. "Well, goodnight."

"Wait." Blade reached into his cloak, extracting a small leather bundle. "I have something for you."

He handed it to her, and Mouse turned the weighty object over in her hands. She felt for the end, finding something hilt-like and solid in her grip. Mouse fumbled with the bundle, uncovering a soft, greenish blue glow at the base. The glow grew brighter as it slid easily from the leather case, revealing a short, curved, and sharp blade. Breathtaking, intricate designs spread along each edge of it, flowering out in remarkable detail from the hilt to the tip. Mouse traced the patterns lightly, careful not to catch her fingers on the blade's razor-like points.

"Whoa," she whispered. "What is this?"

"It is a ceremonial dagger. Only the Masters and the Keepers would carry these."

Mouse continued to examine the piece closely, its shimmer illuminating everything around her. "You were a Warrior, though, right? How do you have one?"

"It belonged to Theana." Blade reached out and gently took the dagger in one hand, running his own fingers across the engraved designs fondly with the other. "It was a gift, from her mother, who had been a Keeper."

"I don't know what to say," Mouse said. "Thank you."

"It does not make sense for me to hold on to it," Blade replied, giving it back. "I think Theana would have wanted you to have it."

Mouse carefully put the dagger back into the leather pouch and placed it inside her jacket. As she did so, Blade nodded, turned, and a made a quick stride toward the camp.

"Theana wasn't just your friend," Mouse stated quietly. "Was she?"

He paused, his back to her as he answered. "You are perceptive. No, we were betrothed."

"I'm... so sorry."

Blade remained in that spot, standing at a short distance from Mouse. Though it was dark, she could see his silhouette shift, his shoulders slumping against the low light of the fire.

"As am I," he finally replied. Without another word, he continued on his way.

Mouse watched in silence for a while before turning to climb up the rock. There was a pang of guilt in her curiosity about the Guardian Theana, but she could not say the question had not been in her mind since Blade had first mentioned her. Indeed, their relationship explained much about Blade. The way that he seemed to blame himself for everything, his revoking of his Guardian status, his protectiveness over her and Toma – it made sense.

She clambered onto the flattest part of the boulder and sat down toward the edge that looked out ahead of their camp. Mouse strained to see the forest in front of her, but nothing was distinguishable. Even the trees ceased their swaying, and Mouse was alone. Her hand wandered to the pocket where she had placed the dagger, and she absentmindedly tugged at it.

Unlike any other weapons she had handled, it was warm, hot even, through the leather pouch. Had it not been cool to the touch just moments before? Curious, she slipped the dagger out of her pocket to examine it.

There was a soft glow, even through the pouch, that seemed to intensify the longer she held it in the flat of her hands. Amazed, she pulled the pouch away, illuminating the forest in a wide arc. She held the dagger tightly in her left hand and waved it in front of her. It hummed through the air softly with every flourish, and despite her own clumsiness, remained precise and graceful. Mouse held the blade aloft before her eyes. *How could a weapon be so well balanced, so perfect, as this, even after years of disuse?* She wondered if Blade had done anything to keep it so, but she suspected he had not touched it since Theana's passing.

The dagger's bluish glow mesmerized her, and she laid it down on her thigh as the emanation intensified. *Fascinating.* Blade's swords had always remained a definite shade of green – eerie, ghostlike, and unchanging even when she or Toma had handled them. This dagger, however, which had been a muted green-blue when given to her, became a different shade altogether, more blue now than green, and alive, it seemed, with her touch.

The thought of life within the weapon disconcerted her as she handled it distractedly. Nothing she knew was quite like this. She couldn't help but wonder, as irrational as it seemed – *does it…see? Does it know who I am, better than I can know myself?* Unnerved, Mouse put the dagger away hastily. Her surroundings returned to shadow. Still, even out of sight, she felt it, its presence paradoxically comforting despite the disorienting darkness. For the first time, she could not readily recall a reason to be afraid.

CHAPTER TWENTY-FOUR

An icy mist crowded the base of the northern Jagged Jaw Mountains as the bounty hunter, Fox, reached the valley that would lead her to Thunder Run. There was a cold wind, carrying with it the whispers of the coming winter as it forced its way through the narrow corridor beside the mountains. She pulled her cowl tightly around her mouth, cursing the brevity of autumn in the north. It was pleasant enough in the summer months, especially since the mists touched very little of the area, but autumn would fade quickly into a bitter winter that stubbornly held its grasp until mid-spring. If all went well, she would not have to endure it. The black mare she sat upon shuddered a bit in the gust and stomped impatiently.

"Steady," Fox murmured, patting the mare's damp neck. "Quietly, now."

She scanned the surrounding area before coaxing the horse forward. The tall tree trunks of the Swaying Forest stood on the sloping hill to her left, and the craggy maws of the mountains ran steeply along her right. At a distance, she could see the valley flattened out and the forest edge fell away from the mountains. It was there, only a few miles ahead, that Thunder Run would reveal itself, exploding from an underground cistern and pouring into a deep chasm within the mountain chain. Fox rode discreetly through the low valley between mountain and forest, her horse's footfalls muffled by the springy undergrowth of the field. This pleased her; if she were to come upon this supposed Syndicate smuggler, she needed to see him before he could see her.

I'll kill that sewer-dwelling lout if he's wrong about this. It was not like her to rely so heavily upon intel gathered by another, as she was an excellent tracker without it, but to her great displeasure, her targets had been meticulously stealthy. *A Guardian, indeed.* After a few days following a barren trail with no leads, she had run out of options and could not waste any more time. There was, however, one resource she had not explored: Myergo.

Yes, she knew Myergo. Seasons ago, in the time when Fox first began taking contracts, he had hired her for a hit on a disobedient drug mule in Maiendell. It was among the first of her kill jobs, and she had completed it neatly. When she returned for her compensation, Myergo refused to pay his promised price. In those days, Fox was as naïve as she was hot-headed and bold, and that latent fire of aggression reared its ugly and impulsive head as she challenged Myergo over this slight. Indeed, he had accepted the challenge, but Fox had not known Myergo was a criminal among criminals – cruel, cunning, and codeless save for the rule of his own strength. The blaze of her temper was never a match for the overwhelming power of Myergo's forces, which he sent to hound her when he dismissed her. She had barely escaped his labyrinthine domain with her life.

Many seasons had passed since then, and Myergo had never pursued her beyond his kingdom. He'd done it to teach her a lesson, but there was no doubt if she crossed him again, he would not hesitate to kill her. Requesting an audience with Myergo was the last thing she had wanted to do, but Fox was desperate. If she waited any longer, the girl and this Guardian would surely have found a way into Elmnas. There was no time. This needed to be done.

She found Myergo's contact in his usual place, smugly smoking blackleaf among the smokestacks of the industrial district. Fox approached him openly, allowing the man to size her up as she strode slowly toward him.

"Dervish," she said as soon as he was within earshot.

"Who's asking?" he replied, squinting warily at her as she approached.

Fox lowered her traveling hood and cowl and pressed a gold piece into his hand.

"Someone looking for information."

"Why, don't you look familiar," Dervish muttered, studying her thoughtfully. A mocking grin suddenly spread his lips. "I do believe I remember you. You coming back for more?"

"Tell me what you know about the Coalition city-wide drill from a few weeks ago," Fox demanded, ignoring the comment pointedly.

"Alright, alright, don't have to be pushy about it." Dervish took a long drag from his pipe before continuing. "Well, it wasn't a drill, I can tell you that much. They were looking for someone. Don't know who, though. Heard word it was a Guardian they were after."

"Any idea where he was headed?"

"Couldn't tell you that." He shrugged. "But if you find him, Myergo'll want to hear about it."

"And why would that be?" Fox asked.

Dervish simply shrugged again. "Don't know the details, really. If only I had somethin' to refresh my memory..."

Fox growled, stifling a string of threats before pressing another gold piece into Dervish's outstretched hand.

"Ah, it's coming back to me now. If I had to guess, I'd say it has something to do with the mill incident."

"Explain."

"We had mill down south we used to process and package... eh... product. Great location for it, too. Locals didn't know much about it, Coats kept their hands off. Well, a few weeks ago, the mill got hit. The whole place'd been burned to the ground. Well, we know it wasn't any Coats that did it. The party officials wouldn't dare. Only clue was one body, left just outside the back. No burns from the fire or an energy pistol, just two big stab holes straight through his chest, and a note pinned to him."

Here Dervish crossed his arms sarcastically. "The blood of the innocent cries for justice, it said, or some nonsense like that."

"Hmm. Stabbed, you say," Fox mused.

Dervish nodded to the blades slung over Fox's shoulders. "Only a few people who kill with swords around here, and I'm guessin' it wasn't you."

"No," Fox confirmed, a disingenuous smirk stretching her crimson lips. "Not this time."

"Ah. So where does that leave us?" Dervish prodded.

"I want an audience with Myergo," she continued, flipping him another gold piece. "You go be a good messenger boy and tell him. I'll be at the Twin Lions, waiting."

Dervish hastily shoved the pipe into his mouth as he caught the coin with both hands.

"Yes, ma'am," he said, and with a smile and a nod, he hurried off into the smokestacks.

Dervish's shrewd, pinched face appeared briefly in the soot-stained window, disappearing again as he slouched toward the inn's entrance. Fox had tucked herself into one of the smoky corners, watching the door and pondering what serious lack of judgment had given her target and the boy the idea of coming here. The Twin Lions was a place for the blue-collar crowd, filtering in and drowning their sorrows after a long day of toil. It was no wonder the Coats had so easily picked out the two young out-of-towners on a mission to Elmnas. Dervish's arrival, however, was much less conspicuous. He slipped quietly behind the large wooden door, his shifty eyes darting around the room until they rested on her.

"Looks like you got the boss man's attention, then," he said, sidling up to her table.

"Just like that?" Fox replied, taking a polite sip from her cup of mead. "Hmm."

"Yeah," he muttered. "He'll see you, just as long as you can part with your... uh, tools, for the meeting."

"I hope you do not take me for a fool, Dervish," Fox bristled, placing the cup down. "I do not have time to die today."

"Well, neither does he." Dervish shrugged. "Look, he's a busy man. If he really wanted you dead, we wouldn't be talking. As it is though, you were right. He's got that Guardian on his mind, not you."

Fox considered the offer carefully, thumbing one of the many daggers holstered to her side.

"Very well," she agreed, pushing herself back from the table. "I will comply."

Dervish smiled impishly and made a sweeping gesture of mock chivalry. "After you."

The route Dervish took to Myergo's fortress under the streets was much different from the one Fox could remember. They wound throughout the city, in between the smokestacks, and deep into the industrial district.

Dervish nodded as factory workers shuffled past them in misery, occasionally lifting their weary heads to stare blankly at the odd pair weaving through the courtyards. Indeed, an odd pair they were – Fox, who towered a good head above Dervish, fiercely beautiful and heavily armed, was an imposing sight among the bowed heads of the tired masses. Dervish, on the other hand, was hardly distinguishable from the gray faces of the changing shifts. Of course, this is what lent Dervish to doing his job well. He made a quick turn toward a back entrance of one of the buildings, Fox following in stride.

Hot air and the strange smell of mixed chemicals struck them as Dervish swung the door open. Fox followed behind him as he picked his way through a room crowded with clinking machines, boxes, and workers. No one took notice, however, as they moved among the machinery and to another doorway on the far side. The pig-nosed woman guarding it narrowed one black eye at Fox contemptuously; the other eye, a scarlet glass ball, listed in its scarred socket. She acknowledged Dervish with a nod, the gold rings adorning her ears clinking, and stepped aside. Fox glared back until they were behind the door, which the woman slammed behind them. Wet, stagnant air and silence replaced the heat, the smell, and the noise of the factory.

"Here we are," Dervish said, pulling a lantern from a rack behind the door. "Now watch your step and follow me."

A dim, dank passage stretched before them, its slick walls

glistening in the lantern's glow. It sloped downward and they descended quickly, each step wetter than the last as they entered the bowels of Lilien's sewer system. Reflexively, Fox placed a hand on one of her pistols. Dervish might have told her she was in no immediate danger, but instinct always warned her otherwise.

After a while, they reached a lighted passage, which ended abruptly in darkness. Dervish took the lead, carefully picking his way through it. By the light of his lantern, Fox could see they had reached the edge of a precipice that overlooked an enormous cavern. She recognized this immediately as the courtyard of Myergo's stronghold.

Accidentally discovered when a crew of Myergo's men unwittingly dug through its ceiling and plummeted into the earth below, the vast underground cave now contained the greatest riches of his exploits. Fox gazed over the edge cautiously.

His cavern was a sight to behold. Flourishing bioluminescent plants, lanterns, and campfires winked up from the cavern floor, illuminating its activity. It resembled something like a small city, with an economic and social climate distinctly its own. Various people, many of whom wore more arms than clothing, milled about on irregular slabs of rock that formed the streets. Hulking silhouettes congregated around open fires or large tents, weapons glinting in the firelight. Mercenaries, from what Fox could guess. Aside from the mercs, the congregation within the cavern appeared to be rather akin to normal city life. Vendors manned stalls and booths along these crude paths, peddling goods from the city above. A few children darted in and out of crowds. Fox spotted goats and chickens scattered among the makeshift dwellings. Someone had even erected public bathhouses since her last visit. Myergo had built an empire for himself here, and even Fox had to admit it was impressive.

Dervish proceeded to lead Fox down a rough staircase hewn from the cavern wall. They made their way down the steep steps slowly, careful not to tread too close to the bare edge beside them. Whether from the steepness of the steps or the lack of faith in their support, the pair made their descent swiftly. With great relief, Fox found the damp, spongy ground of the cavern floor.

"Alright," Dervish puffed, wiping his brow as his feet found safety.

"You know the drill. Just make your way to the gatehouse and they'll hold your things there. As for me, it's time for some good ol' cave brew.

"Oh, and good luck," he added before shuffling off with a wary and telling look in his eye.

CHAPTER TWENTY-FIVE

F ox followed the path up to the gatehouse where she was met, as promised, by a group of armed guards. There she surrendered her weapons and they took her deeper into the cavern, where it spidered out into a maze of natural tunnels. Myergo's lair sat within the labyrinth, down a cramped shaft only his guards could navigate. Countless passages branched out from this one, spreading far and deep into the earth. Fox noted it was not the same route she had taken before, as well as a different set of guards. She could not help smirking at this – Myergo was ever wary, ever watchful, and never trusting of even his own inner circle. This network had saved Fox's life during her last visit, though it could have just as easily taken it from her. One wrong turn to the right or the left, or one turn too many, and Fox would have never seen the world above again. Whether by miracle or fortune, however, she had managed to escape, and she had little interest in discerning the cause. There were times her mind returned to the tunnels, wondering if it might have been better to have died there in the darkness those many years ago. It was with morbid amusement she walked these same tunnels now.

After they trudged on for a while, the guards finally brought Fox to an opening. The tunnel they were in dropped out suddenly, sloping into a large room where all the webbed passages connected. Lit sconces made of bone and rock lined the cold, dripping walls, permeating what would otherwise be an impenetrable darkness. The mixture of burning tar and melting animal fat filled the cavern with smoke, making the stagnant air thick and hard to breathe. Fox had the fleeting impression the cave was not home to a man, but rather a fire-breathing leviathan devouring the last charred bits of some poor, wayward soul.

The room sloped slightly as Fox's escorts lead the way to Myergo's Great Hall, hidden even deeper within. Fox vaguely remembered this part of the procession, although Myergo had made quite a few improvements since their last meeting. Fit for the king Myergo fancied he was, the antechamber had been chiseled out and crafted into a throne-room. Mercenaries stood stoically throughout the hall, watching her with sharp, suspicious eyes. At its far end, Myergo waited. He lounged in a large chair draped in thick animal pelts and ceremoniously raised on a platform of hewn stone. Two great antlers spread from the back of the chair, while horns and bones of other creatures decorated its arms and legs. The throne, a new feature, came with another addition since her last visit – the crown adorning Myergo's closely shaven head. Fashioned of worked metal and overlaid with ornately carved bone, it seemed rather unconventional, but the large, twinkling Cardanthium stone mounted on it proclaimed Myergo's explicit message well.

So they have made him a king. Fox resisted the urge to shake her head. Of course, she understood why. Massive in size and even crueler in comparison, Myergo could be very persuasive. Even she had forgotten the immensity of his stature. Sitting down, he dwarfed the two men standing beside his throne. Fox wondered how the chair managed to support the pounds of sheer muscle atop it. *He is still but a man*, she reminded herself. Even so, Myergo seemed more bestial than anything as he sprawled lazily over it, watching smugly with black eyes as cold and empty as the abyss.

"Ah, look who comes back to me," he rasped, his voice a deep and chilling. "The fox returns to the hole."

Fox's mouth grew taut as curses threatened to spew from it, a fire long dormant now burning in her belly. Her fingers twitched involuntarily toward her waist where her pistol should have been.

"Hello, Myergo," she replied instead, reining in her itching hands and folding them behind her back. Myergo burst into a cruel laugh.

"Ah, how your words are tempered, oh fiery one! Good, very good. You are... teachable, yes? I had hoped I would not have to kill you today."

"Such a kind observation," Fox quipped flatly. "I am, however, more interested in business."

"Yes, of course." He righted himself in his throne and leaned forward, his giant hands folded just under his chin, index fingers steepling. "It has come to my attention that you hunt a Guardian."

"Yes, as well as this girl and boy he is traveling with." Fox removed the dossiers from her cloak. "I'm looking for information, if you have any."

"Companions?" Myergo mused. "This is news."

He motioned to the guard beside him, who retrieved the files from Fox's extended hand.

"The Guardian is acting as their guide," she explained. "I believe he is attempting to find them a way into Elmnas."

"How... interesting," Myergo remarked, studying the images thoughtfully. "There have been reports of a girl matching this description here... in the sewers. It was not too long ago. Heynor, my guard captain, would know. He watches the Jackal Syndicate for me, you see, keeps their new recruits in check."

"She was here," Fox replied, stating a fact more than asking. She rubbed her chin, frowning. "What was she doing with a group of petty thieves?"

"Ah. This, we shall soon know." Myergo grinned, exposing yellow, pointed teeth. "Heynor! Bring me the thief."

One of the guards who had escorted Fox inside nodded curtly before disappearing into the darkness of the cavern. Fox watched as he left, only to find Myergo openly leering at her when she looked back.

"Yes?" She said, doing little to hide her disgust.

Myergo sneered in response. "While we wait, there is something I must know."

He lifted himself slowly from his throne, his massive frame uncoiling like a snake as he rose. There was a mottled black and gray pelt of some monstrous beast tied about his neck, and it followed him as he stood. He cast his crude cape behind him with pomp before lumbering off the platform, eyeing her with twisted amusement. The warlord stroked his face thoughtfully, his heavy steps echoing around the chamber as he approached her.

"After our last... encounter, I expected you would not dare to return. I am impressed, yes, at your... courage, but I wonder why you chance it? Perhaps there is another reason."

"I have no hidden agenda," Fox replied, cocking her head. "The reason is clear enough. I needed more information, and apparently, you need me. The arrangement is mutually beneficial."

By this time, Myergo had reached her. Every sinew in her body tensed to flee, but Fox stubbornly rejected the urge. She crossed her arms over her chest and fixed a brazen glare on the towering menace. To her displeasure, Myergo lifted a colossal hand and touched her face. She flinched as he traced the scars on her chin.

"I had always wished you had not been so impetuous," he said, drawing closer. "Such a waste it would be to kill you."

Fox smiled coldly. "Do not fear, Myergo, my talents have not gone to waste."

He smiled as well, but his eyes remained mirthless. "Not your talents, no. But that was not my concern. Your beauty, however..." Myergo licked his lips. "I am sure we could come to a mutually beneficial arrangement that would make good use of it."

"Being eaten alive by Mistwolves sounds more pleasurable," Fox retorted, pulling away sharply.

Myergo lurched forward angrily, his hand raised to strike her, but he quickly composed himself. His hand fell limp, and he let out a hollow laugh.

"I shall remember that, huntress. We shall see."

At that moment, Heynor returned, dragging a wretched and dirty prisoner behind him. The captive was a young man – clearly, a new Syndicate recruit fresh from the streets. He coughed weakly, his battered body shivering pitifully beneath deteriorating rags. His bleary eyes roved the room in terror. She hopped out of the way gingerly as the guard flung the prisoner at Myergo's feet.

"Ah," Myergo chuckled in delight, prodding the prisoner with his foot. "Our guest here wandered too far from his home, his… den, they call it? Yes, he has learned why little scavengers do not go where Myergo has forbidden."

"Please," the man implored, wheezing. "It was an honest mistake, I swear."

"It is possible," Myergo considered, placing his boot on the Syndicate member's face. "But it is more likely you are one of Woldyff's spies, seeking to undermine my authority."

He ground his heel into the man's cheek, pinning him painfully to the floor.

"No, I would never – please – just tell me what you want!"

Myergo relented. The prisoner sputtered feebly and curled into a ball. Myergo knelt down beside him, grabbed a fistful of the prisoner's hair, and jerked his head off the ground.

"Tell me about the Guardian," he said calmly.

"A Guardian? They don't exist! I know nothing!" the man cried.

"You lie!" Heynor interrupted, kicking the prisoner in his side.

"Wait!" Myergo raised a large hand, effectively stopping Heynor mid-kick. "I believe this may be a case of simple… misunderstanding."

Myergo laid the image of Mouse on the floor and turned the thief's head toward it. Do you recognize this girl?"

The prisoner's eyes grew wide. As much as he could, he nodded. "I… I've seen her, yes."

"She had companions, yes?"

Again, the prisoner nodded, and sputtered, "A boy, about her age, and… another man. Tall, cloaked. Woldyff kept calling him the King of the Shadows."

"Ha!" Myergo laughed, dropping the captive's head to slap his knee. It hit the stone floor with a sickening crack. "Blade, the King of the Shadows, is my Guardian? Ha!"

"You know him?" Fox interjected.

"I know enough," Myergo said coldly. He turned his attention back to the captive, who whimpered. "I am not unmerciful, friend.

You may leave today with your life. It would be wise to go before I change my mind."

Feebly, the prisoner hobbled to his feet and limped off as quickly as he could. Myergo watched with disinterest as the prisoner faded into shadow, his dragging steps echoing after him.

"Do you think the cave will have mercy?" Myergo drawled lazily to no one in particular. He stroked his chin again, staring off into the darkness. "I doubt it."

Fox scowled nastily, not bothering to hide her growing impatience. "Where does this leave us, Myergo? I have to find this Guardian."

"Yes, yes…" Myergo answered slowly. "It will not be difficult. He is an old member of the Syndicate, and so there is only one place he will go to enter Elmnas. He will cross at Thunder Run, in the far north above the Swaying Forest."

"And what makes you so sure?" Fox asked skeptically.

"Because it is the only way for someone like him," Myergo answered. "He will be meeting a Syndicate smuggler, who will ferry him down the river. You get to him before they cross, and you will have the girl. But this you must do for me…"

Myergo leaned in close to Fox, his black eyes full of malice. "Capture the Guardian alive. I have a surprise for him."

"I am already delivering the girl," Fox said, annoyed. "How do you expect me to transport the Guardian as well? And am I to work for nothing?"

"You may leave him where he falls. I will send someone to receive him myself." Here Myergo's eyes flashed with cruelty. "And, my little vixen, I expect you to have learned. I have helped you, and so you shall help me. Would you like to see the surprise?"

Fox would have said nothing, but Myergo didn't give her an opportunity to answer. He let out a low whistle, which was answered by the sound of rumbling. A large door on the side of the hall swung open with a loud bang. Behind it, four men pushed a great metal cage on wheels. Fox held her breath as she beheld the immense beast imprisoned inside. The creature bared wicked daggers of yellow teeth and voiced a tortured howl. At this the guards flinched, and soon the light of the hall revealed the rest of the monster's shaggy frame. It heaved against its shackles, growling in frustration as the chains rubbed open sores on its raw limbs. The beast barked and gnawed at its restraints with renewed fervor. It raised its great snout to taste the room, black eyes glazed and useless in the light.

"A Mistwolf," Fox said in disbelief. "You must be mad."

Myergo approached the beast's cage with a fond smile. It turned its head sharply at his approach, emitting guttural snarls as if cursing under its breath. Without a hint of fear, the man wrapped his hand around a bar on the cage and turned to speak.

"It is incredible, isn't it? The Mistwolf is so cunning, so powerful, so… matchlessly vicious. And yet, no one knows where it comes from. As if the very soil of Reidara spawned it to undo us. An enigma." Myergo studied the beast. "Yes. This is a thing of nightmares, and I possess it. In my hands, it is nothing more than a trophy for my showcase."

He sniggered at this, watching gleefully as the creature snapped its massive, dripping jaws.

"No, I am not mad, my lovely huntress, but those who defy me must be," Myergo said, eyeing her coldly as he stepped away from the cage. "Capture the Guardian. My trophy is hungry."

This was enough. With a silent, terse nod, she backed away, her desire to be as far from that beast as possible overriding any sense of pride she harbored. As it were, pride in Myergo's presence had only brought her trouble. Myergo was polite enough, beckoning the guard to escort her back through the tunnels as she turned to leave. How troubling it was, however, to feel his eyes upon her as she walked, penetrating her with that inhuman, hungry gaze not even the meanest creatures carried in them.

"Oh, and Fox," Myergo called after her, the lazy, unconcerned drawl resurfacing. "I am hopeful you do not prefer this beast over me. For, if I do not get the Guardian, I will certainly make you choose."

To halt her steps would be to acknowledge Myergo's upper hand in the situation, so she neither paused nor spoke until she was clear out of the tunnels themselves. Fox ached for the comfort of a cool pistol or a warm blade to soothe her restless fingers, which had felt intolerably impotent during the meeting. Though, as Myergo had suggested, the consequences of her failure would be distressing, she had no desire or inclination to consider it. It was a pointless thought; one that required her to contemplate failure. She would not fail.

Using the Coalition resources at her disposal, Fox acquired transport as far north as she dared – a few miles below the rendezvous point at Filk. There was no telling where her quarry now roamed, and the increasingly impassable terrain made hovercraft travel cumbersome and too conspicuous. No matter. A few days of hard riding brought her near enough to the river.

Fox and her mare plodded slowly along the base of the mountains as she scanned the horizon for any hint of movement. A bitter gust accosted her as she rode, scourging her with the cold and filling her nostrils with the smell of wind-scattered smoke. This was all the hint that she needed – she was close. Instinctively, Fox brought the horse to a trot and guided her into a nearby alcove that jutted into the valley from the mountain chain. In one swift movement, she dismounted, and nimbly picked her way along the rocky outcropping. The scent, as well as the distant and distinct roar of flowing water, grew stronger as she hastened forward under the mountain's shadow.

She came to a larger clearing, the space between the forest and the mountains widening into a low vale. With hawk-like intensity, she scoured the scene and pinpointed a destitute little shack by the forest's edge. It was a dreary-looking place, with deformed boards crudely nailed together to form a pitiful excuse for a wall. Vines grew unchecked along the building's sides, prying their way in between the dilapidated slats. Fox would have thought it abandoned, but a smoldering cooking pit told her otherwise.

She hunkered down into a well-hidden cleft, prepared to wait the entire night for the smuggler to show himself, but she didn't have to wait for long. Moments later he poked out of the dwelling's opening with a bundle of laden sacks, which he lassoed together and tossed into an old cart he had dragged from the shack's far side. Apparently satisfied with his work, he nodded and trotted to the building's backside, shortly reappearing with a sturdy draft horse in tow. After hooking the horse into the rickety cart, he hopped spryly into the back and hollered a passionless "Hyah!", effectively goading the beast forward. Cautiously, Fox watched as the man made labored progress toward the mountain pass until he disappeared behind protruding walls of rock and into the pass beyond.

Surveying her immediate surroundings, Fox took in the numerous rocky formations spilling into the valley. She stalked among the boulders, noting the position of the shack in reference to Thunder Run. The conclusion was clear. If the Guardian would come to meet the smuggler here, his troupe would necessarily be funneled directly into this inescapable pass.

It was all the advantage she could ask for. Pleased, she prepared herself, gauging all the routes and possible vantage points for the most effective ambush. Much better than she had hoped, a plan was quickly falling into place.

All that was left now was to wait.

CHAPTER TWENTY-SIX

Mouse lay awake long before dawn could creep dismally off the horizon, fixing her eyes upon the swaying arms of the trees above. The night had been long, woefully devoid of the rest Blade was so keen on her gaining, but she doubted he would be able to tell. She was more alert now than she had ever been, anxiously roused by the knot coiling in her stomach. As the restlessness mounted, Mouse did her best to remain motionless, concentrating on the sound of the now waking forest. A lonely, spectral wail was the first voice Mouse heard, coming faintly to her from a far, dark corner of the wood. It was answered by a drowsy call closer by, and then another, until all manner of life awakened around her. There was a peace in this, and so she lay listening, careful not to disturb the rising chorus of mournful voices reverberating through the heavy air. She drank it in, allowing its grievous beauty to fill her with a sorrow she did not understand, much like old songs Toma would sing for her on occasion, or Blade's campfire tales of ancient glories long forgotten by the living.

Toma yawned loudly, interrupting the moment. "Guess I'm up."

Startled chatter erupted from the treetops as Toma stretched out and stumbled into an upright position. Winged silhouettes flapped away frantically, leaving them once more in total silence. He kicked at the fire's cold embers with the toe of his boot lethargically, sending a few rogue sparks into the air. Mouse sighed and propped herself up.

"Oh! You're up," he whispered needlessly. "Didn't mean to wake you."

"You didn't," she replied, shaking her head. "I've been up for a while."

"Ah, that's too bad." He plopped down onto a nearby stump and shuddered with the early morning cold, his breath hanging in ethereal wisps in front of him. Mouse had huddled herself up near what remained of the fire, hoping to glean some warmth that her blankets had not provided. She shivered, and for a fleeting moment, hoped Toma might notice. The thought was immediately replaced with irrational mortification, and she dared a panicked glance at him to see if he had observed it. To her relief, he had not, and was instead staring blankly in the opposite direction.

"Any idea where Blade's got to?" Toma blurted suddenly.

Mouse shook her head slowly, glad for the distraction.

"Well, I hope he's found breakfast," Toma continued. "S'pose I could get a fire going for whatever he's got."

"No time for that, Toma," Blade's voice came from somewhere in the predawn shadows.

Toma jerked backward, nearly toppling off the stump. Mouse suppressed a giggle as Blade materialized out of the thicket behind them, his gear packed and resting on his shoulder. She quickly stifled it when Blade's expression did not soften, but remained frozen in inscrutable sobriety.

"Once we pack camp, we need to be going," he stated. "I would prefer to start moving while the night yet lingers. It is our best cover."

"Are you expecting that we'll need cover?" Toma ventured timidly.

"Not necessarily, no. But let us not take needless chances."

After a few hurried minutes of packing, everything was ready for their departure. Since Blade had taken the liberty of packing most of the supplies while they slept, Mouse and Toma were left to care only for their own personal items. Mouse tucked her new dagger, case and all, into an improvised belt loop for easy access. Not that she had much of an idea of how to effectively wield it, but its closeness brought her some small comfort as they prepared to set out. Blade offered them a few of their slightly stale provisions, and they were soon on their way, hastening silently out of the dark forest.

Morning wore on, and the shadows of the night before morphed into a cold, gray haze that hung on the ground and swirled around their knees as they walked. The sight of it unnerved Mouse, conjuring up unpleasant recollections of past experiences, but the distinctive lack of the telling sulfurous taste in her mouth was enough to set her mind at ease. She continued in step next to Toma, hoping she would not have to experience that fear again. It had been a long time since she felt it – the saturating panic that made her heart race and her legs numb – and she was surprised at how suddenly it came upon her. When she was alone, fear was a natural state, but with Toma and now Blade, she had stumbled upon a sense of security that allowed her to let her guard down, enjoy this new life and discover what it held with unbound curiosity. But every fear was quick to remind her this security was a false one. Against otherworldly things, like Mistwolves and slave-creating evils, even Blade and Toma could not overcome. Mouse shook the thought away. How she could do without this primal feeling!

They soon came to a spacious part of the woods, where orange needles covered the flat ground, and Mouse could see the clearing Blade had promised. Several paces ahead, the backside of a gnarled old shack, bleached and worn with the many seasons it had seen, appeared before them. The entire structure sagged dangerously to the side where the wood had rotted or fallen out, and Mouse was sure the next wind to come barreling down the valley would flatten it. It was an ugly blight on an otherwise scenic landscape – the last, decaying evidence of man in a manless country. Nature, having realized this, had already begun to aid in the destruction of the old building as vines wedged themselves between the shack's rickety slats and conquered the assortment of rusty, mangled equipment laying haphazardly against and around it.

Blade signaled for them to stop moving, and he crouched down silently in the remaining tree line. Obediently, Mouse imitated him and stooped behind him. Toma fell in beside her.

"Are you sure this is it?" Mouse whispered anxiously. "It looks like no one's been here for ages."

"That precisely is the point." Blade cupped his hands around his mouth and emitted a rather convincing birdcall, a warble that fell somewhere between a whistle and a chirp. This he repeated, each time waiting attentively for what Mouse guessed would be some sort of response. Only the rustling of the wind in the tree limbs above answered the keening call. Just when Mouse began to doubt Blade's certainty, a similar whistling chirp echoed faintly back to them from somewhere to their right.

Blade wheeled sharply toward the sound and chirruped again. The echo came back clearer now, and the dull thud of footsteps followed shortly after. In time, Mouse spotted a large, brown draft horse weaving its way around the trees. Atop it was a weathered, middle-aged man with wide shoulders and a grizzled beard. He wore a heavy fur coat, high, sturdy boots, and a broad hat that tipped just above his shrewd, brown eyes. When he reached them, he stopped his horse begrudgingly and inspected them with skepticism.

"Blade, I presume," he said gruffly, nodding.

"And you must be our ferryman, Dane," Blade answered warmly. "We thank you for your trouble."

Dane scoffed. "Well if yer too much trouble, Woldyff can forget it. I don't owe him nearly enough to be gettin' killed today."

"Any reason for that thought?" Blade asked seriously, his hands tensing upon his sword hilts.

"It's a feeling I have. My gut hasn't steered me wrong in forty odd years, I ain't ignoring it now." He spit and gestured behind him as he spoke. "I came up in yon tree line and stay clear o' the shack 'til now because of it."

Blade nodded, peering out past the shack into the valley below. "There is no cover, then, from here to the river."

"None t' speak of," Dane affirmed.

"Then we shall have to move as fast as possible. I see nothing, but I'm not quick to dismiss your instinct, either."

"Good boy," Dane said caustically. "Well, yer all on foot, so you'll have to keep up best you can. I'll let you tie up your gear on ol' Sunshine here iffen you'll move better."

They loaded their things onto Dane's mare and followed him. The group tread cautiously into the field, uncomfortably aware of the gaping, open space before them. Mouse kept her eyes on the mountains that loomed ahead, close enough, it seemed, for them to reach before any besetting dangers. A whipping wind began to blow across the valley, so Mouse took refuge on the far side of the horse, keeping close to Dane's stirrup. Toma was content enough, despite the bitter wind, to walk on the other side, while Blade trotted ahead of them, swords in hand.

Their careful steps lead them safely across the valley and into a gradually rockier terrain. Mouse looked over her shoulder. The field sloped gently away until stopping short of the murky forest behind the shack. All was still, to her surprise, as even the wind had halted its attack on the narrow valley. Ahead, the mountains rose up to wall them in, funneling the group into a tapering, jagged corridor. The noise of rushing water echoed down the pass, and the walls vibrated with the great river's life. It built as they moved along, drowning out Mouse's thoughts of anything else. No wonder many regarded Thunder Run as a dead end. From the sound of it, the river could pound a hovercraft to pieces.

A low rumbling reverberated throughout the corridor. Mouse peered about anxiously as Blade held up a hand, halting them. It was not of the river; no, the sound was deeper, heavier, and closer. The ground began to quake, unrelenting even as Mouse attempted to steady herself. She tottered unnaturally, unable to gain her bearings. Sunshine whinnied and stamped nervously.

"Look!" Toma shouted, pointing behind them.

It was the walls of the pass. They buckled, trembling in ripples like water rolling out from the shore. Then, with one terrible shudder, they began to crumble, and all at once, the juggernaut of rock barreled toward them.

"Move!" Blade cried, barely audible over the enormous crashing of mountain against mountain.

Mouse found her feet propelling her forward, stumbling but flying over the shifting ground. Gravel pelted her back, but she didn't dare glance back lest the avalanche overtake her. Clouds of dust billowed in violent torrents around her, threatening to choke the breath from her lungs. Every step was a leap of faith, every breath promising to be her last. Air rushed in sonic blasts, heralding the bearing down of the mountains intent on burying her. Mouse charged on. She was lost in the chaos, she knew it, but she would not die willingly. It would have to claim her.

As rapidly as it had started, the quaking ceased with one final boom. Though blinded by the dust, Mouse could taste fresh air. Free of the suffocating grains, she collapsed, coughing. There was sputtering and hacking around her, and when she could, she opened her eyes. Toma laid beside her on the ground, clearing his lungs forcefully. Gray with dust, he shook out some of the larger shards of rubble lodged into the mess of his hair. Ahead, Blade rose slowly from the ground, wincing noticeably. Dane had managed to remain unscathed, saved by the speed of his mount. Only a little debris dusted his clothes and the rump of the beast. Dane shook his head irritably and gestured angrily at the wall of crushed rock behind them.

"Look what yer stampedin' feet have done! How am I s'posed to do my job now?"

Indeed, as the dust settled, it was clear the entire pass had caved, barricading the way back indefinitely.

"Do not be foolish, friend. This was not the result of anyone's clumsiness." Blade closed his eyes briefly, grappling with the pain of an unseen wound, but held his swords at the ready. He overcame it to search what remained of the mountain's walls. "This... this is purposeful. We need to move, now."

A crackling beam of light rent the air over Mouse's head, sizzling with a familiar searing heat as it tore through Dane. She watched in horror as he slumped forward on the mare's neck, who whinnied frantically. With a "Whoa, Sunshine!" Toma rushed toward the horse and grabbed its reins. The spooked beast calmed at his touch, and though her rider's limp body dangled in the saddle, it did not fall to the ground.

"Where did that come from?" Toma yelled, yanking his energy

pistol from its holster. Mouse followed suit, grabbing her own and pointing it uselessly in random directions.

"I'm not sure! Stay behind me!" Blade cried, leaping forward with swords raised. A sudden, unnerving silence followed, all of them whirling around confusedly to find the source of the blast. Her weapon raised, Mouse tiptoed back to the horse as the standoff continued. She found Toma holding the reins with one trembling hand, whispering soothingly to the horse, and aiming his gun unsteadily with the other. His wide eyes darted toward her as she came around the horse.

"You're okay," he said weakly.

"Yes," Mouse said, regaining her own wits as well. "Can you tell if Dane's alive?"

"I... I haven't checked." Toma shifted nervously, unwilling to let his gaze wander from the corridor's walls for even a moment. "I... would you?"

Mouse obliged, doing her best to assess the fallen man. Dane was lying, as in sleep, on the horse's neck. There was a ghastly hole torn through his right shoulder, but his chest rose and fell slightly with breath. *Life!* Mouse exhaled in relief and searched the saddlebag for something to bandage him. Finding a cotton shirt, Mouse pulled back Dane's garments around the wound. There was little blood – the blast had seared its mark – but the sickening smell of charred flesh filled her nostrils. She gagged and stuffed the fabric into the gaping hole.

"Is he alive?" Blade asked, still posturing defensively in front of them.

"He's breathing," Mouse answered. "But he's in a bad way."

"We need him," Toma stammered. "We're stuck here between a maniac with a gun and a landslide otherwise!"

As if on command, a fresh barrage of fire erupted upon them. This time, Blade was ready. With steady and masterful swings of his swords, Blade fended off every shot. Sparks and flashes of light crashed into the rocks, exploding on contact and raining bits of rubble upon them. Mouse watched in amazement as Blade moved fluidly against the assault, his cloak swirling about him with every parry. Even his blades flared anew, glowing brightly as if they themselves were impassioned by the battle.

The terrible fireworks display ceased, and all but Blade's cloak came to rest. Ready for whatever came next, he held the twin swords above his head. It seemed to Mouse they were alive, burning with unmatched brilliance.

A disembodied female voice echoed down the corridor.

"You are better than I thought," the voice said.

"What were you expecting?" Blade answered, a hint of weariness in his own.

Their assailant emerged from behind a large boulder ahead of them, stepping delicately from a natural shelf in the rock face. It was the tallest, most terrifying woman Mouse had ever seen.

"That you, Guardian, would prove to be as useless as the rest of your kind," she drawled.

The woman bounded gracefully down the rock wall, her two large-barreled energy pistols pointed steadily at them as she approached. They smoked unapologetically with their recent use. Mouse took in the details of their hunter as she came closer. She carried herself with the regal pride of a Coalition Party Representative, and even with the three large scars stretching down her face, her exceedingly attractive features arrested Mouse. Rounding on them with the pistols and an arrogant grin, she sniggered.

"Well, I see now that these are not going to accomplish anything. No use in wasting my ammunition, anyway."

To Mouse's surprise, she holstered the pistols. Blade lowered his swords as well.

"A bounty hunter," Blade observed. "I am not surprised. Let us hear your demands."

"My demands?" the woman scoffed. "No, this is your situation. You are trapped between me and a giant wall of rock. Even if I was not standing before you, your guide is clearly incapacitated, and all hope of navigating the river disappears with him. Unless, of course, you are suicidal, which I deem you are not. This is what you will do. You will give me the girl, and I will be gracious enough to let the two of you live."

She smiled as she spoke, but her eyes were ablaze with barely contained hostility. Mouse looked to Blade, who to her great astonishment, laughed.

"But of course a Coalition's slave would expect all to be as gutless as she! No, friend, I do not bow at the altar of fear. Or, in your case, gold."

"Very well," she sneered. "I can kill the boy slowly before your eyes for that."

"I don't think so!" Toma interjected, and with that, he fired upon her.

Instead of exploding in flames, the woman produced two blazing Cardanthium blades of her own, staving off the blast furiously just as Blade had before.

"Stupid boy," she hissed, and with maddening speed flung her swords at Blade. He resisted her advance, his swords singing as they met hers. The woman moved as fluidly as he did, rushing and withdrawing like the storm-driven tide. He answered with the same spectacular speed, and Mouse followed the battle by the shimmer of their blades – his, still a ghostly green against her hot, almost neon glow. She flipped acrobatically off the rock face. Blade leapt from place to place like a shadow, there one moment and gone the next. Their dangerous dance ranged the terrain. The huntress lunged, surprised to find herself thrusting into the air. Blade, however, did not have a complete advantage. Even Mouse sensed his strength waned, his movements becoming heavier with each of the bounty hunter's ceaseless blows. She appeared to gain strength and speed as they grappled, vitalized by the passion of the battle. Mouse gasped as he miss-stepped. The woman fell upon him like a wild beast, viciously searching for his gut with the tip of her sword. Blade blocked it. With a roar he staggered her, his heels grinding into the dirt.

The battle continued in this way as Mouse and Toma stood by helplessly, afraid to injure Blade in joining the fray. Mouse, for her part, reached for her dagger and brandished it angrily, unwilling to simply watch as Blade's strength failed. She lurched forward, but Toma caught hold of her before she could do anything.

"No! He can handle this!" Toma shouted.

"I won't wait here to watch him fall!" Mouse screamed back, ripping herself away.

Toma reached out and caught her again. "You don't know what you're doing! She'll kill you!"

Mouse made to escape again, but Blade pinned the woman against the rock. They were stuck in a horrible standstill, Blade forcing his swords down and she fought with every ounce of her will to fend him off.

"Get to the river, now!" Blade managed. "Wake Dane! Go!"

"Get on!" Toma demanded, pushing Mouse toward the horse.

"But Blade!" she cried, resisting.

"This is our only chance! He'll meet us there! Come on!"

Mouse's body went rigid, rooting her to the spot as she watched Blade struggle against the hunter. Toma's strong arms hoisted her from the ground and jerked her over the saddle. He hopped on behind her, kicking the mare hard as he landed. It galloped forward, darting past the two locked figures. Mouse witnessed the woman escape Blade's hold as they rushed away, bellowing and fighting with renewed fury. The battle, and the sound of clashing metal, disappeared as they rounded a bend in the pass.

Here, the pass sloped precipitously downward, leading them to the deep gorge where Thunder Run frothed along. Toma dug into Sunshine's sides, but his awkward position on her back and loose grip on the reins had them skidding to a rough stop right before the riverbed. When they had settled, Mouse was relieved to see the skiff sitting on the shore, tied to a stake for good measure. She looked hesitantly at the river in front of them, which eddied about and rushed on with terrifying speed.

"We have to get him conscious," Toma said resolutely.

With that, he pulled Dane off the horse. Mouse winced as Dane's body hit the sand with a dull thud. Toma took no notice of this, and instead proceeded to shake him and shout his name.

"It's not working," Mouse said after Toma slapped Dane's face in desperation.

"Maybe this will," Toma said grimly. Brusquely, he jammed his finger into Dane's fresh wound.

"Gaaah!" Dane howled, gasping for breath. "Stop killing me!"

"We need you to get us out of here!" Toma shouted. "Or that crazy assassin is going to murder us!"

"What are you on about, boy?" Dane panted, his eyes rolling around his head.

"Long story," Mouse interjected. "She's the one who shot you."

"What'd I tell yah!" Dane gasped. "The gut never lies!"

"Can you get us out of here?" Toma repeated, enunciating every word.

"I can't... I ain't able to steer, boy," he wheezed.

"We can do it." Mouse said.

"What now?" Toma blurted.

"Dane, can you direct us while we do all the heavy lifting?" Mouse clarified.

Dane rolled his head weakly to look at Mouse.

"Is that the only shot we got?"

Mouse nodded. "Even if Blade kills her, we're stuck in this pass. You need a healer as soon as we can find one. I'm pretty sure the Coalition knows we're here."

"If they don't, then someone just as bad does," Toma added.

Dane fluttered his eyelids briefly and groaned in pain. "I don't wanna die in the river, but it's better than dying here."

"Great, let's get this boat ready," Toma said. He pushed the boat into the water, its strong current raging against the rope. They did their best to gently lift a loudly complaining Dane into the skiff. From the bottom of the craft, Dane grunted terse instructions to the pair.

"Looks like we're ready," Toma said, moving to untie the rope that anchored them to shore.

"Wait!" Mouse shouted, staying his hand. "We're not leaving without Blade."

A lone figure rounded the bend and came sprinting down the slope. Long, raven-black hair flew behind her, the pulsing light of her blades darkened by freshly drawn blood.

CHAPTER TWENTY-SEVEN

A strangled sob caught in Mouse's throat as the woman approached. She wore an arrogant sneer as she ran, her eyes boring into Mouse with triumph. Angry, hot tears stained Mouse's cheeks as she wrenched her dagger from her waist.

"Come on!" she roared, brandishing the blade.

"Mouse, no!" Toma said, putting his hand on her arm. "Don't make his sacrifice worthless."

Breaking her vengeful trance, Toma's touch brought Mouse to her senses. With a quick swing of the dagger, she severed their tether. The boat rushed into Thunder Run. Mouse watched the woman reach the shore. She lowered her swords in frustration as they sped away. Rage returned and filled Mouse, burning in her stomach, making her sick with hate. In one smooth motion, she drew her energy pistol and fired remorselessly at the mercenary, as many times as her clip would allow. To her dismay, the woman blocked them with little effort. Mouse registered, however, one fleeting look of amazement, the fire in her eyes replaced with... something else. Was it empathy?

"Mouse! Sit down!" Toma shouted, panic in his voice. "And maybe a little help here!"

"Oh," Mouse said stupidly, the danger of her precarious position dawning on her emotion-numbed mind. She sat down immediately, narrowly avoiding being tossed out of the skiff by the sudden eddy that followed.

"This was your idea, young lady," Dane grumbled crossly. "Now get workin' so we don't die."

Mouse listened attentively as Dane doled out jobs. While Dane could easily handle the boat on his own, he kept a spare set of oars in the boat just in case. He instructed Mouse to pull the extra set out and use them in the front of the boat.

Dane jabbed a finger at Toma. "I don't doubt his strength, but he ain't got the reflexes to do it on his own. You two will get us in some tight spots, so you'll need all the power you can to get us out. Alive," he added condescendingly.

For as gruff as Dane was, he certainly didn't lie. The current carried them along with merciless rapidity, constantly pushing them toward the deadly waters in the middle. It was a deep river, caged in on both sides by impassable cliffs. Too far in the middle, and they would lose control and drown in its relentless pull, but too far on the sides, and they would be crushed against the gorge walls. Neither, Mouse decided, would be pleasant.

Toma and Mouse fought the river apprehensively, Dane the whole time shouting and cursing at their every move. Mouse could hardly see for the spray that rained down on them, the freezing water slapping her smartly as they rowed. The river quickly became shallow and the current slowed. The boat rocked gently along. Unsure of just how they managed to survive, Mouse looked about in amazement. She caught Toma's eye, who sighed in relief. Dane simply sniggered as he lay pale and motionless on the bottom of the boat.

"Don' get your hopes up yet, boy. Look up yonder!"

Large, white-tipped waves crested ominously ahead. As they came closer, Mouse saw they were big enough to crash onto the boat, surely overturning them if they got caught.

"Wooo-eee!" Dane whooped. "Here we go! Leeeft!"

Mouse did her best to make the boat veer left, just missing the full fury of the white cap. Toma groaned with effort as the back of the boat caught in the wave, threatening to go into a fatal backspin.

"Well, come on now boy, put your back innit!" Dane cried delightedly.

Toma grunted and puffed as he put all his might into saving the boat. It turned enough to escape the fatal current.

"He's insane!" Toma wheezed.

"He's got to be in shock," Mouse answered, puffing as well. "Delirious, probably."

"What's shockin' is we're still alive!" Dane hollered. "Riiight!"

This eddy, though smaller, caught Mouse by surprise, and the boat suddenly faced the wrong way.

"Turn it around!" Toma cried.

"I'm trying!" Mouse replied frantically. She stuck her oar in the water, attempting to get the boat to spin about. It turned the boat into the current instead.

"Oh no!" she gasped as water lapped over the side.

"Aaagh!" Toma exclaimed as his pack bounced into the river. Before he could reach out to grab it, the water sucked it under. And in that agonizing moment, Mouse realized they would soon follow.

Blind rage returned, brimming inside her until she felt it render every other emotion dead. Anger at Toma for making her leave, anger at Blade for dying for her, anger at herself for killing them here. Most of all, her anger burned at the cruelty of this brutal world – one that created lives full of nothing but suffering, only to end in the same horrendous way. Her life, Blade's death, this journey; all of it had been so unjustly meaningless, and now she would cost the lives of two more who did not deserve it. Tears stung her eyes. Like the waves of the river, self-pity washed over her. Maybe if she had just kept to herself, maybe, just maybe if she had lived out her time at Misty Summit in quiet, Red, Blade, Toma, and Dane could have been fine with quiet lives until the end of their days…

A blazing radiance encompassed her, embracing her with a warmth she had forgotten. Mouse looked ahead, aware that whatever it was, it was in front of her. The river was gone, the boat was gone, and now she was drawn to the light, the all-consuming presence of something she could feel but could not quite see. She squinted into the luminous horizon. A wing, she saw, gilded in flame, itself rising out of the light.

Deep shame reared up as the light touched her, exposing, as it were, every foolish feeling of the moments before, which seemed so exceedingly remote now. Her anger, her sorrow, her fear, her shame – all these were bathed in light inaccessible, and suddenly, they were gone.

Mouse blinked and rubbed her eyes, aware of the slight rocking of a gentle current. She swiveled around to get her bearings, only to find herself still in the boat. Toma was there, dumbfounded and staring at her as his mouth hung wide open. Here also was Dane, and he was laughing, his entire body shaking with glee despite his still tender wound.

"What?" Mouse asked after the laughing fit finally subsided.

Before Toma could conjure up words, he gesticulated wildly, flailing in apparent distress.

"What do you mean, 'what?' We just about *died* back there, and then all of a sudden you become this expert white-water rafter, and you ask 'what' like it's no big deal?!"

Toma threw up his arms in exasperation. "Who are you?"

"Well, would you look at that," Dane said, wiping tears from his eyes. "We're here."

With a gentle bump, the boat ran aground a shallow shore sparkling with smooth, obsidian pebbles. Mouse gasped in awe as the landscape unfolded before her eyes. Dark peaks spread along the entire horizon, casting great shadows over the soft hills rolling endlessly beyond them. It was beautiful but for its one blemish; the deep, black scar cutting a swathe through the forests ahead. Sinister, gray mists stretched out from the scar, striking both wonder and fear into her very core.

"Elmnas," she whispered.

ABOUT THE AUTHOR

Kaylena Radcliff is a magazine editor, pastor's wife, mother, and indefatigable world builder. As such, she subsists almost entirely on coffee and prayer. A voracious reader and prolific writer from an early age, Kaylena was deeply influenced by the likes of C.S. Lewis, J.R.R. Tolkien, and Flannery O'Connor. She dabbles in many genres, but most loves writing and reading speculative and fantasy fiction. Aside from writing, Kaylena loves discussing history, theology, and all things nerdy. You might also find her unsuccessfully attempting to relive the glory days as a collegiate athlete on the community soccer field. Despite extended trips abroad and the passport to prove it, she never did manage to escape her Pennsylvanian hometown. In true hobbit fashion, she happily resides there with her husband and two young children. https://kaylenaradcliff.wordpress.com/

 facebook.com/kaylenaradcliff

 instagram.com/kaylenaradcliff